Copyright© 2006 by Dion Jones

ISBN#: 0-9774103-2-3

Cover concept/artwork by Dion Jones/Bruce
Gadson (Waaliy)
Cover design by Sandy Petrie, Zig Zag Design
Studio

Penhouse Publishing
P.O. Box 820
Lovejoy, GA 30250

Printed in the United States of America
November, 2006

DEDICATION

To all those who share in the experience of a triad relationship. Not the cheaters, or those who are out on the creep, but those of us who put it out front and let it be known what it is from the start.

PLAYER, CHEATER
OR
DAMN FOOL

CHAPTER LIST

Prelude

Desiree Was Staring out the front window of the truck, when Angie climbed back in. She looked over at her wondering how it was she had no problem whatsoever with Davonte's illogically perverse orders time after time.

"You know," Desiree said, becoming serious, *"When we get back, I got some words for him."*

"I hear ya," Angie said, continuing to prepare herself for the task at hand. *"When we get back, you can talk to him about whatever you want. However, right now, you need to be getting it together so we can get this party on the road.* Desiree looked over at Angie and smacked her lips, *"You act like this shit is normal!"*

"No!" Angie said holding up her hand letting Desiree know to say no more, *"For your information what it is, I act like I'm going to do what he told me he wanted me to do. If I wasn't or felt as though I had a problem with it, I would have let it be known the very moment he said what he wanted done."*

"Bitch right," Desiree thought, *"You wouldn't have told him shit. You ain't been telling him nothing."*

"Now, are you telling me you ain't gonna do it?" Angie asked, knowing good and well what the answer would be.

Desiree thought for a second and figured if she turned back now, it would just cause problems later.

"No, that's not what I'm saying," she answered, hating it all the same.

"Alrighty then," Angie chimed, *"Let's get it. He's counting on us!"*

"Yeah, he's counting on us alright," Desiree mimicked, wondering how the hell it was that Angie was so happy. *"Let's get this preposterous shit over with,"* she snapped. *"Oh, and just so you know, I am a bit perturbed."*

DION JONES

PLAYER

CHAPTER ONE

"GOT IT MADE"

Davonte **L**ooked **O**ver at his cell phone, it was 9:30 and it had been ringing since 7am. Desiree lay there beside him, watching, waiting for him to answer it. She was tired of the ringing and him pretending he didn't hear it. She let out a sigh, then elbowed Davonte in the side.

"Get your phone please. You know you hear it."

He smacked his lips and reached for the phone. As he flipped it open, he hadn't even got it to his ear good before the voice on the other end came through loud and clear.

"Bout time you picked up! Mannn! What you doing? I know you heard the phone ringing. Where you at?"

Before he could respond, Desiree sat up in bed and looked him in the face.

"Go ahead, tell her where you at."

"Nevermind," the voice said through the phone, *"You don't have to answer, I heard her."*

Davonte looked at Desiree with a warning look, *"Don't start,"* he told her. Then proceeded to talk into the phone.

"And you little lady need to calm down."

"Whatever," Desiree snapped jumping out the bed. *"It seems like we can't get no quality time,"* she said speaking loud enough so she could be heard through the phone.

"Stop it," he said pointing a finger at her. *"Now, what's up with you?"* He spoke into the phone.

"Nooothing," Angie chimed, *"I just wanted to hear my baby's voice."*

"I talked to you last night before I went to bed," Davonte told her in a semi-frustrated tone.

"Anyway," Angie said, *"You mean before you gave her a piece of Big Ben and the twins."*

Davonte didn't respond.

"Didn't you?!?" Angie asked. Still he didn't answer. *"Well, Davonte?"*

"Well, what?" He said finally, responding to her interrogation.

"Did you give her some of the 'Honey Dripper' or not?!?"

Davonte spoke calmly, yet in a stern tone, *"Listen Angie, you know what it is. We've been through this."*

"Yeah, you know what it is!" Desiree yelled over her shoulder, walking out of the room.

"I'm sorry baby," Angie whined, *"You mad at me?"*

"Naa," Davonte answered, *"You just need to get a grip and stop trying to go there with me. Now, what's up, what's good?"*

"Nothing much," she told him, *"I've been up all night studying. I'll be glad when I graduate."*

"I know you will baby," Davonte told her.

"Just hang in there, you'll be okay. Just think, you only have a couple more months."

"Yeah, I know," she said with more enthusiasm than before. *"So, you coming up this way next weekend or what?"*

Before he could answer, Angie snapped, *"Don't play Davonte! You promised and I'm looking forward to seeing you."*

"I told you I'll be there and I will. As a matter of fact, why don't you come get me?" Davonte asked.

Angie thought for a minute. The long drive up and back, not once, but twice and the second ride back would be by herself.

"Naa, that's okay," she told Davonte while listening close to detect whether there was a change in his attitude.

"Okay, that's cool," Davonte responded. *"Now, if you don't mind, I need to take a shower and get dressed."*

Just as quickly as Angie turned herself onto snap mode, she turned herself off.

"Yeah, you do that," she told him, *"And wash good, make sure you get all of her off of you,"* sounding as sarcastic as she possibly could.

Davonte began laughing, *"You silly, you know that?"*

Angie recognized an opening and took advantage of it.

"Davonte, you love me don't you baby?"

"Yesss, Angie," Davonte responded.

"Tell me, tell me you love me," she pleaded.

"I love you," he said in between his thoughts of her and Desiree.

"Are you in love with me?" Her tone went from whiny to being inquisitive just that fast.

Davonte caught it, *"Look baby, I told you I love you and I mean it. Now, I need to be getting dressed and I mean that too."*

"Davonte," Angie said, attempting to sound seductive, *"Tell me you love me one more time. I need to hear it."*

Davonte started becoming frustrated with Angie's little game. It was one played only too often by her and Desiree whenever he was with the other.

"I love you," he said in a slightly angered tone, *"Now, I'll talk to you later."*

Angie knew she wouldn't be able to take the conversation any further. Besides, she had done what she'd set out to do, call and wake him and Desiree up with the sound of her voice and get the man she loved to express his love for her while lying in Desiree's bed.

"Okay baby," she said, *"Call me later."*

"I will," he assured her, then hung up.

But not before she quickly yelled out, *"I love you, baby!"*

As he placed the phone on the nightstand, Desiree walked back into the bedroom.

"Tell me you love me," she mimicked as she lay on the bed beside him.

"You wrong," he told her.

"How you figure?" She asked with a surprised look on her face.

"Eavesdropping on my phone conversation," he told her.

"What?!" She exclaimed. *"Let me make sure I follow this correctly. You in my house, in my bedroom mind you, talking to her and I ain't supposed to hear?!? Yeah, right,"* she said.

Davonte didn't answer, he was in deep thought.

Desiree stared into his eyes, wondering what was going through his mind.

"Man," she thought to herself, as she took in the visual of this man whom she loved dearly. His bedroom eyes, with his sexy big nose and sexy lips made for a near perfect face. His light-caramel complexion, broad shoulders, along with his nice chest, showed just above the covers. He had a stocky physique, and although it was well shaped, it didn't look as though he had worked hard for it, more natural looking than anything. His baldhead made him look sexy and powerful. She let her eyes travel down his shoulders over his strong arms. As she did, Desiree became turned on. She reached over and began rubbing her hand along the sheet, just between Davonte's inner thigh.

"Baby," she whined, interrupting his thoughts, *"Why don't you hook a sister up?!?"*

He looked her over and smiled. It was a nice thought and to get busy first thing in the morning was an enjoyable treat. He turned to face her and began softly caressing her shoulders and arm. His touch was so pleasing to her, she simply laid back and looked up at him with flames of desire kindled in her eyes. Davonte leaned in and kissed her forehead while allowing his hand to brush across her nipple, which instantly became aroused. Davonte kissed

6

the tip of her nose, then a soft peck on the lips followed. As she opened her mouth to receive his tongue, she also parted her legs in order that his hand may invitingly explore her pleasure zone. At that moment, Davonte pulled the sheet off of him and jumped up out the bed.

"I don't think so," he said standing beside the bed. *"I hooked you up last night, yesterday evening and the night before that. You getting spoiled."*

Desiree laid there partly in shock looking at his naked body standing there, his strong looking thighs with that long, fat meat hanging between them.

"You'll be alright," he said as he turned and headed for the bathroom.

Desiree stared at his 5'10" frame with his wide back and tight ass with the dents in the sides. Her mouth watered and she jumped up out the bed swallowing.

"O...oh no you didn't!" She yelled chasing behind him, only to reach the bathroom door too late, as she jiggled the doorknob to see that it was locked. *"I got your spoiled!"* She yelled through the door.

"I know you do," Davonte barked back at her.

As she heard the shower come on, it dawned on her she really wasn't getting any. She hit the door with the side of her fist.

"I don't care. I'm straight anyway!" She said yelling through the door once again.

"Okay straight!" Davonte yelled with laughter in his voice.

Desiree walked back to the bedroom, flopped on the bed and let out a sigh.

"It ain't got me spoiled," she told herself.

Then a voice in her head told her, *"No, it got you sprung like a mutha fucka."*

"Who said that?" She questioned, as she turned her head quickly to her left and right. *"Oh, that was me,"* she said

7

as she busted out laughing. *"I'm in here talking to myself.
Damn!"* She thought as she placed her hands between her
legs and cuffed her coochie. *"Shit got me going crazy, him
and that thang of his…fucking froggy style and that pole to
the wall coochie crawl. Aaaarrrrhhhh!"* She yelled out as
she began rolling back and forth on the bed like a big kid.
"He could've given me some. Ole stinky punk!"

Davonte stood in the shower letting the hot water run
down his body. He couldn't help but to think of his present
situation, two women, both knowing of the other, both
loving him. Each having their own unique individual
quality about themselves that brought about the
balancement he felt he needed. And although it may have
been thought to be impossible, he honestly loved them
both. And it seemed that once he'd put things out front and
told each of them about the other, they began loving him
even more. They had only heard each other's voice over
the phone, never once meeting face to face. However, the
fact that they knew of one another did make things run
smoother. No sneaking around. He wondered if the two of
them meeting in person would be possible without any
drama.

At times, they made comments of how they weren't sure
if this was what they wanted for their lives and even had
moments where they attempted to pry him away from the
other with a range of harsh to soothing words. Davonte
thought deep on that and questioned himself on whether or
not he would ever leave one for the other? His thoughts
slipped into weighing the pros and the cons of the matter.
Their education was equally matched as for them both
taking it upon themselves to acquire more than a high
school diploma, both having college experience. Desiree a
nurse and Angie graduating in a couple more months and
becoming a Certified Executive Chef.

When in the presence of either of them, they catered to him with love and true devotion. Although, at times, Desiree was hard headed and had to be told to do things twice or more. Not to mention, Angie had her moments of coming fly out the mouth. Those were dislikes he didn't care for, but tolerated, quickly putting them in their place when these acts of rudeness arose. He tried his best to remain humble about the situation and not get the 'big head'. Being fully aware that it was more than a matter of simply having two pieces of pussy at his disposal. Strangely enough, Davonte came to realize the two women kept him grounded in reality, something Black men very much needed in this day and time. Yet, he had to admit to himself, when he thought of how attractive they both were, he couldn't help but toot his own horn.

Desiree was a smooth chocolate complexion, with full juicy lips. And although she was very much into her Nubian ethnicity, wearing a natural hairstyle of twists and braids, no perms; her eyes held a mysterious look of worldly seduction. This, along with her long legs, causing her to stand at 5'8", protruding hips and small waist that offset her full 36D breast made her ever so tantalizing. And her buttocks helped make her body measurements a lovely eye-pleasing 36-27-43. She had a little tummy on her, but hey, the rump caused it to go unnoticed. Yes, it proudly carried the title 'Ba-dunk-ka-dunk! Bless her heart.

Now, Angie was in some ways opposite of Desiree, however, equally as beautiful. She was petite, yet, had meat on her. She stood about 5'4" with large, sexy almond shaped eyes. When she blinked, it brought you to mind of an innocent little baby. She had a slender, yet very distinctive jaw line, nice pink lips, and long curly hair that easily hung to the middle of her back. Her thighs and calves were well shaped, like an athlete who ran track. Angie was hairier than the average female, but in all the right places and it added to her eroticness. Her skin complexion was fair, she was what is considered in the south a 'redbone'.

If you looked into either Angie or Desiree's eyes long enough you would swear they were undressing you or asking you to get undressed.

"Leave one of them for the other?" He questioned in his mind. *"Hell, to the nah!"* He couldn't see it.

The water in the shower began to turn cold, so he hurriedly scrubbed his body, rinsed and got out. As he dried off, he realized he had to go back into the bedroom naked and really wasn't in the mood for frolicking with Desiree at this point. He meant what he said she was getting spoiled. Plus, he had to save up for his visit with Angie next weekend. She liked a full load. Not to mention, her being a wild 'thundercat' in the bed.

"Oh well," he thought, *"If Desiree starts I'll just have to say no!"*

He opened the bathroom door and made his way briskly down the hall to the bedroom. When he entered the bedroom, it appeared Desiree was asleep, until she spoke from under the sheet she had over her head.

"So, I see you managed to use up all the hot water again."

She popped her head out from under the cover to register his reaction. To her surprise, Davonte was quickly sliding into his clothes.

"Oh, it's like that?!" She asked.

"Don't start," he told her, *"I have to be getting a move on and handle a few things and I can't do that lying in the bed all day with you."*

She pulled the sheet back over her head and sounding disappointed told him, *"I'm straight. Like I said before, you took so long in the shower, I hooked myself up."* She lied and he knew it, but decided to rub it in.

"Good for you!" He said being sarcastic.

She gritted her teeth under the sheet. They both knew she wanted it, but she had been learned, 'no' meant 'no' with Davonte. There had been only one other time he'd said 'no' and gave in.

Refusing to be outdone, she popped her head out, *"Well, just so you know...,"* she paused waiting for him to look up from putting his shoes on.

When he didn't, she continued, *"Your girl called while you was in the shower, so I answered the phone to see what she wanted just in case it was an emergency or something."*

She knew his cell phone was a soft spot as with most men who had one.

With his eyes squinted from the anger building up inside of him, he stood up.

"You did what!?" He questioned as he made his way over to his cell phone. *"What'd I tell you about my phone?!?"* Picking it up off the nightstand. He looked over to Desiree, waiting for her response. *"Answer me!"* He scolded. As he looked at the screen, he noticed no calls had come through. He turned to see the 'I got you' grin on Desiree's face.

"You lied," he snapped.

"Yeah, but you believed it. You was ready to trip. I don't know why you don't want us to talk." She said to him, while raising a curious eyebrow. *"It's not like we don't know about each other."*

Davonte leaned over and gave her a kiss on the forehead, *"I gotta go. I'll give you a call later."*

"You didn't answer me," Desiree told him.

"About what?" Davonte asked all the while heading out the bedroom to leave.

"Why don't you want us to talk or why haven't you introduced us in person? Hey! You hear me!?" She yelled out to him.

He didn't answer. Truthfully, she knew he wouldn't. It wasn't the first time she'd asked the question. What it was about this other female had become an enigma for Desiree and oddly enough, it was part of the reason she put up with the relationship. She tried figuring it out. He had enough balls to come clean about his seeing both of them. Okay, he gets one point for honesty. Outside of that, letting them know why he wanted it this way and how it was he loved both of them, he didn't go into and left no room for discussion.

"This is how it is, and this is how it's going to be," is all he would say, along with letting them both know they are to see no one else.

"Okay, cool," Desiree said at the time, *"Let's see how it all plays out."*

But the fact that it had been a year and they still hadn't met face to face nor talked to each other on the phone other than if one of them answered the cell phone and at that, he only allowed brief 'Hello's' and 'Hi's'.

"What was it?" Desiree was becoming fed up with the, *"You need to be with me having another woman, but you can't meet her,"* shit. Know about her, sure. But meet her? No. *"To hell with that,"* she thought. *"He need to figure out how he gonna play this shit out."*

Desiree took a deep breath as she continued her thoughts. She was ego tripping and knew it. Davonte had been very clear on how things were going to be and he wasn't like most men who said one thing and did something else. No, not at all, if he called it that's what it was. No ifs, ands or buts, at no point did he ever show signs of being confused about the decisions he made.

"Maybe, I ought to leave him," she told herself. *"Tell him its over,"* she paused for a second. *"Give up and let some other chick have my man? Nah, that's not an option."*

Plenty of thoughts flooded Desiree's head. However, none were able to outweigh the thought of how much she loved Davonte. And although there was another female in the picture, things between them were fine. Not to mention, he took good care of her. He wasn't rich, but she wanted for nothing. He kept it simple, but still, she had.

"Damn," she thought, *"Honestly, all was good, but doesn't every woman deserve her man to herself?"* That is the question.

As **D**avonte **D**rove through the morning traffic, he thought on how content he was with his present situation. And although the ladies couldn't quite overstand how it was he loved them both, he did, and a great deal. So much so, he had made the decision that no matter what, he would always have them. He was well aware of their concerns and did his best to be as sensitive to their feelings as he possibly could. Unfortunately, no matter how open the lines of communications were, he remained unable to answer the infamous questions they both would frequently ask, *"Why? Why it is he felt the need for two women? Isn't one enough for you? Ain't I enough for you?"*

He was unable to answer these questions. Even he wasn't totally sure of the answers. Was it was lust, greed or the failed relationship between he and his mother? *That...* was the question. Either way, he desired to have them both in his life. Whatever the reason, it created the balance he needed and caused him to feel complete and loved. Because of that, he refused to let either of them go. At one point, he had talked to both of them about their past relationships and from what he gathered, although they were sharing him, they were better off. There was no mental and physical abuse, he did nothing behind their backs. He gave what financial support he could, when he could, although he still had bills of his own. He was also a rather decent lover. Neither ever complained. They referred to him as a 'Super Freak' from time to time, but never a complaint. Ironically though, they both shared the same concerns about the one conversation that did warrant attention, the marriage…children…my biological clock, conversation. He overstood where they were coming from seeing they were both in their early thirties, Desiree, being 32, and Angie 30. He also couldn't deny the fact they were both perfect for marriage, ideal wife material, knowing how to maintain a home and be supportive of their mate.

Davonte also was aware of them both being beautiful black women, with a great deal to offer to a man and a relationship. He also knew from his present situation, that at the age of 26, he had a great deal to learn.

"Rest assure," he told himself, *"In time, I'll experience all I need to and learn just as much. But for now, they will have to continue loving me and be patient."*

In his mind, he felt he was able to deliver them both total satisfaction and happiness. For Davonte, the thought of him without them and they without him, was not an option and *that* he was sure of. As long as things continued the way it was, from what he could see, all was good and he had it made.

CHAPTER TWO

"ON MY WAY"

Desiree **M**ade **H**er way into the house shutting the door behind her. She hurried over to the couch and flopped down. It had been a long week at the hospital. Not only did the patients wear on her last nerves throughout the week, her boss, Dr. Scott really had her pissed with his failure to keep appointments she had scheduled with the patients. Some mess about him having to be in court all week for a malpractice case with another doctor, leaving her with no other option but to call all 19 patients and re-schedule them, which caused tempers to flare. She was as overstanding as she could be, for the most part, however, a couple folks caused her to get a bit heated. No doubt she lived in Atlanta, the A.T.L as it is referred to as, but make no mistake Desiree was from Philly! Philadelphia, PA, and when pissed off, it came out a few times, all the way out! Now that she thought about it, she hoped she hadn't lost her job behind it.

"Oh well," she thought. *"I'll know come Monday morning."*

Taking a deep breath, she questioned herself on why she had allowed the patients to get under her skin seeing she usually handled things pretty well at the hospital.

'Calmly and professionally' was her motto, yet, this week and especially today she failed to apply her little golden rule.

"But, why?" She questioned, as she slipped off her white Reebok Classic tennis shoes. *"Don't play games with yourself."* She mumbled under her breath as she stood up and slid down her purple scrub pants to her ankles.

Stepping out of them, she reached back and pulled her white cotton panties out the crack of her butt.

"You know damn well what's wrong." Her thoughts continued as she sat back on the couch and reached for the envelope that contained the cable bill. Opening the envelope and pulling out the bill, she unconsciously did a quick scan. Her brain not registering what her eyes saw for she was preoccupied with her thoughts. The thought of Davonte leaving out today to go spend time with Angie in Ohio where she attended college. Although this had been going on for a little over a year now, she hadn't got used to it and figured she probably never would.

The amount of the cable bill suddenly caught her attention. As she stood and made her way down the hall, her long brown legs moved gracefully causing her hips to sway, creating a slight jiggle and a subtle bounce in her large butt cheeks. Entering the bathroom, she didn't bother to turn on the light, she just slid her panties over her hips and let them drop to the floor. She sat on the toilet and took another look at the cable bill.

"Eighty one dollars."

She couldn't believe it. The bill on the average was only thirty-six dollars, but upon looking over the pages, she began to see why it was so high. Davonte had ordered a fight on pay-per-view.

"His ass paying for that!" She said out loud.

Then she noticed a few late-night X-rated movies that he'd ordered. *"Freak!! He paying for those too."*

She laughed remembering how a few times he had made mention of them having a threesome.

"Ménage à trois my ass! And why the hell hasn't he called me? I know his butt ain't get on the highway without calling me. As soon as I'm done I'll be calling his punk butt."

Her mood quickly went from anger to happiness as she thought for the thousandth time of how much she loved Davonte.

"Peeeuuw!" She exclaimed. *"It stinks in here! Where's my incense, air freshener, something?! My goodness!!"* She said while frantically looking around the bathroom with a hand placed over her nose.

Angie Stood In the doorway of her bedroom in nothing but a soft pink tank top staring at Davonte's naked body. His well shaped physique, with large shoulders and soft sexy lips. To her, Davonte was a beautiful creature who she had the pleasure of loving. The sight of him sent chills down her entire body and made her pussy tingle from the inside out. Without even looking in her direction he raised his hand and with one finger, motioned for her to come. She made her way over to the bed wearing a smile from ear to ear. Knowing what was in store for her, the hairy muffin between her legs was already seriously wet. Reaching the side of the bed, she slid off her tank top exposing her perky round breasts. Her nipples were a dead give away of her bodies yearning. She allowed her eyes to travel from the top of his head down his body. She enjoyed the sight of every inch of him. When she reached his mid-section where his manhood lay, she had to take a deep breath, as she became excited. As Angie looked at his tool, her heart picked up it's pace. There it was, long and fat. Many guys bragged on what they were "supposed" to have, how large it was, what they could do, but not Davonte. He rarely spoke of his piece or his abilities. But if by chance he did indulge in a conversation about it, he spoke nothing but the truth. His balls resembled golf balls, they were extremely large. Her eyes scanned the length, right up past his navel. The man had a real live ten inches and the girth made it something fierce. Angie reached over and began rubbing

Davonte's chest as she leaned forward and kissed the shaft of his meat. Her eye's shot him a seductive glance as she slid her tongue up towards the head of his penis, which she gladly gave a soft wet kiss.

"Baby, can I?" Angie requested. Davonte gave her a smile of approval and she crawled onto the bed and straddled him. She grabbed for his pipe with her thumb and index finger, misjudging it's size and quickly being reminded of it as it slipped out of her grasp and fell back on his stomach with a thump.

This time she reached for it, grabbing it with her whole hand. With a nice grip on it, she began rubbing the head up and down the opening of her vagina preparing the orifice. With Davonte there was no rushing, he had to be mounted right; slowly, carefully, inch by pulsating inch. As she worked the head around and heard the smacking noise of her own happy juices, Angie started kissing and sucking on Davonte's body. Thoughts of what was taking place went through her mind, his love-making was so powerful and intense it caused her to always want more.

Although he easily wore her out time and time again, she was never able to get enough. It was always so much, so overwhelming. Angie began to lower herself onto Davonte's love muscle.

As she felt the head probe her soft lips, she let out a deep moan, it remained all that to her. Even after the many hot lovemaking sessions they'd shared, it still took up all the space in her love pocket.

Davonte placed his hands on her hips preparing her for what he had to offer.

Before he'd even started, her toes curled and her legs shook slightly. Her mind and body already knew what was in store.

Davonte knew her body well, every spot and what she once may have liked, she now loved. She slid up and down, slowly on his meat. She could feel the pleasure of his penetration all the way from the opening of her vagina through her butt cheeks, and lower back. She could feel the sensation of his stroke throughout her body. Davonte took her earlobe into his mouth and gently sucked on it.

He softly whispered in her ear and asked, *"You ready baby?"*

Angie just nodded her head barely hearing his words, already in a state of ecstasy.

"I guess that means yes," Davonte said getting a firmer grip on her hips, pulling her down as he lifted his hips and thrusted upward.

What started as a stimulating suck on his chest, turned into an erotic bite. It was all she could do to help her take what was being given. The more Davonte stroked, the further she sunk her teeth into his chest.

"Oh, so you want to play dirty?" Davonte asked.

As he used her hips to move her up and down faster, deeper, the bouncing motion made her ass cheeks jump. However, she hadn't heard a word he said. Angie's eyes rolled back in her head and although she could feel the pleasure of what was taking place. Her mind was blank. She was unable to think or hear, she only felt. And the pleasure she felt consumed her entire being.

Suddenly, a bell went off in her head causing distraction. She began to bounce and grind faster, harder so it would go away. Angie moaned, in an attempt to outdo the noise of the bell ringing in her head. She opened her eyes to look at Davonte and to ask him to make the noise go away.

To her surprise, there was no Davonte, only a wet spot on her sheet where her mouth had been. She looked down between her legs to see a pillow gripped tightly between her thighs.

"What the...?" She questioned, then realizing it was a dream, frustratingly took a wild swing, slapping her alarm

clock off the nearby nightstand sending it crashing to the floor. She pushed the pillow up between her legs, figuring she would finish the dream, then just as quickly, realized it wouldn't be the same. She pulled the pillow from between her thighs, taking notice of the wet spot on the satin pillowcase.

She thought, *"Damn, I done messed my pillow up."*

Angie placed her hand between her legs and let out a little giggle.

"I need a cold shower," she told herself, *"And I also need to get in some study time before Davonte gets here."*

Because she knew once he arrived, there would be no time to study, especially after a dream like the one she just had.

Removing her hand from between her legs, she smelled her finger, *"Oh, but no,"* she said climbing out of bed. *"Let me hit the shower. But first, let me call my baby and see where he's at."*

Davonte **S**at **B**ehind the wheel of the truck listening to his cousin Harry babble on about the women he had and how they were getting on his nerves.

Davonte had been driving Harry around all day, doing one thing or another. And all day, he had been listening to Harry's complaints about his relationships. Davonte knew the greater part of Harry's problem lied in the fact that he was a cheater, pretending to be a player.

"Listen cousin, and listen close, in order that you don't get the words mixed up. The problem you're having is based on your failure to be honest and true to what you're doing. You see, a cheater runs around having more than one lady, yet none of them knows of the other. He doesn't keep it honest. Now, the player, simply put, is a man who lets each of his women know of one another and he also lets them know their place in his life."

Davonte's cell phone began ringing as he spoke.

"Yeah, yeah," Harry mumbled not trying to hear Davonte because, telling *his* ladies about each other was one thing he wasn't about to do.

Davonte took a look at the number on his phone, it was Desiree, he already knew what she wanted. Why hadn't he called or stopped by would be her questions. Before he could flip open the phone to talk, another call came through.

It was Angie, *"Where you at? When you leaving?"* Would be her questions and damn good ones too. Seeing that he had to leave out, drive eight hours from Atlanta to Ohio and he still hadn't packed his clothes for the trip. The phone continued to ring, now with both numbers flashing back and forth on the screen.

"Damn! Player, honest man or whatever you are," Harry said sarcastically, *"You need be answering that, don't you?"*

Davonte gave him a crazy look out the corner of his eye, then answered his phone.

"Yes, Desiree baby, how can I help you?"

"I'll tell you how you can help me!" She snapped into the phone, *"First, you can stop taking so long to answer the phone when I call. I know my number comes up, so I know you know it's me. Secondly, I know you ain't left yet, so you need to be stopping by here before you do."*

As she spoke, Davonte's caller ID continued to blink with Angie's number on the screen.

"Okay baby," he said, *"I'll be by there before I leave."*

"You'd better Davonte. Don't just be telling me that to get me off the phone."

Davonte took a deep breath to calm himself.

As Desiree talked into the phone it dawned on him he had to drop Harry off, go by his place to get packed and make his way over to Desiree's before pulling out. It was already five p.m. So, that meant he'd be driving all night.

"Did you hear me?" Desiree questioned, interrupting his thoughts.

"Yeah, I hear you. Give me a minute and I'm on my way, alright? Now bye. I love you," he said quickly, hitting the end button, then send button to catch the other call.

Before he said a word Angie started in, *"Davonte you gonna stop letting the phone ring ninety times before you pick up. I'm sure you did that because you were unable to get a signal as you passed through some mountains on your way here, right?!?"*

"Not quite," Davonte told her, *"However, I'll be leaving out in a little bit and be on my way."*

"Damn!" Angie exclaimed with a sound of disappointment in her voice, *"You ain't even left yet? I mean that's really messed up."*

"Yeah, I know," Davonte said, picking up on her disappointment. *"But don't worry, when I get there I'm gonna make up for it."*

Angie liked the sound of that.

"Oh, are you?!?" She questioned, *"And just how are you going to do that?"*

"Don't worry about that," he told her, lowering his voice so not to be heard by Harry. *"You know Daddy got you. I'ma let you play with Big Ben and the twins all night."*

At the sound of his words and the thought of what he'd just told her, Angie's mouth began to water and she smiled on the other end of the phone.

"You better," she purred.

"Don't worry," Davonte assured her, *"I got you. Now let me go, so I can be on my way. I'll call you while I'm on the road. Okay?"*

"Okay," Angie said, *"And you'd better hurry up."*

"Alright, I will," Davonte told her, *"Now, bye. I love you."* Without waiting for a response, he hung up the phone.

"Well damn, Mr. Romance," Harry said, *"I see you got your two women, telling them you love them and all. Got them both thinking you on your way."*

Davonte paid Harry no mind, truth was, he would have been handled his business of being packed and stopping by to see Desiree had he not been fooling around with him all day ripping and running up and down the road.

"Let me ask you something," Harry said with a curious look on his face.

"Make it quick," Davonte told him, *"Cuz it's bout time to drop you off, I gots things to do."*

"Yeah, I hear you," Harry said, *"Drop me off, but not before we make one more stop and you take me by the Jamaican spot to get something to eat. You know I'm hooked on that red beans and rice with extra sauce."*

Davonte just looked at him while shaking his head. That's all Harry ever wanted to do, eat. And he ate too much, everyday, all day. Davonte watched how Harry rubbed his belly as he spoke on the beans and rice. Harry was only five-foot six inches, rather short for a man, but not a bad looking fellow. Dark complected with a goatee, he kept his haircut fresh and could dress decent. However, he weighed about two hundred and seventy pounds and the majority of his weight was in his stomach. Davonte figured if he would pay more attention to his health, he would more than likely not have problems with the ladies.

Unfortunately, Harry didn't give a care about his health and eating habits, and for that, he had to pay like he weighed.

"Did you hear me?" Harry asked.

"Nah," Davonte told him, *"What did you say?"*

"I said, how is it you feel you love both of them? Or are you running that straight player game on them?"

Davonte took a deep breath. Stopping at a red light, he looked over at Harry. He didn't really care for the question and the fact that Harry referred to his feelings for Desiree and Angie as some straight player crap, kinda pissed him off. Yet, he tried to overstand the mind state of the Black male in today's society, where being a player or a pimp was idolized in 2006 and black peoples minds were on some impoverished lifestyle from the 70's.

"Like I have told you before," he began, while staring directly into Harry's eyes, *"I do and very much so love Angie and Desiree both deeply. It's because of the two of them that I have a true peace of mind. Something that many a Black man do not have today. At no point do I take the relationship I have with the two of them lightly. They are who and what I need in order for my life to be complete."*

Harry watched as Davonte spoke and realized that his cousin was very serious about what he was saying. They had been hanging together since they were knee high, and he'd seen many a things Davonte had been through, and being honest with himself, he'd taken notice of the mental change that had taken place with Davonte the very moment he started seeing the two ladies. And the moment he told them of each other, it was like he'd gone up a notch as far as manhood was concerned. It worked for him, and he would simply respect that. Harry decided from this point on, he wouldn't question his cousins' feelings for the two ladies.

Tuning back into Davonte. He was finishing up his response to Harry's question.

"...So, all in all," Davonte said, *"I apologize if you don't overstand, but it is what it is. So if you would, just respect it."*

Harry was cool with what was said, he wasn't tripping in the first place, he just wondered how it was possible. Now, here Davonte sat looking at him waiting for a response and the light had changed green. The people in the car behind them had started blowing the horn.

"Alright player," Harry said, realizing Davonte wasn't planning on driving unless he gave a response. *"Now, go ahead and drive. No need to draw attention to us."*

Davonte took his foot off the break, put his foot on the gas and began easing forward. The Ford Explorer crept across the intersection. Davonte looked over at Harry wondering why he looked noided and made the comment about drawing attention.

"Alright cuz," Davonte spoke, *"I've got things to do, so we need be wrapping things up."*

"That's cool," Harry agreed, *"Let's make one more stop, grab some food and you can drop me off."*

"As long as this one more stop is close, we good," Davonte said. *"If not, you won't be making it."*

After Rubbing On her Vanilla Jasmine lotion from Bath & Body Works, Desiree stood up and slid into her red lace boy-cut panties from Victoria's Secret. She grabbed the matching top and slid it over her head while making her way over to the mirror that hung on the back of the bedroom door. Staring in the mirror, she couldn't help but to smile. Turning to get a look at her ass from the side she mumbled to herself, *"Bitch, you look good."*

The boy-cut panties fit lovely and rode perfectly above her hips as they allowed just enough of her lower ass to hang out the back. In the front you got a glimpse of her coochie hairs through the lace and the print of her lips showed up good. She observed how the lace top let you see her large nipples as she practiced a couple of seductive stances. Everything she had on (which wasn't much) was Davonte's favorite.

"A little lipstick and gloss and I'm set." Desiree had plans on wearing Davonte out when he got there, she didn't care what he was talking about. As soon as he came through the door she would be on him kissing, hugging and caressing. She knew he would more than likely put up a fuss, especially if he had to put in any work, so she had already done her leg stretches and prepared her vagina and stomach muscles. Desiree was going to ride Davonte like a wild bronco, getting hers and giving him his. Then, she planned on sucking him dry until there was nothing left.

"Maybe I can't stop you from going, but I guarantee it won't be much left to give her when you get there. Damn straight!" She snapped as she turned up a glass of Long Island Iced Tea. Searching on her dresser for her lipstick, she giggled knowing Davonte would be on his way soon and she'd be ready.

Angie Changed Her pillowcase then lay across the bed. She estimated that Davonte would take no longer than nine hours to arrive, which would make it 2 a.m. when he'd get there. She set her alarm clock for 11 p.m., figuring she would hit the grocery store, come back, take a power nap, wake up in time to study a little and do a couple menus in her homework assignment, straighten up a bit, take a nice hot bath, get sexy and be ready to get broke off by the man she loved so much.

Angie lay there thinking of Davonte. He was no doubt the most wonderful thing that had ever happened to her. The thought of him just sent chills down her spine. His words and guidance were all she needed to get her through. With these thoughts, she got up from the bed and slid into some jeans and a T-shirt. When Davonte got there she would not only have her way with him, but also awaiting will be his favorite meal; large jumbo shrimp simmered in a sherry and cheddar sauce with fresh spinach all tossed with linguine, just the way he liked it. She even decided that while she was out she'd pick up something new for the two of them, something nice, something sexy.

Davonte **D**rove **T**he white Ford truck quickly in and out of traffic, heading towards Harry's house in north Georgia in a little place called Sandy Springs. Harry sat in the passengers seat chewing on a piece of curried chicken listening to Davonte fuss about how he had taken up his whole day and put him behind on what he had to do.

All Harry could say was *"My fault, man."*

There were two things keeping him a little preoccupied to the point that he heard Davonte talking but wasn't listening to him. That was, the curried chicken and red beans and rice that sat on his lap, which he continued to wolf down barely chewing as he ate. The other thing was the car he noticed in the side-view mirror that had been following them, with what appeared to be two white men in it. As they slowed down to turn into Harry's apartment complex, the car sped up on the side of them and went speeding in front.

"What the hell they doing!?!" Davonte yelled as he pressed down on the horn to make the driver of the passing car aware of his disapproval. No sooner than he'd done that the car turned in front of him, cutting him off. Davonte slammed on the brakes and threw the truck in park, he reached for the door handle ready to jump out and curse out the reckless driver but before he could do that police cars with sirens blasting came from every imaginable direction. All you heard was guns clicking and cops yelling, *"Freeze! Put your hands where we can see them!"*

As they were pulled from the truck, Davonte repeatedly asked, *"What did we do??"* He looked over at Harry, who said absolutely nothing, he just stared at the spilled food on the ground. As they were both walked to separate police cars, Davonte gave Harry a quick glance and it was then that he realized that Harry had to have known what this was all about. In the back of the police car Davonte's cell phone began to ring. With hands cuffed behind his back, he twisted his body so he could get a peek at the screen, undoubtedly Angie, calling to see if he was on his way. And he was on his way all right, on his way to jail.

CHAPTER THREE

"DECISIONS, DECISIONS"

Davonte **S**at **A**cross the table handcuffed to a chair listening to a Drug Task Force detective run down how he and Harry had been followed most of the day. He couldn't believe what he was hearing. The detective laid out everywhere they had stopped and what had taken place, even the incident when he paused at the traffic light while talking to Harry.

"Well," the detective said. *"I'm sure you find this to be a bit overwhelming."*

Davonte said nothing, he simply nodded his head in agreement with the detectives words.

"However," the detective said as he leaned forward on the table, looking directly into Davonte's eyes, *"You can make this easy on yourself. You see, we know what Harry's been doing, we were going to bust him anyway. You just happened to come along at the wrong time, if you know what I mean?"* He added sarcastically. *"So what I'll be willing to do is cut you some slack if you just help us out a little bit, if you know what I mean?"*

Davonte sat looking at the detective thinking, *"Ain't this some shit! You gonna straight tell me, in so many words, you know I ain't have nothing to do with his dealings, yet you want me to tell?!"*

Truthfully, Davonte did know Harry hustled, but to what extent he didn't. During the whole time of running Harry around he didn't think to stop and ask him just what he was up to. Harry could have at least told him he was dirty. Although he felt played by Harry because he never told him what was up, deciding whether or not he was going to tell was a no brainer! Being from the streets he already knew, 'stick to the code by applying the rules' was the motto.

"Well officer, I don't think I'll be of any assistance to you. With that, you can let me go or take me to a cell."

The detective looked at Davonte for a moment before he spoke.

"Listen son, don't throw your life away behind this foolishness. Why don't you take a little time to think about it..."

Cutting him off, Davonte told him, *"There's nothing to think about. I'm unable to help. Unfortunately for you, if you know what I mean?"* Davonte added, giving him the same corny look of sarcasm he was given only a few moments ago.

"Suit yourself," the detective said, showing signs of temperament. *"In that case, you'll be charged as a co-conspirator with intent to distribute, among other drug related charges."*

Davonte's eyes became wide as he stared at the detective in disbelief.

"Hey, don't look at me all bug eyed," he said with a large mimicking smile on his face.

"It was your choice, now live with it."

After **B**eing **F**ingerprinted, psychologically screened and taking a brief medical exam, Davonte was finally placed in a cell amongst other inmates. It stunk and was so noisy that it was ridiculous. Some of the inmates were walking around in their boxers, some were doing push-ups, and one guy was sitting on the toilet taking a dump. The fact that the guy was in plain view wasn't too difficult to deal with, seeing they were in jail and it wasn't like the facility was going to put up some type of privacy partition. What blew the scene away for Davonte was how the guy on the toilet was holding a conversation with a guy who sat on the floor directly in front of him. The guy on the toilet even grunted here and there between words. Davonte dropped the worn out mat and blanket they'd given him on the floor and took a seat at the metal table that reminded him of a picnic table in a park. Carved into the table were all kinds of things, from gang names to Jack loves Jill, even scriptural quotes. One read John 3:16, "God so loved the world that he gave his only begotten son." Under it someone had carved, "If God loved the world so much, why doesn't he just get rid of the devil?"

"Damn," Davonte thought, *"That's harsh but a damn good question."* Davonte raised his head up from reading the writings and noticed a couple guys staring at him. It was his first time in jail, however, he wasn't scared. Instead of playing the game of staring each other down and mean mugging, Davonte allowed his thoughts to be occupied with how he was going to handle his present situation. As far as he saw it, he hadn't done anything and didn't deserve to be there.

The **P**hone **R**ang a second time before Desiree opened her eyes. She had fallen asleep awaiting Davonte. Moving her hand from between her legs in her panties, she sat up on the couch knocking over the half empty glass of Long Island iced tea as she did. Looking at the clock, she realized it was a little past 10 p.m. and immediately became pissed off. She just knew it was Davonte calling to tell her he had left out heading to Ohio without stopping by to see her. She reached for the phone ready to go off.

"Hello!" She snapped as she placed the receiver to her ear.

As the recording played letting her know it was a collect call from Davonte in jail, her anger began to mix with worry. She pressed 9 to accept the call.

"Desiree!?!" Davonte's voice came through the phone as the recording stopped.

"What's going on, why are you calling me from jail?"
Desiree asked, attempting to calm herself.

"Just be calm," Davonte said as he began telling her what
had taken place.

Desiree's eyes began to tear up as Davonte spoke. She
had no idea of what jail was like, she'd only heard rumors
and had occasionally watched the T.V. series "OZ", with
that she couldn't help but to think the worst.

As Davonte talked, a recording interrupted saying there
was one minute left on the call.

Desiree heard it and asked Davonte what it meant, he
informed her the phone calls were timed and only allowed
for 30-minute conversations.

She began stuttering as she realized the phone was about
to cut off and the man she loved so much was in jail.

*"C..c..call right back Davonte. R..r..right back, so you
can tell me what I need to do to help, what I need to do to
get you out of there."*

"Okay, just be cool, I'll call and we'll talk, okay?"

Before Desiree could respond, the phone cut off. She
hung up the receiver and leaned back on the couch instantly
feeling depressed. The thought of Davonte in jail was
unreal to her. Sure he was rough around the edges, but
jail!?! That surely wasn't a place for him.

Desiree thought of the conversations she would have with
the girls at work from time to time. Some of them had
dated guys who'd either went to jail, just got out of jail, or
were always in and out of jail.

They would say things like, *"Ain't nothing like getting a
piece from a brother fresh out."* Or how a brother in jail
would write letters and poems saying the sweetest things.
But what she remembered most were the more mature
females. They spoke of how it seemed like once a brother
started going to jail he couldn't stop. He would begin to be

unsuccessful in avoiding the traps and pitfalls of the system.

Desiree took a deep breath and told herself that wasn't the case with Davonte. She looked over at the clock, ten minutes had passed and Davonte hadn't called back yet. Wondering what was taking him so long she decided to call the jail and see what they were charging him with and what she could do to get him out.

Davonte **S**at **T**here in a slight dilemma, no sooner than he'd hung up the phone with Desiree, a voice came over the loud speaker announcing that the phones would be cut off in ten minutes.

"Just great!" He thought. He told Desiree he would call her right back, but now he also needed to call Angie and let her know what had taken place and that he wasn't on his way. Davonte figured it would be best to play fair and balance things out the way he always did with the two of them. He already called Desiree, and thought it only right to call Angie and let her know what was up. He'd just call Desiree back in the morning.

Angie **H**ung **U**p the phone and sat at the edge of her bed with tears streaming down her face. Davonte's collect call from jail was totally unexpected. Truthfully, she was so overwhelmed by the call, she couldn't quite get her bearings together enough to clearly grasp what Davonte was saying had taken place, causing him to end up in jail. She had questions, not only on what happened, but what should she do? Davonte couldn't be in jail, he was supposed to be on his way to see her, to be with her, so she could hold him, feed him, make love to him, feel him inside of her.

"This can't be real," she thought, *"It has to be a nightmare!"*

After **H**anging **U**p the phone, Davonte made his way over to a bare spot on the floor. He unrolled the thin piece of plastic that was to be used for a mat.

"How the hell these people keep locking people up," Davonte thought. *"And they ain't even got bunks to lay on. Got people laying on the floor."*

He covered the mat with a worn out sheet. As he lay back, he noticed the peering eyes along with a couple scrunched up faces trying to come across tough. Davonte didn't have time for whatever foolishness may have been going on through their minds.

"Don't start nothing and y'all niggas will be alright," Davonte thought to himself.

He hadn't been in such an environment before, however, he wasn't afraid. To the ladies, he may have come across as a sexy brother who was a little rough around the edges. His appearance at times caused many to underestimate him. Truth be told, Davonte was very intelligent and attractive, but had no problem throwing hands if the situation presented itself. His fight game was steps above average and many had learned that the hard way.

Davonte's motto was, *"I don't bother nobody, so the moment someone pushes my buttons, clock mode is a must. I'll do a Mike Tyson and bite a ear off,"* he laughed to himself. Refusing to let the silly thought remain, he placed his hands behind his head, stared up at the ceiling and began to think about his two ladies.

In the early stages, he used to go back and forth between the two of them, torn between the unique prodigious degrees of love they both showered him with. Often disappearing back and forth between the both of them for days at a time. These were his days of being mendacious; he never tried to completely convince himself that what he was doing was right. Yet, he didn't hesitate to justify it by telling himself it was all he could do at the time to keep the only two people who truly loved him.

Despite all the lies, Desiree knew there was someone else. She was nosey and would snoop through his things while he slept. She looked through everything from his wallet and pants pockets, to the glove compartment and trunk of his car. Occasionally finding receipts to hotels and restaurants she'd never been to and if she had been to either with him, the dates didn't match up. There were even purchases for lingerie that she never saw. She wouldn't say anything direct, only asked questions here and there in a roundabout way. That's when he would take it upon himself to become a prevaricator.

However, enough became enough, when she decided one day to give him a special treat and hook him up. After going through silly little changes to get his pants down, she found lipstick stains on his boxers. Not to mention on a pair she bought. Someone else had beaten her to the pleasurable task of draining the honey dripper. That was the last straw for Desiree. She let it be known he needed to be coming clean on what had been transpiring.

Basically, she already knew. Now, it was time to hear it from his mouth.

He remembered like it was yesterday, what she said.

"Tell me who she is and what's up between the two of you. It's the least you could do, since you got us both drinking from the same pipe."

Now Angie, she knew, or she assumed for some time, but didn't have the nerve to go through his things as Desiree did. However, she had no problem asking him on a regular basis was there anyone else.

That's when he would kiss her softly, gently, with pure passion and tell her, *"No, there's no one else. I love you."*

Her heart would tell her one thing, her mind would say something altogether different. She wanted to believe him so she did. Her heart, along with the raw fire and energy he put into making love to her caused Angie to believe he loved her dearly and that she was the only one (imagine). Love her dearly, he did, and with all his heart, but the only one she wasn't.

After the lipstick encounter and the continuous questioning from Desiree, along with innocent look of love and desire in Angie's eyes, he decided to tell them both the truth.

An argument broke out between two other guys and the clamor interrupted Davonte's thought of his two beautiful women. That's when he decided he'd better get some sleep. They would be calling him out for court in the morning. He figured they'd give him a public defender, better known as a public pretender. Whatever the case, he was aware they had nothing on him because he'd honestly done nothing, so he should be let go or given a very low bond that would allow him to get out. With those thoughts, he took a deep breath and drifted off to sleep.

Angie Sat With her hands in her lap, thinking of the long distance call she'd made to the county jail in Georgia where Davonte was being held. The jail clerk gladly gave her whatever information she wanted to know about Davonte's situation. Even volunteered information that another female by the name of Desiree calling. That pissed Angie off. Not that the lady told her Desiree called, but the fact that Desiree had called before her, meaning Davonte called her first. Angie had intentions of letting him know how she felt about that when he called again. As she sat on the side of her bed, the thought of Davonte being in jail began to really eat at her. Then it hit her, the question of, was she the blame? He asked her to come get him. Had she gone, she would have arrived early in the morning and no sooner than she'd got there they would have left. Therefore, he wouldn't have ended up riding around with his cousin and going to jail. But instead, she said, *"No."* No to going to get the man she loved. Now he was not only not on his way, but also in jail. Angie laid her hands upon her face and began to cry hard as she placed blame on herself for Davonte's misfortune.

Desiree **M**ade **H**er way across the courthouse parking lot. Her face showed signs of no sleep, the look of fatigue was accompanied by signs of sadness.

Davonte's court hearing only lasted five minutes and was in no way what they expected. Climbing into her car and shutting the door, she looked at herself in the rear view mirror.

"Pull it together," she said under her breath in an audible tone. Things have to be taken care of. Davonte's truck has to be gotten out of the police pound. Desiree sat thinking, should she wait to get the truck out on her payday, which wasn't until the end of next week. Quickly, she decided against that thought, realizing if she waited that long it would be that much more costly. Instead, she told herself she'd get it after work. Besides, she would need another person to drive her car.

Starting her car up and putting it in drive, she figured she would be able to have things worked out by the time she got off.

"What's Up Man? So, how'd it go?" A couple guys in the cell asked as Davonte returned and made his way over to his mat on the floor. Although his face didn't show it, he was furious on the inside.

"How in the hell these knuckle heads gonna ask me anything concerning my situation?" Nosey people, he couldn't stand them.

And how in the hell was the judge going to deny him a bond? Talking about 'further investigations of the case'. Then, gonna tell him he was more than welcome to come back in 90 days for another bond hearing.

"Ain't that about nothing?!?" He thought as his anger fueled even more as he tried to figure out what the hell his cousin had gotten him into. Ninety days, what was he supposed to do in jail for ninety days? And what about his truck note? Rent at the apartment?

"Mutha fuck," Davonte thought, laying back staring at the same spot on the ceiling he stared at the night before, noticing a nasty piece of dried toilet paper, someone slapped up there. He began brainstorming, something he had always been good at. Davonte remembered when he would get into tight situations, his mother would tell him, *"I ain't gonna help you, for what?!? You do your best when you're under pressure."*

And ironically he did, every time. He smiled for a second as he thought of the old cliché, "Mother knows best." No sooner than the smile had come across his face, it was gone. His mind was racing with thoughts. Thoughts jumped back and forth from the financial responsibilities he had, to the two women he loved.

Desiree was here and Angie was far away, *"Not a good combination,"* he told himself. Whatever the case, he made himself a promise that he'd have things figured out by the next morning.

Davonte Let Three days pass before he decided to contact Desiree and Angie. He told himself he had a lot of thinking to do in order to handle the situation. Truth be told, he was drunk from what had taken place and slipped into a brief depression. He snapped back into reality when an inmate trustee who was responsible for sweeping the floors throughout the jail brought him a note from his cousin.

It read, *"Just hang in there, we'll have to wait it out. Don't worry, they have nothing."*

He didn't know how to take the note seeing that he already knew they had nothing on him from the start.

During the course of his brainstorming, he came to a rather absurd idea to keep and maintain his belongings and financial obligations. However, as far-fetched as it seemed, it was the most logical thing he could think of. Davonte decided to bring Desiree and Angie together. Actually, letting them not only meet in person, but possibly live together. It would help out all three of them. Now, he was well aware that the two of them may find it abstruse at first. However, he was determined to work them through it and past whatever they thought they may not overstand. He would have to stay at them until they were able to see the big picture.

Davonte knew it wouldn't be an easy task. He also knew he had to come correct and on point when he presented the idea to them. Because as the saying goes, *"How you start is how you'll end up."*

Exactly how he would do things, was a good question and a careful decision to be made. They talking without him around meant the opening up of a can of worms. He knew once he started this and gave the green light, he had no control over how things may turn out. Not from jail anyway – or did he?!?

*"**What The Fuck!** Davonte, do you hear yourself? I mean do you really hear yourself?"*

Davonte paused before he spoke again.

"Baby, just think about it. It will make things easier on all of us for now."

"How!?" Desiree snapped. *How in the hell do you figure that?"*

"Financially," Davonte responded, *"Plus it'll give the two of you a chance to get to know each other and possibly become good friends."*

Davonte stopped talking and thought for a second on whether he should have said these last words. Not sure if them being close is really what he wanted at this time.

"Oh well," he told himself, *"You done said it now."*

"Listen, Davonte," Desiree began to speak slowly, calmly. *"I love you. God knows I do, I mean, with all my heart. At times I've even asked myself what would I do without you, or if I could even live without you? Over the years, you have asked me some very tripped out things, from would I do a threesome to whether or not I was willing to die for you? All was taken into consideration. Now, in being honest I never thought on ever really coming face to face with those situations. When you first told me about you and Angie's dealings, I was pissed. I already knew there was someone else, let's just say my woman's intuition has yet to fail me. In respect of your honesty and finally coming clean with it, I accepted it. It was hard, trust me, it was and at times it still is. Yet, I deal with it by telling myself things like… At least he came clean with it, he could've been like other men who claim to be players, but are actually cheaters because the women they deal with never know of one another. I also tell myself, maybe it won't last long. She's just some female he done come across and having a fling with. It's been over a year now, but hey, I still have my hopes. Like I said these are ways I deal with it, as if that's not hard enough. Now, here you are asking me to not only attempt to become 'close friends' with the 'other woman', but to also allow her to move into my house with me. Now, Davonte if I may say so myself, and I must, that's some shit! And on top of that, of course if you don't mind I would like to ask you, **Who the fuck do you think I am!?"***

"You have one minute left," the recording announced before Davonte could answer her question, not that he really had a response at the moment.

"Well, look babe," he spoke sweetly, *"The phone is about to hang up. If you would please, just think about it."*

"I've thought about it, Davonte!" Desiree snapped.

"Well, think about it some more please and I'll call you later, okay?!? I love you, bye."

Just as he'd gotten the words out, the phone hung up. The thirty-minute collect calls from jail were something Davonte was going to have to get used to. Every time it seems you're about to get into a good conversation, its time to hang up.

Although Desiree hung up the phone slowly, calmly, her heart rate was well above normal.

"The nerve of that nigga."

Desiree made her way over to her little home bar, grabbed a glass and the bottle of Long Island Iced Tea. Setting the glass on the coffee table, she flopped down on the couch and screwed the top off the bottle. Holding the bottle up, she took notice of it being half full.

"Oh, to hell with it," she mumbled as she turned the bottle up to her mouth and began downing its contents.

"*It's Whatever You want, Davonte*," Angie said with very little enthusiasm in her voice.

"It's like I have always told you, if it makes you happy then I'm with it. You just need to make sure you have it all figured out, so it goes the way you want it to. Also, I'll be finished with school and graduating in a matter of weeks, at which time, I'll be..." Angie paused as it suddenly dawned on her that Davonte would be unable to attend her college graduation. Not only was he very supportive and for that she felt that he deserved to be there, but now she would be in a situation where her family would be

expecting him to be there and what she was going to tell them about his whereabouts, she had no idea. The thought of him not being there caused her to feel sad and pissed off at the same time.

"Helllooo, are you there?" Davonte asked, wondering what warranted the sudden moment of silence.

"Yeah, I'm here," Angie said.

"Well," Davonte told her, *"You can continue with what you were saying."*

"I was saying, once I graduate I'll be looking to move, so you need to have things together however you gonna have them." Angie's thoughts took over again.

"Davonte!" she snapped, *"How you gonna up and go to jail now! And I hope to God you're not blaming me. I mean true enough, had I come and got you, you may not have ended up there, but I just hope you're not turning this into being my fault."*

Truthfully, Davonte hadn't looked at it that way but now listening to Angie and knowing her the way he did, it was clear to him she was placing blame on herself whether he was or not.

"First of all," Davonte said slowly and calmly, making sure he had her attention. *"I would greatly appreciate if you wouldn't yell while speaking to me, I haven't done anything to you to deserve that..."*

"You're right," Angie told him, *"I'm sorry baby. I'm just upset over this and..."*

"As I was saying," Davonte interrupted realizing had he not, Angie would have undoubtedly went on an emotional tangent.

"Sure, had you come to get me this more than likely would not have happened, but seeing that it has, it is now necessary to go about devising a plan to make sure things turn out okay, do you hear me?" Davonte asked, placing emphasis on the last words.

"Yes!" Angie quickly responded.

"Well then," Davonte responded. *"It's as simple as that. I'll arrange for you and Desiree to speak on the phone in order for the two of you to get a feel for one another. Got it?"*

"Okay, Davonte," Angie solemnly responded. *"You just need to make sure that at no point am I in danger."*

"Don't worry, I would never place you in harm's way. Desiree is sweet and nice like you and I truly think that once you two talk everything will be fine. Hell, ya'll might even become the best of friends."

"I hear you, 'best of friends'," Angie said with a scrunched up face and in a tone that faded before getting the words all the way out. The two of them slipped into their thoughts, causing a brief silence. Angie thought of how much she loved Davonte and how she would do anything for him, while Davonte thought on whether he was making the correct decision for the three of them. He was trying to get them to see the bigger picture as far as working together for a common goal, which at this point was to help maintain his material possessions, as well as, getting their finances in order so they could save up to get him out on bond, if that was needed. The automated recording came on interrupting both of their thoughts.

"Baby," Angie said in a melancholy tone.

"I'm here," Davonte answered.

"It said we had one minute." When Angie said that it made Davonte want to break out like "duhhh!" but instead he remained calm, wondering if she thought he had failed to hear the recording.

"Yeah babe, I heard it." Angie hated the recording coming on and signaling that they only had one minute left to talk, one minute left on the phone with her precious baby.

"So, are you calling back?" she eagerly questioned wanting to know if she was going to get to continue to talk to the man she loved.

"Maybe a little later babe, I'ma get some rest," Davonte told her. Angie became instantly saddened by his response.

"So, you don't want to talk to me?" Davonte took a deep breath, aware of her need to talk to him.

"It's not that," he said, knowing there could only be seconds left on the call he hurriedly told her, *"Just think on what we talked about, okay? I love you."*

"I will, and I..." the phone cut off before she could finish *"...love you too,"* she said softly to no one.

Though They Both sat in their individual spaces in the world, they each shared in the same line of thought. Desiree was unable to believe what was being asked of her by Davonte, yet she knew very well that he was serious about his request and would be looking for an answer the next time they talked. He was like that, when he wanted something he wanted it *NOW*, no ifs, ands or buts. That aggressive thinking and lack of patience is what kept Desiree telling him time and time again, *"Don't cut your nose off to spite your face."* Now, whether or not he listened was a horse of a different color.

Angie stared off into space. She continued to beat herself up mentally for not going to get Davonte, now here he was in jail, locked up away from her. She took a deep breath and shrugged her shoulders.

"Don't worry baby, I'ma do what you want and need me to do in order to show you how much I love you." With that said her mood changed, knowing she would once again make Davonte happy by doing what he asked.

Davonte sat on his mat on the floor thinking of the conversation he'd shared with his ladies. Now that the seed was planted he only needed to help it grow and he was convinced that he most definitely would, he just hoped he had made the right move.

Knowing that Desiree could be difficult at times, she became his main concern in the matter. Angie just wanted to be assured that no matter what, everything would be alright between them. She oftentimes lived in an optimistic world created in her own mind, which at times could be good, but also could be dangerous.

Davonte's stomach began to make bubbly noises, which reminded him of the fact that he hadn't had a bowel movement in three days. He looked over at the toilet then looked around the cell at the other guys who occupied it. Some were sleeping, others reading books or writing letters. A devilish grin came across his face as he began rubbing his stomach while getting up and making his way to the toilet. There was no doubt that he was constipated, still he was about to blow it up and knew it.

"What better way to break the guys in," He thought to himself.

CHAPTER FOUR

"SEDUCTIVE PERSUASSION"

Davonte **L**aid **O**n his mat and crossed a line through the four other lines he had made on the wall by him. The five lines represented another week that had passed since he'd been in jail. He'd been there a month now and each time he made a line at the end of the day he became that much angrier. The fact that his cousin did nothing more than send him notes telling him to 'hold on' and 'be patient' didn't help any. His plan with Angie and Desiree was almost spoiled. Desiree got his truck out of the impound for him which he was thankful for. However, with the situation at hand he had thought no more of it.

Desiree cunningly waited two weeks before springing her little surprise on him. He had been running his little spiel on her about how cool things would be with her and Angie, then out of nowhere Desiree asked him, *"So when were you going to tell me your truck is in her name or is it hers?"*

The question had caught him off guard. Davonte had forgotten to mention it, more so on purpose. At the time, he didn't feel that the conversation about the truck was of any importance, what he had overlooked was the fact that he was dealing with a black woman and anything, at anytime concerning her man and another woman was of the greatest importance. Desiree let it be known as she snapped and went off on a tangent about how she didn't appreciate him and Angie keeping secrets from her. Davonte realized that it wasn't the time for a foolish pretext, so he simply told her how he had had the money to put down on it but the lot was giving him a hassle about his credit. Though it wasn't bad, he didn't have enough credit history, so Angie had come through for him and put her name on it so he wouldn't miss out on the deal on the truck.

It took Desiree a minute to calm down, but she did. Once she had, she and Davonte got right back to business at hand, her and Angie coming together. He had been speaking back and forth to each of them about the other, telling them both how they had said nice things about the other and how one was looking forward to meeting the other. Truth be told, neither of them had said such. In fact, when he told one what the other had supposedly said, all he would get from either was a *"Hhmmm"* or *"I hear you"*. It was this that caused him to go inside himself, he had to keep in mind that he was dealing with women and not just any women at that, but the world renown, most sought after –black women.

Black women are very much mental and there hasn't been one yet who didn't like to be challenged mentally. The 'big game' is what they are all secretly after. Davonte decided he would be just that, even from where he was. It was all a matter of keeping them in check and focused on him while he figured out which direction he would take things. Would he come off as a Puritan, making himself one to extol or should he deal with them in a less graceful manner? Whatever the case, he would take their mind away from the reality of where he was and create a more pleasurable vision they could enjoy. At least until he could return home to them. Davonte wasn't sure what force was driving him to entertain the thoughts he was having, but he was sure it had to be love along with his refusal to lose either of them.

"Yeah, that's what it is," he told himself. *"I can't let this place take them or in any way cause me to lose them."*

Davonte sat totally consumed in his thoughts on what his next move would be. He couldn't wait to call and have them both on the phone. This would allow him to determine just how possible his plan would be. The way they interact would surely tell it all.

Davonte **S**at **H**olding the phone listening to Angie and Desiree talk. When he first called Desiree and had her call Angie on the three-way, the conversation started out rather slow. However, Davonte kept at it, initiating different topics for discussion. Finally, after having Desiree call Angie back two more times, they opened up and began asking this and that about one another. Job related questions, age, more so the normal 'feel a person out' questions. Which was all that was needed for Angie, she was one to talk. It was as if she liked to hear herself talk, that's how much she talked once she got started. On top of that, she was eager to please Davonte by trying to make things work out between her and Desiree.

Davonte's eyes scanned the sixteen-man cell that unfortunately, at the time, held twenty-nine men. He took notice of the cell door opening up and inmate number thirty was making his way in. He was a tall fellow, about 6'4" and though he was very slender, his shoulders were noticeably broad. There was a look about him that said he wasn't the average-thinking man, whatever he knew, showed on his face. His walk was more of a smooth glide and a look of confidence showed in the smile he wore, with his hair pulled back in a ponytail. He was a clean brotha.

The man quickly took notice of Davonte noticing him, they locked eyes for a moment and before breaking the gaze, the man greeted Davonte by giving him the head nod that all brothas were only too familiar with, the one that simply said 'what's up?' Davonte returned the nod and proceeded in listening to Desiree and Angie's one-sided conversation.

The recording broke in interrupting Angie's, *"I remember one time..."* speech and announced the end of another phone call.

"Davonte you calling back?" Desiree asked.

"Yeah, baby, you calling back?" Angie added.

Davonte thought for a second, then decided he'd let things go a little further.

"No, I'm not going to call back, why don't you two go ahead and talk some more without me? I'll call back tomorrow, okay?"

"You sure?" Desiree asked.

Angie didn't know what to say.

"Yeah, I'm sure," Davonte responded. *"I'm also sure the two of you may have some things you'd like to talk about without me."*

Desiree held the phone to her ear not saying a word but nodding her head up and down.

"Sure as hell do," she thought to herself.

"Well, the phone will be cutting off any second now, I'll talk to you two later."

"Okay baby, I love you," Angie said with sheer happiness in her voice.

Her words caught Desiree off guard, *"I love you!?! What the hell!!"* She thought.

"I love you too," Davonte told her. *"And I love you too, Desiree."* Noticing the hesitance in her response he asked Desiree did she hear him.

Still stuck on the thought of Angie saying she loved him, she simply blurted out, *"Yeah, okay, bye."* The phone hung up. Davonte could tell from her tone that Desiree wasn't with Angie saying she loved him.

"Oh well," he thought, *"It'll be something she'll have to get used to."*

Before walking away from the phone he searched his thoughts for his reasoning, he questioned what he had done and wondered whether or not he would regret letting them talk so soon without him there to mediate. It was an act of foolish boldness but he was willing to wait patiently to see how things played out.

"Well, well, well," the gentleman who had just arrived said. *"Looks like you're entertaining thoughts in my field of expertise."*

Davonte looked at the man sitting at the table and wondered what his deal was. Everyone who had come through the door in the last few weeks, himself included, wasn't much for socializing when they first arrived. It was a matter of being drunk off of the reality of where they were, at least for a few days. But not this gentleman, instead he sat at the table as if all was good and this was no set back for him.

"So, am I right?" He asked Davonte with a big smile on his face.

"About what?" Davonte questioned coming across nonchalant.

"About your thoughts, young blood. I'm right about your thoughts, ain't I? They're down the lines of my profession."

"And just what might your profession be?" Davonte asked, feeling a little slighted at the idea of the gentleman picking him to talk to out of all the people in the cell. If the man had intentions of probing, he surely wasn't in the mood for it.

"Women!" The man responded proudly in a bold manner. *"I specialize in the ladies."*

"And what makes you think that's where my thoughts were?" Davonte asked the man as he began to walk towards his mat on the floor, not really caring to chit-chat.

"Let's just say I've been around and in my travels I've come to learn there's only one thing that causes a man,

especially a young man, to think so hard his forehead wrinkles and that's a woman."

"And what makes you an expert on such an issue, or as you say 'a professional'!?! Davonte said, attempting to mimic the guy.

The gentleman placed his elbows on the table and took a couple of mental notes on Davonte's demeanor. He once again brandished his signature smile and responded to his new pupil, *"I guess you could say I am a man of leisure."*

"A what?" Davonte questioned more from the fact that he didn't quite hear him, not because he didn't overstand.

"I'm a man of leisure," he gladly repeated.

Davonte gave him a quick glance with a raised eyebrow. *"Could you be a little more terse?"* Davonte asked him, causing the man to look at him, only now he wore the raised eyebrow.

"Concise," Davonte explained, realizing he didn't overstand his terminology.

"You know, a little more layman!"

"Dig that!" The gentleman thought to himself as he began rubbing his chin. *"The young man has a little vernacular about himself."*

"A little more layman you say? Okay, try this on for size young blood, I'ma pimp!"

Angie And Desiree spent their weekend calling each other on the phone. Desiree called the most, seeing her phone plan consisted of free unlimited long distance. At first it had started out a bit rocky, Desiree caught Angie off guard with her first question.

"So, when did ya'll start fucking?" Desiree asked.

Angie tried to act as though she wasn't surprised, however, she wasn't sure just how she should go about answering the question. Being a female herself and knowing exactly where Desiree was headed with the questioning, Angie attempted to keep things kosher. She had told herself she would do that for Davonte. It was a matter of finding a timeframe close to when he had told them about one another so it didn't look so bad. Although she knew Davonte had been laying it to the both of them for some time before he fessed up to it. For some reason she didn't care, to her another woman was a small thing to deal with when it came to Davonte. To her, he was beautiful and just what a woman wanted in a man. He was intelligent, attractive and every time she thought of how he would sex her, she would cream her panties.

Davonte **H**adn't **C**alled all weekend. This was done intentionally knowing it would cause them to continue to call each other and talk more if for no other reason but to milk one another for information. It would either push them apart or begin to bring them closer. Hopefully, it was the latter of the two.

Davonte **S**at **B**ack on his mat patiently waiting for one of the two guys to get off either of the phones. He had a sneaky grin on his face that he wasn't even aware of due to his thoughts concerning the conversation he was going to have with his two ladies he loved so dearly. Some of his ideas were undoubtedly a bit much, however, at this point after talking to the pimp who went by the name 'Mr. Wonderful', he felt he had no choice but to step his game up. Mr. Wonderful had begun by breaking down what he claimed were 'The Golden Rules' never to be forgotten by a true player.

Davonte recalled Mr. Wonderful's words, *"A pimp should always keep his emotions to himself. Realize this young blood... as a pimp, you just a bitch that has reversed the game. Make sure you come across as Prince Charming to dem broads. They should think you're god. No matter what, young blood, control the whole female. It's important that you be the boss of her life, even her thoughts. It's what she wants anyway, please believe! Always be serious with dem there split backs, ya dig?"*

Sometimes, Davonte felt Mr. Wonderful's words were a bit harsh, yet as he continued to talk, Davonte continued to listen.

"Don't forget to use a great deal of pressure, they need it. That's what keeps them moving. If they fine, pretty females young blood, you got to keep your game tight cause they gonna try you. They gonna look for that weakness. The way you start with her is the way you'll end with her. Pimp hard from the start. If you chase a female you get a weak one, if you stalk her you get a strong one. Find out what makes them tick."

Mr. Wonderful went on and on for the entire weekend.

"Last but not least, remember, there isn't a female you can't live without. It's like a game of chess baby, think before you move."

After all that, he had asked Davonte if he overstood his words. Davonte let him know that he overstood well, however, he wasn't trying to become a pimp. He just wanted to keep the two ladies he loved. When Davonte told him that, Mr. Wonderful burst out with laughter. He laughed so hard his eyes teared up and he caused other men in the cell to begin laughing too, although, they had no ideal what they were laughing for. As though he had an automatic switch to turn the laughter off, Mr. Wonderful stopped and became real serious. He looked at Davonte with piercing eyes and began to speak slowly.

"It don't matter if the relationship is girlfriend/boyfriend, husband/mutha fuckin' wife, them funky cunt broads is all the same, so you make sure you apply the rules when dealing with them. Even if you have to play things out in your mind and not tell them a damn thang. You make sure

you establish the pimp/hoe relationship if ya don't, you'll wish you had."

As one of the phones became available Davonte made his way over. The words Mr. Wonderful said continued to permeate Davonte's mind. He was from the streets and had heard the rumors about pimps and how they got down when it came to their women. Now, he had met one face to face.

As Davonte picked up the phone and started to dial Desiree's number, he knew he would use some of the rules to what Mr. Wonderful referred to as 'Whoreology 101'. He told himself he had a plan of his own and that he wasn't trying to become a pimp. Even though the thought of it sent chills down his spine. The phone rang in his ear and the last thought that went through Davonte's mind before Desiree picked up were the words of Mr. Wonderful saying, *"You have to be Prince Charming to dem. Control not just their bodies but also their mutha fuckin thoughts!"*

"Hey, hold up!" Desiree said, cutting into Angie's conversation, *"That's Davonte calling on the other line."* Desiree clicked over, she didn't wait for the recording to announce it was a collect call she quickly pushed the button to accept.

"Thank you for using Correctional Billing, go ahead with your call," the automated recording instructed.

Davonte hadn't called all weekend and although Desiree was mad about that, she was equally glad to hear from him.

"Hey negro, why you just now calling?" Davonte purposely paused for a second before talking, he took a deep breath, smiled and dove right in.

"Hey baby," He spoke smoothly, calmly. *"How's my sexy brown lady with her beautiful self?"* The words, the tone, Desiree felt her self melt on the inside.

"F..f..fine," she stammered.

Davonte held the phone tightly up against his ear, listening intently to Desiree. He heard her swallow; her mouth was watering. The words had caught her off guard. From that, Davonte was in control and they both knew it. That's where he wanted to be and subconsciously it was where Desiree wanted him.

She held the phone to her ear waiting for the words that would follow that seducing hello, the words that made her melt even more and caused her to hand her heart and mind over to Davonte to do whatever he damn well pleased.

"Listen baby... Are you listening?" Davonte asked. Desiree didn't say a word, but indeed she was listening. Davonte didn't hear a response, although on the other end Desiree was slowly shaking her head 'yes'. Davonte wasn't waiting for an answer anyway as he continued.

"Sweetheart, baby, this is how it's gonna be..."

Angie **W**alked **A**round in her room getting clothes out and preparing for the next day. There was an air of excitement about her. She'd just got off the phone with Davonte and Desiree. They'd talked on the phone for three hours. Angie found it to be an interesting phone conversation. Davonte had them share with him how things had gone with the two of them talking on the phone over the weekend. They both agreed that at first it was somewhat awkward, but they got over it.

"Yeah," Angie said, *"For you, we put aside whatever ill feelings we may have had based on sharing our man and made it work."*

"That's right," Desiree added. *"We did it for you."*

Once they filled him in on their weekend chitchat, he proceeded in letting them know what would be what with the three of them. It was what he told them and how he delivered it that made Angie so excited. Davonte always had something different, something new for her. Along with keeping her living on the edge of life, he kept her feeling as though she was floating on a cloud. Angie loved how Davonte kept her mind stimulated in one way or another with something new, something so out of the norm. He had her asking questions and entertaining the thought of things that had never crossed her mind before. For her, it was a thrill to be with Davonte and today's conversation proved to make things even more tantalizing for her.

Desiree Turned The lamp off on her glass nightstand beside the bed and slid under the cover. *"Davonte",* that was her thought. The conversation the three of them had was something else. He'd never ceased to amaze her over the years. He has spoken to her about some of everything, from starting businesses to selling drugs, having threesomes and a whole lot more. Desiree had simply looked at it as part of his creative and incredibly vivid imagination. It was very seldom that he actually opted to do any of it except the times he attempted to start his own businesses. The carpet cleaning company was a good idea, he just couldn't keep up with the clientele by himself and he needed more equipment to handle the bigger jobs. Then there was the home remodeling which was fine until he installed some faulty wiring and a ceiling fan caught a lady's bedroom on fire. Then there was the escort service, which for some reason he felt she should be the first employee. Yeah, Davonte was something else and he knew it too. But, this latest ordeal may possibly top them all. Being able to finally become acquainted with Angie, her man's *other* woman, was cool and it was about time. But she had to admit the conversation he injected into them in the last hour of their phone call was something else and with her knowing him the way she did, there was no doubt in her mind that he had already planned and mapped it out in his head. What tripped Desiree out even more was how she was willing to go through with it. Was it him, the way he presented his ideas for their arrangement, or what? She wasn't very sure, but in the back of her mind something had her thinking strongly about it. Even though she had led Davonte to believe she was reluctant to do so. *"Davonte"*, she thought once again. *"The man I love. Check that out."*

Davonte **L**aid **B**ack on his mat thinking of the phone conversation he just shared with his ladies. Initially, upon calling them he wasn't too sure about how things were going to go seeing that it would be based on how well they had gotten along with their phone calls. When he finally called them he took notice that throughout the phone call they would both quickly agree on things as well as a couple times they called themselves teaming up on him. That's when he knew it was all to the good. Davonte had listened to the girls talk back and forth, it was moreso idle conversation than anything else. He could tell that by allowing them to talk over the weekend without him it caused them to open up to each other. They told him they were willing to get along basically for him and to make things easier considering the present situation. Since things had come this far, them talking on the phone and all, Davonte suggested they should hang out and get to know how each other was in person.

"How we gonna do that?" Desiree asked. *"She in Ohio and I'm in Georgia."*

"Yeah baby," Angie had added. *"How we gonna work that out?"*

Davonte responded quickly, *"Angie, you gonna drive down next weekend and spend three days at the house with Desiree."*

"Damn," Desiree thought, *"How he gonna tell her to just up and drive seven hundred and some-odd miles to hang out with me for the weekend."*

"Davonte, tell me something," Desiree inquired. *"First of all, how you know she doesn't have things to do next*

*weekend? Second of all, even if she don't, how you know
she wants to spend it driving on the highway for hours?"*

*"Because I know her schedule, as well as, I know she'll
do what I ask her. Right Angie?!?"*

Without any hesitation Angie responded, *"Yes baby! As
long as my money is straight for gas, I'll be there."*

Now, although Desiree had just heard for herself
Davonte's suggestion for Angie and Angie's willing
response, there was something about it that came across a
little strange to her. From there the conversation between
them all continued on. They discussed different things,
from Davonte being in jail to Angie being in the last couple
weeks of school. It was when Desiree said she couldn't
wait until Davonte returned home that the conversation
made a complete and unexpected change in direction. At
least it was unexpected for Desiree and Angie, for Davonte
it was exactly the direction he wanted it to go.

Desiree went into what she was going to do once he came
home, she spoke of a hot bath, cooking for him, a massage
and how she was going to jump his bones giving him the
ride of his life until they both came heavily.

Angie listened and decided she was not going to be
outdone, she boldly went straight to telling them how she
was going to caress and stroke Davonte's manhood with
her lips and tongue until he released his whole load and at
that point she would drink it all up.

"That's right, the honeydripper's all mine!"

Davonte listened while they went back and forth about
what they were going to do. Cutting them off in the middle
of their erotic 'I'ma do this, I'ma do that' spat. He told
them, *"How about that, it sounds to me that the two of you
may be in need of some sexual healing."*

Thinking on what he said, Angie realized she was
somewhat horny and had been holding back on the thought
of it so she wouldn't put her finger to work and play with

herself. She wanted to save it all for Davonte's return home. She had already imagined him bringing it all out on her; his skilled technique with his massive tool would surely cause her river to overflow multiple times.

Desiree couldn't help but to also realize her sexual pent up frustration. It was then that she took note of how spoiled Davonte had her. Hitting her off at least 4-5 times a week with no questions asked and if through the week 'she behaved herself', as he put it, he had no problem with dropping a marathon performance on her at least once during the weekend. Which was fine with her, because it usually took a hot bath with aromatherapy candles and a half-day of sleep to re-coup from those.

Davonte was an animal with a large pipe and an enormous sexual appetite, which led to some all out hot sweaty funky nights. Some nights ended with some of everything from her hair being sweated out and matted to her face, to strawberries and chocolate being smeared on the mattress since the sheets popped off. Hell, one Sunday evening things got so wild they had started in the kitchen but woke up on the bathroom floor. Their clothes made a trail from one end of the house to the other. The couch somehow, was pushed away from the wall, a chair from the dining room table was turned over in the hallway. Davonte felt bad about that night, he had went to town on Desiree causing her coochie lips to swell to the point that they appeared to be inside out. She had to wear a pad and wasn't even near being on her period. Desiree came off as one of those 'supposed to be' quiet good girls, truthfully a closet freak on the low. However, Davonte brought it all out to the fullest, he caused her long legs to experience the shakes on plenty of occasions.

It had now been a month or better and Desiree hadn't had any of 'Big Ben and the twins'. She hadn't had to go that long since they had been together, maybe a week, if things were hectic in their schedules, or maybe two weeks if he was upset with her for some reason. In those cases, knowing how it would be once he got over his anger made it worth the wait.

Desiree and Angie both sat on the phone silent, panties becoming soaked from their thoughts before Davonte continued on.

"So, I take it I'm correct? The two of you could use a little nookie?!?"

Desiree answered first, *"Yeah, right about now a sister could stand for a warm embrace."*

"Shhhiit!" Angie exclaimed. *"Some mutha fuckin dick is what would hit the spot! Your dick, that is."*

"For real!" Desiree had agreed.

"Damn, I'm sorry ladies," Davonte replied, sounding sincere at the moment. *"I'm in here and ya'll out there needing to release. Ya'll know, if I was there, how I would do it?!?"*

As they listened, he poured on about how he would do different pleasure-delivering techniques to them both using the right words to create a vivid picture in their minds. His narration caused a rise in their nipples and a throbbing pulsation in the love button between their thighs. His words turned them both on to the point that Desiree was lying on the bed on her stomach with a pillow between her legs softly grinding away. And Angie, she simply slid her panties off, laid back and put her hand between her legs and began probing her finger in and out of her hairy snatch.

Davonte knew them both and knew them well. As he spoke, he was positive that not only were they visualizing what he was saying but they were also, in one way or another, doing something to tease their own little pussies. Knowing that was how far he had taken them, out of nowhere he said, *"Just think of if the two of you hooked up and took care of one another?"*

Angie held the phone to her ear as a devilish grin came across her face, she shook her head as if to say, 'no he didn't!'.

It took a moment for Desiree to catch on to what he was saying, even once she did, she wasn't sure if she'd heard right. Davonte wasted no time continuing on with his plan for seduction.

"I'm saying, it's been a while for the both of you, so some pleasure wouldn't hurt."

Angie had now pulled her finger out of her vagina and began to suck on it.

"So, what you saying baby," she asked. *"You want me and Desiree to fuck?"*

Davonte knew this wasn't the time to stutter, so he kept it coming, *"Yeah, that's exactly what I'm saying."*

"Damn baby, you stay on some freaky shit," Angie said sounding unaffected by the sexual request.

"Davonte," Desiree spoke up, clearing her throat as she did. *"You know you're asking two women to have sex with each other, don't you?!? I mean, I don't know about Angie, but not only am I not a lesbian, I can't say I've ever even entertained the thought of having sex with another female."*

Davonte didn't want Desiree's words to create an air of uncertainty in them so he went into over-drive with it.

"First," he said, *"You don't have to be a lesbian to experiment the act of enjoying another woman. Also, you have to keep in mind if at any point you and I would have indulged in a threesome, chances are you may or may not have lightweight indulged in some foreplay with the participating female, if nothing else."*

"That would have been different," she told him.

That was all he needed to hear, that at some point she would have been willing based on the timing and circumstance. From there he made the whole idea of them sexing each other fair seeming, telling them different things they could try, speaking to them as though he just knew they were going to do it. He even went as far as using reverse psychology.

"Just think," he told them, *"A woman knows what she likes and how she likes it; how and where to touch, caress, the whole nine yards. And seeing that the two of you are mature women, it should not only be very simple, but also very enjoyable for the both of you. Knowing exactly what the other wants will generate the most desirable degree of pleasure, especially when it comes to foreplay. Now, let's be honest,"* he continued, *"Being a woman, wouldn't that allow you to know how to please another woman?!?"*

They both responded, *"Yeah."*

"Well, you would or should think so," Davonte said. *"So, is it on or what?"*

Desiree was still very reluctant and she let it be known by telling Davonte, *"Just because we're women and know what the other may like doesn't mean we should fuck Davonte. I'm saying you a man and no doubt may know what a man would enjoy when it comes to sex but does that mean you want to suck a dick?"*

Truthfully, the statement really pissed Davonte off but he rolled with it and rolled with it well.

"First off, don't ever come at me like that again in your life."

"I'm just saying," Desiree attempted to protest.

"Don't just say a thing!" Davonte snapped. *"And furthermore, we are talking about something I am asking you to do for me, now can you handle it or what?!?"*

Not waiting for an answer he continued, *"Let's do it like this, Angie will come for the weekend as I said and if the two of you find each other attractive then give it a try, alright? Fair enough?"*

Angie was gun ho, *"Okay baby,"* she said to Davonte, *"I'll go there and turn Desiree's pussy out for you."*

"Desiree?" Davonte inquired, *"Deal or what?"*

"Doesn't seem like I really have a choice," she mumbled under her breath. *"Yeah, okay,"* she responded as one sounding the least bit enthused. Still to her, something just didn't sit right with her and it wasn't just Davonte's request. At the moment she couldn't place her finger on it but she would.

"That was that," Davonte told them, *"And don't worry,"* he added, *"I know both of ya'll and I think you will not only enjoy each others company but also all else that you share."*

When he hung up the phone from talking with them he entertained a couple of thoughts. First he gloated and told himself the pimp world would be proud of him. Then, he made a mental note to use the entire week leading up to Angie's arrival to convince them that what was taking place was all good. Then, just before he laid back on his mat to check off another day on the wall, he asked himself the question, *"Why? Why am I doing this? Love?"* Was that it, why he was doing it? Was he that afraid of losing them that he was willing to go to the extreme?

63

CHAPTER FIVE

"CURIOSITY CRAVED THE CAT"

Saturday 9:45pm

The Week Went by relatively fast for Desiree and it was full of phone calls from Davonte making sure that, as he would say… "her head was on right." The truth of the matter was, he was just making sure she wasn't gonna trip on his other woman once she got there. Along with the fact she hadn't given him a different answer on whether or not she was going to sleep with Angie. The thought of it still hadn't quite set in. It was like, he was saying she was pretty with long hair, really trying to embellish the chick, but when Angie spoke of herself, she was like, *"Oh, I'm very average, nothing special, take me or leave me."* That to Desiree wasn't too appealing. Then, there was the question of, how is it that they had gone from being two women sharing a man, to two women going to live together to help out the man, to two women going to have sex for the man's benefit? Davonte's ass was very adamant about the whole situation, he not only called all week talking about it, but he also brought it up the two times she came to visit this week at the jail. Desiree eventually had to admit to herself, Davonte had truly sold her on the idea of sexing Angie with all the talk about the different sexual positions they should try and the fact that they being women should make it that much easier to please one another, knowing what women liked. Davonte told her, *"Desiree babe, be honest, you know you a freak and a good hard orgasm is right up your alley."*

Yeah, true enough she was on some behind the scenes freaky shit, but this was more than she'd ever thought to do. Yet, all in all, in the back of her mind she did entertain the thought of… if she did go through with it, how it might be?

What approach would she take? Was it true what they say about a female knows best when it come to working the pearl tongue? Those thoughts did cause her to be lightweight curious. However, more than anything, she couldn't wait to be face to face with the chick she had been sharing her man with, so she could ask her the ultimate question once again. *"When the fuck did you start sleeping with Davonte!?"*

Desiree's phone began to ring, she looked at the clock and let out a sigh. It was 10pm, Angie's arrival time. She figured there was no turning back now; the weekend would be what it would be. She picked up the phone and sounding as chipper as possible, said, *"Heelllo."*

"Hi," Angie said into the phone, *"I followed your directions the best I could and if I did right, I think I'm right out in front of your house."*

"The Phones Will be cut off in 15 minutes," one of the deputy's announced over the jail intercom.

Davonte looked at the phone and asked himself whether or not he should call Desiree's to see if Angie had made it into town? Naaah, he would wait, as a matter of fact, he would wait the entire weekend, giving them time to get to know one another as well as other things. The way Davonte saw it, all that was taking place as far as their willingness to carry out his request was not only because of their love for him, but also because they were no doubt eager to meet one another to see who was who. Those two elements mixed with his teasingly erotic persuasion should lead to a rather interesting weekend. And although Desiree was still very reluctant and carrying on like she wasn't sure, Davonte was certain she more than likely would go through with it. Especially, since Angie was more than a willing participant, talking about what all she would do to Desiree and how she was going to do it. She talked so much about it, Davonte had to ask her was she trying to turn Desiree out?

"No," she said, *"Not unless you want me to. It's just that my whole thing is…if I'm going to do it, might as well enjoy it and do it good. Plus, I hate doing something then later be thinking how I should have done more of this and that."*

Davonte agreed and told her he overstood and if that's how she was thinking, that was smart and she'd better put it down for him and work Desiree. She promised that she would. With those thoughts, Davonte figured why call? Things gonna go down or should, at least, and being familiar with both of their freaky sides he raised the curiosity in both their minds to the point if they did nothing else, they would at least kiss.

Tuesday 3am

As Angie Made her way onto interstate 75 headed north out of Georgia, she thought of her interesting weekend at Desiree's. Upon her arrival, she had to admit the one level 3 bedroom, 2 bath, 2-car garage home impressed her. She was really taken aback by the large bedrooms, but the kitchen was her favorite, it was large with lots of cabinet space. The golden brown cabinets went around the entire kitchen. The stove was gas with the matching refrigerator. There was also plenty floor space in the kitchen for a nice dinette set or her chef's island. Angie thought of how she would decorate things once she moved there. Not that Desiree had done a bad job with her Egiptian style layout. It was just that Angie felt if she was going to be living there, her style and presence had to be displayed also. It was a nice house, the living room could have been a bit larger, but the fireplace made up for that. She could tell Desiree was proud to show her around the place. It was cool and gave them a way to break the ice and converse without having to be stuck sitting on the couch or

something staring at each other uncomfortably. Angie had
to admit though, the highlight of it all was, how over the
course of the weekend she had partaken in sexual intimacy
with another woman, not once, but five times. She
replayed the events over in her mind. *"Damn,"* she said
out loud as a smile came across her face, revealing how
much she actually enjoyed what had taken place. Angie
found Desiree came across somewhat aggressive during
their sexual escapade. Aggressive, but good, damn good.
Desiree took it upon herself to cater to Angie's body,
delivering little sensational explosions each time they
frolicked. Angie even thought of the performance she
delivered.

  "Pussy don't taste half bad," she told herself. *"A rather
enjoyable treat, I might add. Listen to me,"* she giggled.
"I've been a bad girl." Shifting her Honda Civic into fifth
gear and speeding down the expressway.

  "Damn you Davonte!" She yelled. *"What you got me
out here doing? I mean for real baby, what you got a bitch
doing?"*

Tuesday Evening 6pm
*"Hell Yeah, Damn right I want you to tell me everything
that took place, in detail too!"* Davonte barked into the
phone at Desiree.

  "It was my guidance that put things in motion," he told
her, *"And I want to be sure ya'll followed through on my
instructions. What ya'll think I want to know for?"* He
asked. *"For some form of mental pleasure? Naah baby, I
want to know if ya'll did as I said."*

  Truthfully, he did want to hear the steamy details for his
own gratification, but he wasn't about to let that be known.

  "Okay, okay," Desiree consented, she'd come to realize a
change had taken place as far as how Davonte dealt with
her since he'd been there. Whether it was him dealing with

his insecurities or not she couldn't quite place it. Whatever it was, she would tell him all that had taken place in the hopes that he'd get out of it whatever he was looking for, as well as acknowledge just how much it was that she loved him by carrying out his wishes.

"Well, as you know," she went on to say, *"From your enticing little phone calls you subjected us to over the last week, truthfully, I think it's fair to say that we were both looking forward to this weekends gala. You know she arrived Saturday night and had to leave out on Monday night or last night..."*

"Yeah, yeah," Davonte smirked. *"Just get to what took place."*

"She arrived about 10pm," Desiree spoke slowly. *"And I must say, she is pretty with the long hair and all, but let me tell you..."* Desiree said becoming very excited, *"Your girl talked all that stuff and was straight nervous. I mean I was a bit nervous too, but she was ner-vous! I had to get things started,"* Desiree told him. *"Baby, you would have been proud of me..."*

Davonte held the phone closely to his ear as Desiree delivered the details, blow by blow. You could hear the excitement in Desiree's voice and the eagerness to tell Davonte all that went down. It was easy to tell that Desiree truly enjoyed herself.

Flashback
Saturday 10pm
Desiree Walked To the front door and looked through the peephole at Angie.

"Interesting," she mumbled to herself. She put on her happy face and opened the door.

"Well, hi there!" She said to a smiling Angie, *"So, you made it?"*

Desiree quickly gave Angie a once over; she stood several inches shorter than her, she had a light complexion with longer than average hair. She had on a pair of baggy stone washed jeans, ran down tennis shoes and a tee shirt that had a purple smiley face on it. A gym bag hung from one shoulder and there was a store bag in her hand.

"Okay," Desiree thought to herself, *"Davonte better be glad because I would have been pissed to find out I was sharing my man with some ugly chick."*
In fact, she found Angie to be very pretty.

"I'm sorry, come in," Desiree said as Angie walked through the door past her. She tried to get a glimpse of her body, but couldn't because her clothes were too baggy.

"Put your bag anywhere you like and have a seat."

"Okay," Angie said sounding chipper. *"Here, I brought this."* Angie said while holding out the store bag.

"Oh, treats?" Desiree inquired.

"Yep," Angie said, *"I figured it would help things go smoothly, if you know what I mean."*
Desiree looked in the bag and found a bottle of V.S.O.P. Remy Martin.

"Oh for sure, I know exactly what you mean. Let me put this in the fridge."

As she turned to walk into the kitchen it was Angie's turn to take notice of Desiree and see what was what. Desiree figured this would be the case, so when she turned towards the kitchen she didn't simply walk, she strolled softly and teasingly. She wore a t-shirt along with a pair of peach stretch pants. Angie took notice of how tall Desiree was and she couldn't miss her seductive eyes and smooth brown skin. Desiree had a sexy body; long with a slender waist, she was very hippy but what caught Angie's attention was how large Desiree's ass was, it looked immense compared to her slender frame.

"Damn!" She said out loud, it was a slip up, but she didn't care if Desiree heard her. After a brief chit chat Desiree took Angie on a tour of the house. Everything was good, they talked and laughed, that was until Angie saw a pair of Davonte's shoes in a closet. It wouldn't have been so bad if it hadn't been a pair she'd bought for him, but before she could really get upset over the matter Desiree made a suggestion.

"I'm sure you're tired from the drive, let me run you some bath water and pour a little somethin', somethin' to drink."

"That sounds good to me," Angie commented.

With those words being said and agreed upon they said no more, they simply shared an uncanny smile, one that only two women could overstand, one that said, 'why is it we are about to do what we are about to do?!? I don't know but let's do it!'

During the bath the two of them were very careful with their conversation, making sure to stay away from topics that could rub the other the wrong way. Angie did a great deal of talking, jumping here and there with different scenes of her life, always starting with, *"I remember one time..."* Desiree was amused.

They drank their drinks while bathing, then washed each other's body in very sensual ways, paying close attention to each other's reaction. The bath lasted over an hour. They dried one another off and from there Desiree led Angie to the bedroom. She instructed Angie to lie on the bed as she turned on her little radio and pushed play for the CD. Reaching for her bottle of baby oil from on top of her dresser, Desiree allowed her towel to drop giving Angie a clear and pleasant view of her rump.

"You have a big ass," Angie told her.

Desiree turned with the baby oil in hand, *"You like?"* She asked stepping over to her on the bed. She paused and looked at Angie then pointed at the towel she still had wrapped around her.

"Remove that," she said.

Angie smiled and did as she was told. Desiree climbed on the bed beside her and began what turned into a steamy simultaneous massage. The caressing and rubbing led to them both being extremely turned on. Desiree's breast became erect, allowing Angie to see just how large her nipples were, they were the width of dimes and stuck out like bullets. Desiree could feel Angie's willingness to indulge, but the signs of her nervousness were also visible.

Desiree was hot and horny and figured, *'I've come this far, fuck it'.* Giving Angie no warning she leaned in and pressed her lips upon hers. The second Angie responded it was on. They went at it; kissing and caressing rolling around, grinding.

Desiree became aggressive and took charge, she rolled over on top of Angie and began kissing her neck, nibbling her earlobes. She slowly made her way down Angie's body, she could hear Davonte's voice in her head, *"Ya'll both women... so you should know exactly what each other would enjoy."* She knew Davonte was running game to make evil fair seeming, unfortunately it was true, as a woman she knew just what she liked and what she and other women had spoke on concerning what they enjoyed in bed and what most men failed to do. With those thoughts, something came over her and within her own mind she vowed to put it on Angie's ass, from there a sexual beast was unleashed. She straddled Angie and began having her way with her breast; sucking, licking and tasting. She made her way down applying gentle kisses along Angie's stomach and sides. Raising Angie's legs, she kissed and sucked her inner thigh occasionally glancing at Angie's hairy pussy allowed Desiree to know just how well she was doing. The inner lips of Angie's vagina and the crack of her ass glistened from the out pour of her pleasure juices, not to mention she would jump and moan as Desiree found her hot spots and worked them. For thirty minutes, Desiree gave Angie all over sensations making sure she delivered the slow stimulating foreplay that women yearn for, then suddenly she stopped and looked up into Angie's eyes. She stared at Angie's breasts heaving up and down from her heavy breathing. The sudden stop had caught Angie off guard.

"W..w..what?!? What is it?!?" Angie questioned. *"What's wrong?"*

For Angie, this was not the time to be stopping.

"You want me to do you now? I can, I can do you if that's what you want?"

Desiree said nothing as she pushed Angie's legs up and back spread eagle. From there she dove in and went to work on Angie's muffin. Desiree was all in, sucking both sides of Angie's vagina lips, sliding her tongue up and down the opening of her pussy, slurping and swallowing the juices that poured fourth. Angie moaned deep and grabbed at Desiree's head wanting her to lick her clit for a while. Desiree dodged Angie's efforts and desire to have her cater to her love button. She wanted control and wanted Angie to know she had just that. Even once she made her way to Angie's clit, she performed in a way that sent Angie's eyes back in her head and caused her toes to curl. Licking, sucking, slowly, gently, causing Angie to grind her hips and moan. The pleasure was beyond description! The teasing game Desiree played on her clit had her mind racing, she didn't know whether or not she should curse and yell or say thank you. It sent chills through her spine. Out of nowhere, Desiree place her hands on the back of Angie's thighs, applying enough pressure so they couldn't move, then she began to vigorously work between Angie's legs as if there was a long awaited passion longing to be released. She became so engrossed in what she was doing, even she began to moan along with Angie. The aggressive licking and sucking along with the quick darting in and out of her tongue on Angie's clit caused it to swell and throb. At that moment, Angie felt the floodgates opening and took a deep breath. Desiree felt Angie's body get stiff under her. She wasn't done though. Taking Angie's entire clit between her lips, Desiree began licking and sucking the head of her love button while flicking her tongue all over it. Angie let out a scream of pure delight. Desiree zeroed in on the clit even more and worked it with intense devotion, as if the scream wasn't enough.

Angie cried out, *"Oh my god! Fuck me! Oh my god!"*

Desiree worked Angie's clit and didn't let up until she felt the uncontrollable shaking brought on by a job well done. When Desiree finished, she looked up from between Angie's legs with the same devilish gleam in her eyes she had when she started on Angie.

Angie held out her arms in a inviting way, *"Come, come,"* she said, *"I want to kiss you."*

Desiree quickly slid up to be engulfed in her lover's embrace and to plunge her pussy soaked tongue into Angie's mouth. For a second, it seemed Angie wasn't feeling Desiree's mouth being covered with pussy juice, until, Desiree pulled back and told her, *"How you gonna act like that, it's yours?!?"*

Angie giggled, *"You right,"* she said.

Their lips locked again, and their lust once again took control. Desiree and Angie worked their legs into a scissor position and carried on to the next phase of their merry making. Desiree grinded into Angie until she too exploded with pleasure. That was the first of their five erotic engagements over the 3 night, 2-day visit they shared. By the time they indulged in the last round for the weekend, which took place only moments before Angie pulled out to return to Ohio. The 69 had become the position of choice.

Desiree shared this and how they laughed and joked over the weekend with Davonte. She told him one of the jokes that he thought to be rather corny. Something about… right before they were going to have sex the second or third time, Angie asked Desiree, *"Are you going to use a condom this time?"*

Before getting off the phone with Desiree, she told him that she and Angie definitely became intimate. So much so, she also let it be known it was something she enjoyed, and yes she would do it again, if that was what he wanted. She also spoke of the caressing and embracing they'd done and told him she felt they did that more so because it was needed, rather than just for pleasure. It was the need to be held by someone.

"Do you overstand?" She asked.

"I do," Davonte told her and he did.

"It's your touch we miss, so we substituted it with each others.

Davonte was cool with whatever they felt they had to do as long as they got busy. He wasn't there, but the thought of his two fine ladies getting down, not only gave him an ego boost out of this world, it made his week. Hell, as far as he was concerned, he was the mutha fucking man!

CHAPTER SIX

"ONE'S OWN CONSCIENCE"

Angie Stood In the busy kitchen of Elemental, the restaurant she'd been working at for the last four years. She started out as an intern, waitressing and occasionally working in the kitchen when they were busiest. Now, she ran the restaurant, it didn't matter if the owner John was there or not, whatever she said went. She stood looking at the team she'd put together. Angie had a passion for cooking and everyone she hired had to share in that passion. If not, she felt they could only be a hindrance in her kitchen. Her main cook, Bobby, was a stone cold alcoholic, to the point he not only would show up to work drunk, sometimes if he figured no one was looking, he would sneak shots from the bar. Yet, he could cook his ass off and that's what she hired him for and outside of that, his vice was his vice as long as it didn't affect him serving up those hot dishes.

Angie's cell phone began to vibrate in the front of her checkered chef pants. Truthfully, the rule was, no cell phones in the kitchen, but she refused to miss out on talking to Davonte. She had her home phone forwarded so he could reach her. Quickly making her way towards the ladies room, she reached in her pocket and retrieved the phone.

"Yessss," she said placing the phone to her ear at the same time pushing the restroom door open.

"Hey lady," the voice said, it was her grandmother.

"Hi grandma!" She said while entering one of the stalls.

"Hey baby, how ya doing?"

"I'm good grandma and I'm at work, can't really talk."

"Is that so?" Her grandmother asked, *"Then what you answer the phone for?"*

75

"Well, honestly," Angie spoke before thinking, *"I thought you were someone else."*

"I wonder who could that be?" Her grandmother responded sarcastically. *"Wouldn't have thought it was that Davonte would ya?"*

Angie took a deep breath and said nothing as she pulled her pants down and sat on the toilet.

"I hear he's in jail, what's that all about? What's he done did?"

"Nothing grandma," Angie replied in a jazzy tone due to her not caring to go through this at the moment.

"Oh, that's right...," her grandmother shot back with the same jazzy tone in her voice, *"I did hear they were locking people up for nothing nowadays. Hey, or is it the ole lock up an innocent black man scheme? Cuz you know the white man is the devil and all he trying to do is keep the black man down."*

Angie wanted to yell out, *"YOU DAMN STRAIGHT!"* Because she knew her baby hadn't done nothing wrong.

"Or maybe it was a mistaken identity?" Her grandmother continued on with her sarcasm. *"You know we all look alike?!?"*

Angie had had enough.

"Grandma what?! Stop! I'm sure that's not what you called for."

"You're right it's not. I called about your graduation. If you want you can have something, a party or whatever here at the house and cook up some food and things."

Angie thanked her grandmother, but declined her offer. When asked why she went on to explain how she would be moving to Atlanta to be there for Davonte in his time of need.

"You mean to tell me you're going to move there while he's in jail?" Her grandmother asked, *"And live where?"*

"Davonte has arranged a place for me with one of his friends."

Her grandmother was silent for a moment, she wanted to tell Angie how she felt about what she just shared with her, then decided against it.

"I just hope everything works out for you and this Davonte, you know how you and your relationships go?!?"

"Thanks for reminding me," Angie told her becoming irritated.

"I guess if this doesn't work out, you could always become a lesbian," her grandmother said with a chuckle.

The remark caused Angie to think of her and Desiree's time together.

"Have you ever had sex with another woman?" Her grandmother asked.

"Grandma!" Angie exclaimed.

"What?" Her grandmother retorted with a false sound of innocence, *"Or should I ask, have you ever thought of being with another woman?"*

Angie fidgeted on the toilet for a second.

"I have to go," she told her grandmother abruptly, *"I'll call you later, bye, love you."*

Hanging up the phone, she slid it back into her pants pocket. Rolling the toilet paper from the roll, she again thought of her grandmother's comments. She replayed how she and Desiree had performed, it was something else, something different. The start had been so-so, partly because she had been a little nervous, but after Desiree's continued willingness to get it started, the nervousness was forgotten and they did whatever felt natural. Angie thought of how they had kissed a lot; which was fine with her, she was a kisser and it helped her really get into it each time. Desiree would come off aggressively and kiss the fuck out of her with plenty of tongue, which was her thang. A gentle smile came across her face as she thought of all they

had done during their brief tryst and how relentless Desiree
was once she would start licking her snatch. Angie had to
admit the chick was good at eating some pussy, she came
every time they partook of each others forbidden fruit,
sometimes two or three times. At first it was difficult to get
Desiree off but she got the job done. Angie thought about
the last round right before she left. They were in the 69
position with her on the bottom. She caused Desiree to
cumm so hard that her faced was covered in Desiree's
juices, eyes and all. Her grandmother's voice went through
her head and she momentarily experienced a bit of guilt.

"Shit, what was I supposed to say?" She thought. *"Yeah
grandma, me and Davonte's other woman got busy and she
eats a mean pussy!!?"*

Her conscience began to get the best of her ass. She
thought of how she'd lied to her grandmother, something
she'd only done once before. It was back when she first got
with Davonte and used her grandmother's car to take him
around. Upon returning the car her grandmother asked her
whether or not she had sex in the car or something. There
were footprints on the ceiling and glove compartment. She
told her grandmother no and played dumb when truthfully
Davonte had blown her back out in the car and it actually
was a wonder that they didn't break something. They had
got all the way butt naked and went all the way out.

"And just think," a voice said in her head, *"You lied
about it."*

Placing her hand between her legs to wipe, *"Whatever,"*
she muttered, *"I still ain't no lesbian."*

She pulled the toilet paper from between her legs and
looked at it. It was soaked, and not from pee either.

*"I done sat here thinking about that girl and now my
pussy is drenched! Yeah, and you lied about it too!"* The
voice in her head reminded her.

"So!!" She snapped out loud. *"And I'll do it again!"*

"Angie," one of the waitresses called out, *"They need you in the kitchen. And who are you talking to in there??"*

"Yes Ma'am Mrs. Trever, I'll call you first thing in the morning with your surgery schedule. Okay, you take it easy. Bye."

Hanging up the phone, Desiree let out a sigh of relief. It had been a hectic day of phone calls and the patients were something else. She was dead tired, yet, the day wasn't over for her and wouldn't be until late that evening. Work was one thing, but once she left for the day she had to head up to the jail and stand in line for an hour to visit Davonte who had the nerve to be tripping because Angie hadn't come to see him while in town. They tried explaining to him that people with out of state ID's had to call two weeks in advance to set up a visit. However, they weren't aware of that until she was in town and they called to see if she could come up and visit that day. Desiree felt he should have been happy that the girl even took time out to drive seven hundred miles just for his sake, not to mention what they'd done once she got here.

"Men!" Desiree thought. *"Are they ever satisfied?"* She wondered.

It had been a little over a week since Angie left and soon she would be returning to live in her house as Davonte put it, 'to help out'.

"Help out with what?" Was Desiree's question. Truthfully, she was only with all this 'other woman coming to live with her shit' so she could pump Angie for information about her and Davonte first getting together. Something Davonte and she both seemed to ignore when the topic came up. If they kept it up Desiree was going to bop somebody up side the head. She wasn't in no ways like Angie who she found to be somewhat like an urchin at times and obedient to Davonte's every request.

"You wrong," her conscience told her. *"You and Angie both not only share the same man, you also share in the incumbent task of carrying out his wishes to make him happy and create what he refers to as a balancement in his life."*

Desiree began to experience a slight feeling of guilt from attempting to place her self above Angie when in all honestly they both suffered from the same perplexing, unyielding emotion that all woman became victim to when it involved a man--'love'. Because of that, Davonte was able to induce the two of them not only into sharing him, but also into indulging in what neither of them had ever entertained the thought of doing.

Desiree sat at her desk eyes in a daze with a partial smile on her face, her mind had several thoughts running through it. Davonte led the way when it came to the imagery that occupied her subconscious. There close behind were the visions of Angie and what they had done. Desiree had found it easy to satisfy her little playmate whom she had decided to nick name 'baby girl'. She had picked it up from two chicks who always ate lunch together in the hospital cafeteria.

Yeah, Angie had a sensitive pussy, the lips and all, a little attention to any area and she would cumm. Her clit was a sure shot for an orgasmic explosion.

"Poor girl," she thought as she pictured what she'd do to Angie next time they got together. Oh, she knew Davonte and that little incident with Angie was only the inception, she could hear it in Davonte's voice when she told him how things had transpired between them. It would be imperative that they continued to carry out the activities of his little sex games. Desiree began to fan her legs open and closed by the tingling brought on as the thought of what she was going to do to Angie got the best of her and caused her

honey melon to soak up the inner part of her panties. She giggled as she told herself, *"I'ma turn that little cunt out."*

"What you laughing at?" One of the drug reps asked Desiree interrupting her erotic and stimulating thoughts.

"Nothing," Desiree hurried up and responded hoping she wasn't looking too crazy sitting at her desk absorbed in the fantasy of having her way with another female.

"Don't look like nothing to me," the drug rep said pointing down to Desiree's hand being squeezed between her legs.

The phone rang on her desk and she quickly answered it so she wouldn't have to continue being bothered by the drug rep, who she looked up at with a shoulder shrug and eyes that said, *"What do you want?"*

"Dekalb Medical," she spoke into the phone, *"Desiree speaking, how may I help you?"*

"Chile, let me tell you!" The voice on the other end of the phone said. It was her mother.

"Excuse me," Desiree said to the rep. *"This is an important call."*

The drug rep smacked her lips, spun around and walked away.

"Let you tell me what, mom?" Desiree questioned her mother as she sat in the chair and pulled herself together after being consumed by her steamy thoughts.

"Chile, 'bout this dream I had. I know it ain't true, I don't guess anyway, but it was about you having some crazy affair with some female."

Things **W**ere **G**oing smoothly for Davonte; the girls were on point with what he wanted, they now knew each other personally. He had sent a note to his cousin Harry and explained that since he had gotten him in this mess the least he could do was put a few dollars on his books so he'd be able to make arrangements to get Angie a graduation present.

Surprisingly, Harry came through. Davonte felt all was good, that was until the detective showed up again talking about if he didn't give him some information on Harry he was going to request that he get some more time for withholding evidence and obstructing an officer. Davonte couldn't believe it. He tried figuring out why this was happening because it wasn't like he wasn't out there caught up in no B.S. It was during this time of thought that his conscience tried to get the best of him.

"You used those sister's love to cause them to partake in the forbidden, so hey, here's a little something for you to stress about."

"What the fuck?! I'm straight trippin," Davonte thought, as he wrestled with his conscience of which he felt was a traitor.

CHAPTER SEVEN

"MAKE YOURSELF AT HOME"

"I Mean Seeing that Angie is here now and it'll be the two of you splitting the bills, it's the least we should be able to do."

Angie and Desiree sat listening to Davonte going off about getting him a lawyer. Every since that detective had paid him another visit, Davonte had been a little shook up. He had them calling numbers from the yellow pages and searching the internet, looking for a lawyer. They were both fine with carrying out his wishes and felt that getting a lawyer was a good idea and the best route to go. The only problem was that every penny Desiree had went towards the bills there was nothing extra. Angie had only been there a week and hadn't started working yet. The little money she had was used to pay off bills at the apartment she'd left behind. So, the question was where would they get the money needed to retain a lawyer? They sat on opposite ends of the couch staring at the phone while Davonte's voice came blaring out of the speaker.

Desiree hated when he got upset, that's when he was liable to say anything, not caring who he hurt.

"So, babe, what do you suggest we do?" Desiree asked.

"Yeah," Angie commented. *"Whatever you tell me baby, you know I'll do it."*

Desiree looked over at Angie with beady eyes and thought, *"Now how she gonna say 'Whatever he tell **her** to do, she'll do it' as if I ain't here?"*

"Yeah, I know you will baby," Davonte replied to Angie. That was the straw that broke the camel's back.

"Well damn," Desiree said, *"I guess this conversation is between ya'll?!?*

Innocently Angie looked over at her, Desiree smirked and rolled her eyes hard.

*"Like I said Davonte, what do you suggest we do? And I do place emphasis on **we**,"* Desiree added shooting Angie a sharp look.

"Hell," Davonte barked, *"Do whatever, get a fucking second job."*

"Here comes the curse words," Desiree thought, *"He's upset, no telling what will come out of his mouth next."* She began to fidget.

Angie took notice and became sad and uncomfortable all in one motion. She had never really dealt with Davonte when he was angry, at least not like this. Before, whenever he seemed to become upset or angry with her she'd quickly set out to resolve things, usually by apologizing then giving him unrestrained and aggressive head, this combination was her method to getting back in good with him. At this point, his anger was more than she ever had to deal with and there was no way she could use her sexual tactics. She slid down on the couch deciding to let Desiree handle it. She simply held her head down and pouted.

"Davonte, just tell us what you want us to do," Desiree said once again. *"Whatever you want,"* she insisted, looking over at Angie who was shaking her head in agreement. Desiree made smacking sounds with her lips and looked back towards the phone. There was a pause, then Davonte's voice came through the speaker slowly, calmly. Desiree could feel it and knew whatever it was he was about to say would be fueled by anger and desperation.

"Listen, I don't care what ya'll do but make something happen. I need to make bond, get a lawyer or both. So again, I don't care what ya'll do to pull it off, shit sell some pussy if you have to!"

Angie's mouth dropped open, she couldn't believe what she'd just heard. Desiree sat there shaking her head.

"I'm saying," Davonte continued on not letting them recover from his last statement, *"Use some ingenuity. I'm in here, there's nothing I can do but make suggestions. There's two of ya'll, do something!"*

"You have one minute left." The recording announced.

"Are you going to call back?" Desiree asked, not sure if she really wanted to know the answer.

"No!" Davonte snapped. *"I'll talk to ya'll tomorrow."*

The phone hung up leaving Angie and Desiree sitting there with blank expressions on their faces. Desiree sighed and looked over at Angie who had tears streaming down her cheeks.

She wondered what went wrong? One moment all was good, there was the situation of there being another woman and as odd as it may sound, even that was going smoothly. Then all of a sudden Davonte was in jail and needing help that she wasn't sure she was able to give. And if that wasn't enough, she and the other woman not only end up having sex, yet here she is sitting on her couch and this isn't a visit, she's here to stay.

Desiree looked over at Angie, she had been there a little over a week and what Desiree found to be somewhat surprising was Angie's tendency to walk and sit around butt ass naked. The first day she'd come home from work and saw her stark naked getting something to eat out of the refrigerator she didn't know if she should laugh or go get her a robe. It was something unexpected and here she sat on the other end of the couch but ass naked.

"I can't believe he said that crap about 'go sell some pussy'!" Angie complained, breaking Desiree's train of thought.

Desiree didn't respond.

"Okay, little Ms. 'I'll do anything'," she thought.

"How well do you know Davonte?" Desiree retorted as she stood up from the couch. *"Never mind, don't answer*

85

that," she said heading toward her bedroom. *"I forgot, at a moments notice you up and relocated 700 and some-odd miles for him. You undoubtedly know him very well."* She told Angie, looking back over her shoulder as she disappeared into the hallway.

Desiree entered her room shut the door behind her and flopped down on the bed. The question of what had gone wrong returned. No sooner than the effort of trying to answer it came, then another thought hit her, Davonte's apartment! The rent hadn't been paid and wasn't about to be, who had the money? Unless Davonte still had his last check and even then, what about the next two months? She would have to bring this up when he called tomorrow. Surely, that would only add to the unwanted stress he was already experiencing. Desiree grabbed a pillow and laid it across her chest, hugging it tightly. She pictured Davonte getting upset, apparently he'd forgotten about it because he hadn't made any mention of it. What was she to do?

"And just think, this man up here talking about sell some pussy. Where at and to who?!? She exclaimed letting out a half laugh of sarcasm.

Angie Sat Leaned back with both her feet propped up on the couch. Her thoughts were of Davonte's recent phone call. A lot was said and he and Desiree were both upset behind it, however Angie didn't feel that they had to be, to her, it was only a matter of getting through a negative situation. Fault her if you want, she was an optimist and with that same optimist mind state she was determined to make things happy again. In two more days, she would be able to visit Davonte and didn't want that ruined by gloomy attitudes.

Springing up from the couch, she headed towards Desiree's room, she wore a happy smile brought on by an idea she had. Knocking on the bedroom door, she stood waiting anxiously to share with Desiree what she felt was a start to turning a bitter situation sweet. After a moment or two Desiree called for her to come in. Entering the room, still wearing a cheerful smile, she took notice of Desiree partially sitting, partially laying with her back propped up against the headboard of the bed with a pillow behind her back.

"You just got out the shower?" Angie asked seeing the towel wrapped around Desiree's waist and smelling the fresh scent of soap in the air.

"Yeah," Desiree responded not looking up from filing her nails.

"Well, I need to talk to you," Angie told her hoping she'd look up to see the smile she wore.

Desiree raised her head slowly taking notice of Angie still being naked, her coochie was covered with a mound of long black hair.

"Well, what is it?" Desiree asked returning her chipper smile with a false one.

"I was thinking...," Angie spoke, making her way over to the bed at the same time and glanced under the towel at Desiree's pussy. Straddling over Desiree, she continued to share her thoughts. *"I know all this is difficult for all of us, especially you and me, two women sharing a man. I mean, it would be one thing if we were both just hitting him up for sex every now and then and knew about it. But, we are literally sharing a man, all of him."*

"...And your point is?!?" Desiree thought.

As Angie talked to Desiree, she was definitely happy, for what? Desiree had no idea. Yet and still, she sat attentively listening to her new houseguest, her man's other woman. To her, it was all a matter of getting to know this chick whose life must have been a road paved with marble. She acted as if she'd never experienced a day of hardship. Desiree couldn't help but smile. Truthfully, she wanted to bust out laughing as she wondered to herself, *"What's up with this chick straddled over me stark assed naked, bouncing and just a-talking away."*

"Whaaat?!" Angie squealed, *"What is it?"* She whined, *"Are you laughing at me?"*

"No," Desiree told her, *"Go ahead, I'm listening."*

"All I'm saying," Angie continued, *"Is unless one of us is going to leave, which I doubt, we need to make things work for us, for Davonte, don't you agree?"*

"Why of course," Desiree told her in a mimicking voice.

It was then Angie saw it. *"What?"* Angie asked, this time without the whine. She observed Desiree closely, *"I thought I saw that look,"* she said.

"What you talkin' about?" Desiree questioned, *"What look?"*

"Yeah, okay," the look Angie told her was a look she'd never forget. It was the same look she had seen on Desiree's face that first time they'd messed around. For some reason it was a look that scared her, but turned her on at the same time.

"I have a plan," Angie said, attempting to carry out her conversation and not be deterred.

Desiree placed her hands on Angie's hips and spread her legs slightly, enough for Angie's butt to slide down between them right over her crotch. Angie caught on to the subtle moves.

"What?" She inquired to Desiree as she moved her hips around slowly, *"You want me?"* She asked in a seductive whisper. The gentle rotation of Angie's ass on top of Desiree caused the towel to brush gently across her pubic hairs. It caused Desiree to raise her pelvis and slowly gyrate back. Her eyes became devilish slits as one hand slid up and began to caress one of Angie's breasts.

"Tell me," she said as she pulled and turned Angie's nipple. *"Tell me what your plan is."*

Angie leaned forward just enough to reach and pull the towel down to reveal Desiree's breasts. She moved her hips gently in a circle as she allowed her index finger to outline Desiree's large nipple.

"I want to tell you," she whined, *"But you about to get me."*

"You can tell me, baby girl," Desiree said reaching to pull Angie to her. *"Tell me what it is, tell me what your plan is,"* she told Angie right before grabbing the back of her neck and sliding much tongue down her throat.

Desiree was one to pay close attention to detail during sex, and she'd learned Angie's weakness from the start – 'kissing'. Angie was a kisser. If you got her tongue to yours or even lip to lip for that matter, she was like silly puddy in your hands.

Desiree pulled back for a second. Just long enough to whisper, *"You gonna tell me?"* And slapped Angie on her ass. The kiss and the aggressiveness Desiree exuded had Angie's heart racing and her clit tingling. The slap on the ass brought in a whole other degree of stimulation. As Angie felt the entrance to her vagina becoming wet, she had a flood of thoughts run through her mind; from the idea of this intimate relationship she was now sharing with another woman, to how much she needed this touch, this intimacy, it felt so good. But was this cheating on Davonte, she wondered?

Desiree reached between Angie's legs and began sliding the skin of the hood of her clit up, down and around.

"Oohhh ssssss," moaned Angie.

It felt so good to her, but she had to break the sexual trance Desiree was putting her under. She wanted to be the aggressor this time, the one who took control and delivered the pleasure. Raising her ass in the air to pull her soaked pussy away from Desiree's caring finger, Angie began sucking on Desiree's earlobe and darting the tip of her tongue in and out her ear.

"I got this," she told Desiree in a whisper. Angie worked her way down Desiree's body, kissing and sucking her neck as well as her breast where she played happily with her large nipples, down to her stomach and navel.

Determined not to be outdone by Desiree's last performance, Angie raised Desiree's long legs in the air and slid between them kissing the back of her thighs, she made her way down.

"Ssssss, eeeww!" Gasped Desiree as she felt Angie spread her butt cheeks and let her tongue explore the sensitivity of her booty hole. The soft wet tongue felt oh so good. Angie was now fucking with the true freak in Desiree. Desiree closed her eyes to enjoy what was taking place. She thought of the time Davonte played around and fingered her in the ass.

"Spread them legs and let me get at that brown eye. Not the one that winks, the one that stinks," he'd told her.

Angie paused and looked up at Desiree who was very much enjoying herself. When Desiree opened her eyes to see what the delay was, Angie began licking her honey pot from bottom to top with long licks like a cat lapping up milk. Then with a deep down passion that said, this is definitely for you, Angie commenced to working her tongue all over Desiree's clit head. The immediate and direct assault to Desiree's tender spot caused her to jump with overwhelming pleasure. It was clear that at that moment Angie was determined to declare her sexual eminence. It was fine with Desiree, as she looked down at Angie between her legs and bit down on her bottom lip. It felt good and she wanted to feel more of it, so she took her two fingers and spread her lips exposing the pink of her pussy, while pulling the hood of her clit back at the same time. Without words Angie knew what she wanted.

Pushing Desiree's legs up and back, spread eagle, she worked her tongue all over Desiree's exposed tender spot. She licked, slobbered and sucked. Hot electric sensations shot through Desiree's body. Her breasts swelled and the soles of her feet became warm. There was a destination Angie was trying to reach and Desiree knew in a few moments she'd be glad she'd came. Angie looked up at Desiree to find her looking down at her. Their eyes locked for a few seconds. And once again they shared that womanly stare that had no need for words, for their eyes said it all. They had crossed over into the forbidden garden together once again and partook of the fruit they both secretly enjoyed, and with a split second blink, they agreed to meet there often. From there, Angie lowered her gaze and focussed on the sacred passion she now shared. Sucking Desiree's clit between her lips Angie began licking quickly, softly as she moved her head around in circles going in for the kill.

"Sssss, ohhh, yeaa, yeaaa," Desiree moaned, continuing to hold her lips open. *"That's right, baby girl. Go ahead, taste something, make yourself at home."*

CHAPTER EIGHT

"FLIPPING"

The Drive To visit Davonte was a cheerful one for Angie and Desiree, for that matter, the last couple of days had been as well. They were spent with the two of them bonding and preparing the treat they had for him. Zooming in and out of traffic they shared smiles, glances and girlie chitchat. It was all about making it to the latest visit in the hopes that there would be no other people in the visiting room.

Desiree drove Davonte's truck comfortably, so much so you would have thought it was hers. She wondered why Angie hadn't said anything as of yet concerning her whipping the truck, she figured Angie didn't want to reveal that it was in her name and not Davonte's because it would lead to a discussion of when they'd started fooling around. Whatever the case, Desiree figured if she wasn't going to say anything, neither was she.

"Oh, oh, hold up!" Desiree said gesturing with her hand for Angie to let her speak.

"I got one, listen to this. There was a white man, black man, Hispanic man and a pale Arab, you know one of those Muslims!? They were all standing on top of this high cliff. The Hispanic guy walked to the edge, looked over and said, 'This is for my people, hasta luego!' And jumped over the edge."

"Damn!" Angie exclaimed.

"Shhh, let me finish!" Desiree laughed waving her hand at Angie. *"Then the Muslim guy walked over to the edge, looked over and said, 'This is for my people. Allahu Akbar!' and jumped."* Desiree giggled a little and continued with her joke. *"Now, the black man walks to the edge looks over, takes a deep breath and says, 'This is for*

my people', then he grabs the white man and pushes him over the edge!"

Desiree burst out laughing, she laughed so hard that her eyes began to tear up. Looking over at Angie's expression calmed her laughter as she realized that she wasn't laughing along with her.

"What?" Desiree asked her. *"You didn't find that funny?"*

"My grandmother is white," Angie pouted.

"I'm sorry," Desiree said while reaching over and placing her hand on Angie's thigh, moreso in between her legs close to her crotch. *"It was just a joke baby girl."*

Angie thought for a second then placed her hand on top of the hand Desiree had between her thighs.

"I know," She said allowing a big Kool-Aid smile to come across her face. *"I know you were just joking."*

Leaning over, she gave Desiree a wet kiss on the cheek. Sitting back in the seat she pushed Desiree's hand further between her thighs and began gyrating her hips as if she was grinding her kitty kat on Desiree's hand. Desiree gave her a quick glance and joined her in the flirtatious act.

"Meow, meow, come here kitty kitty," she said while making scratching gestures at Angie's coochie. *"You bad!"* she told her.

"You like it!" Angie shot back.

They entered the parking lot of the county jail both happy as can be, especially Angie since she hadn't seen Davonte in a while and this was her first time seeing him since he had been placed in jail.

Davonte **S**at **W**aiting, watching for his two lovely ladies to walk through the door of the visiting room. This would be a double first for him, first time he'd get to see Angie while in jail and the first time he'd get to see them together. He thought for a second about what was taking place and how it all started.

First there was Desiree, then there was Angie, in time he had told them of each other and explained to them how much he needed them both and how as strange as it may sound to them it was the presence of them both in his life that helped him remain balanced and focused. With that explanation and their love for him, they accepted the idea of there being another woman. Although there was still some reluctance and hesitation, yet in time they would be able to wrap their minds around the reality of how it was and how it was going to be. Now, due an unfortunate situation they came together in support of him. They now not only knew of each other but actually lived together. Davonte rubbed on his go-tee and thought of what Mr. Wonderful had told him.

"You bring two women together black, white or other-wise and they will come together and scheme on you."

Davonte didn't honestly believe that Desiree and Angie would do that to him however, he wasn't going to leave himself open in the event they tried to. He would pay close attention to their every move and conversation, leaving them no room to play and if by chance they foolishly did something he would cut them off, either one or the both of them. It wasn't that he didn't love them, it was quite the contrary, he loved them both dearly, more than anything. It was just a matter of being hurt too many times in the past, bad relationships that had left scars that were equally bad. It left no room for pain in neither his mental or emotional psyche. Not to mention, three of the four chambers of his heart had been destroyed early on in life by women who chose to take advantage of a man who was willing to play fair. His love for Desiree and Angie was fueled by love stored in the one chamber he had left and that's where he embraced both of them tightly, safe and secure. Yet, if they acted up he would let them go without hesitation, again, not because he lacked love for them but, moreso because if that one last chamber was damaged or destroyed it was simple-he would die. He would die from the reality of knowing that once his entire heart had been destroyed he would then have nothing to offer anyone and with that, what would be the purpose of living. Those thoughts carried much weight with him, more than he would ever allow Desiree and Angie to ever know.

The Blur Of two figures in his peripheral vision caused Davonte to snap out of his present thoughts and look up. A smile came across his face as he took notice of Angie and Desiree gliding towards him, they too wore huge smiles of joy. Upon reaching the other side of the plexi-glass window he sat in front of they both stopped, side by side then as if on cue simultaneously they turned slowly as if modeling, giving him a view of their whole bodies, front, side and rear. Davonte waited until they had completed their turns and were facing him once again then he gave a sign of approval by clapping his hands and giving the thumbs up.

Angie sat down and reached for the receiver, *"Hi baby!"* She said cheerfully to Davonte who was already holding the receiver to his ear.

"Well hello there, my pretty lady. How are you?"

"I'm fine now that I'm able to see you," Angie spoke with all the love she had for Davonte showing in her eyes. *"I didn't know they were going to have this glass up here,"* she said with sadness in her voice. *"I thought I would get to touch you."*

"Naah baby, unfortunately not," Davonte told her. *"But it won't be long and you better touch me right."* He said shooting her a naughty look. Angie began to be turned on

and squirm in the seat. The sound of what he said and the vision that came with it brightened her mood even more.

"Well, let me tell you," she said happily. *"I have good news for you and then the both of us have something for you. First, I found a job. Yeaa! Good for me,"* she chimed.

"Yes, it is." Davonte agreed, shaking his head.

While Angie talked, sharing with Davonte the news of her new job as a chef, Desiree watched closely at how the two of them interacted with each other. She found the present situation to be rather strange and uncomfortable. As they talked, she watched Angie giggle and squirm in the seat. Desiree took a deep breath and blinked several times in order to hold back the tears that were attempting to well up in her eyes. The reality of the man she loved sitting here talking to another woman, in conversation he seemed to be definitely enjoying was a lot for her to swallow.

Davonte looked out the corner of his eye and took notice of Desiree's discomfort. There was a hint of sadness and she glanced back and forth at the watch on her wrist impatiently. She wasn't happy at the moment and it showed. Davonte observed as Desiree tapped Angie on the shoulder then signaled to the watch on her wrist. Apparently they decided to split the 30-minute visit up into 15 minutes a piece.

"I love you baby," Angie said before handing the receiver over to Desiree.

Davonte blew her a kiss and she smiled happily.

"Hey," Desiree said into the phone, demanding his attention, *"It's my turn now."*

"Yes, indeed it is," Davonte told her, *"And I must say, you are looking beautiful."*

Desiree smiled and sat up straight.

"Thank you, baby," she cooed, pushing her shoulders back and chest forward she let her eyes drop to her breast then back up to Davonte.

"My, my, my, either I've been in here too long or your breast have gotten bigger," he teased, while looking wide-eyed at her breast and licking his lips.

"I got on my sexy see-thru push up bra," she told him while rubbing a hand across her breast seductively and looking over at Angie.

"Anyway," Angie said, smacking her lips and frowning up her face, *"I can't believe you went there."*

"Well, I did," Desiree shot back.

"Hey," Davonte called out tapping on the glass, *"Are you here to visit me or argue with her?"*

"I'm here to see you," Desiree said assuredly.

Once again her eyes attempted to water up.

"You know it's just hard dealing with this situation sometimes. And I say that for the both of us. You here, her moving in, it just seems to have happened all at once and getting adjusted is a little difficult, you know what I mean?!?

Desiree locked her eyes on Davonte's, she wanted to make sure he really knew where she was coming from.

"I do baby," he told her, *"I truly do. But listen, let's not turn this into a sour moment."*

"Okay," Desiree whimpered, brushing the stream of tears that ran down one side of her face.

For a moment there was a brief silence where they all sat contemplating, pondering the question of what they were doing and where things were headed? Realizing they had reached an uncomfortable moment for the three of them, Davonte broke the silence.

"Uh, excuse me," he said waving his hand to get their attention, *"Didn't y'all have something else to share with me?"*

Desiree sat there for a second then remembered the little treat they prepared for him.

"Oh yeaaah, hold on," placing one hand over the mouthpiece of the phone, she turned her head and spoke with Angie who instantly started smiling and nodding her head yes.

"Okay," Desiree said into the phone, *"We got something for you Big Daddy,"* looking around to see if there was anyone looking, she sat the phone down and stood up. Angie stood beside her and once they had Davonte's complete attention, they both began unbuttoning the dresses they wore. Davonte's eyes became bucked, knowing what they were about to do. With big smiles on their faces, they both opened up their dresses and stood there with their legs shoulder width apart giving Davonte a clear shot to their honey muffins.

Angie had on black thigh high pantyhose with a matching garter. Her pubic hairs were so long, it looked like a black forest. Desiree had on black heels that strapped all the way up her calves. Her thighs and hips looked thunderous!

What really blew him back was, not only was her vagina equally as hairy as Angie's, but she dyed it an almond color that blended superbly with her skin tone. The sight of them standing there showing their nakedness made him become erect. Just when they figured he had seen enough, they spun around, hiked their dresses up in the back showing their bare buff cheeks bent all the way over. And as if that wasn't enough, reaching back they grabbed a handful of their ass cheeks and spread them wide. So wide you could see bootyhole along with the pink of their inner pussy.

"Well, damn!" Davonte yelled, holding himself and squirming in his seat. He said it so loud, it made Desiree and Angie jump up and quickly start to button up. Angie grabbed the phone with one hand while buttoning up with the other.

"Did you like that baby?" She asked cheerfully.

"Did I?!" Davonte exclaimed, *"Man, that was a hellava treat. Y'all went all out for a brother on that one."*

"Anything for you baby," Angie told him with a tone in her voice and a look in her eyes that let it be known she was dead serious.

"That's right baby," Desiree said over Angie's shoulder, *"Anything for you,"* as she displayed the same look of seriousness.

"Man," Davonte thought to himself, *"This is straight, I can't wait to get home to this 'anything for you attitude'."*

The lights blinked on and off twice and a voice came over the loud speaker, *"You have five minutes left for visitation."*
At the sound of those words, Angie showed a look of disappointment on her face. For her, the visit had gone too fast. There was so much she wanted to say. For Davonte she could have stayed there all night. Unable to help herself she began to cry, it hit her all at once, the fact she had to not only leave, but leave Davonte behind.

"Baby, I love you," she said, placing a hand on the glass wanting badly to touch him.

Desiree slid the phone from her hand, she too felt emotionally torn at the moment but managed to hold in the tears. However, there was a trembling of her lips and a cracking in her voice as she spoke.

"You know we love you and will always be here for you no matter what."

Angie sat shaking her head in agreement with what Desiree was saying.

"By the way," Desiree starting to speak in a sort of a whisper, *"There's one more thing…"*

"Okay," Davonte said wondering just what else there could be. He leaned forward, closer to the glass to better see Desiree as she spoke, with a happy grin upon his face.

99

"So, you know me and your girl here has been getting busy... if you know what I mean?!?" She said licking her lips seductively. *"And yes, I've been working that pearl tongue,"* she added flicking her tongue up and down quickly in a sexual manner.

"Yeah," Angie said leaning her head towards the phone to be heard. *"Her name is 'Slick lick'."*

"Well hell," Davonte said, *"Y'all been getting busy doing the do?"*

"That's right baby, for you," Desiree told him.

Davonte took a minute to picture that. A smile came across his face and he saw Angie elbow Desiree.

"Told you he'd be glad," she said.

Mr. Wonderful's voice entered his thoughts.

"You put two females together, they gonna scheme on you."

Remembering those words, the smile disappeared.

"Oh, so y'all think y'all slick!?" He snapped. *"So, y'all hooking each other up without me saying so?! So I take it neither of you don't need me now, y'all got each other!?"*

"What!?" Desiree asked in shock. This wasn't the response she was expecting. *"We thought you'd be happy. We thought that's what you wanted."*

"Shut up!" Davonte snapped. *"Y'all come up here showing me some pussy shots. What is this goodbye?!? Y'all giving me one last peek at what I'll be missing?!?"*

Desiree couldn't believe her ears and looking at him, Davonte was truly upset.

"So let me ask you... how the fuck the two of you bumping clits gonna get me out of here? Tell me that, hunh?!?"

Desiree placed a hand on her chest. He had definitely hit a soft spot because she hadn't figured out what they were going to do to get him out. They were still trying to work up money for a lawyer to represent him when he went to court in a couple of weeks.

"Let me see the phone," Angie said, reaching to pry it out of Desiree's hand who was so upset she didn't even hear Angie who took it as though she was being ignored. *"Let me see the freakin' phone!"* She said snatching it out of Desiree's hand.

That quickly caught her attention.

"Don't be snatching the phone from me!" She barked at Angie.

"Whatever," Angie shot back. *"Baby, listen,"* she said ignoring Desiree and trying to talk to Davonte. *"We wasn't trying to be sneaky and do nothing behind your back. We honestly thought you'd like the fact that we did it."*

"I said don't be snatching from me," Desiree hissed.

"Could you please shut up?!" Angie yelled. *"Can't you see he needs me?"*

"Tell me shut up again and we gonna see who's in need." Desiree was heated.

Angie had stepped on her nigga toe and had the nerve to be trying to front on her in front of Davonte.

"And what is that supposed to mean?" Angie questioned angrily now becoming heated herself. She dropped the phone and stood to face Desiree.

Davonte had flipped the script and now they were flipping out in the visiting room.

"Oh, so what you standing up for?" Desiree asked Angie.

"Don't worry, you about to find out."

"Hey!" Davonte yelled pounding his fist on the plexi-glass. *"I said hey, goddamn it!"*

All the fuss brought two guards rushing through the door, one on the side with Davonte, the other on the side with the girls.

"Let's go guy, visits over," the guard told Davonte.

"Okay ladies, calm down," the other guard told them, *"Unless you don't want to be allowed back or better yet, maybe you want to join him and stay here for awhile?!?"*

With that being said, Desiree and Angie quickly pulled it together. They both walked briskly to exit the visiting room. Neither of them finished buttoning up and the guard noticed as they passed.

"Hey you two," Angie and Desiree turned their heads to look over their shoulders, but didn't break stride. *"He's not worth it, trust me."* The officer said.

Neither of them paid his words much mind. Davonte was the man they loved and who was worth more than anything to them both.

Back in the pod amongst the other inmates, Davonte sat thinking on how he'd just flipped out and wondered how necessary it was, if at all. The thought of what Mr. Wonderful told him was for someone trying to pimp and that he wasn't.

However, on the flip side of that same coin, Mr. Wonderful told him it didn't matter if it was a boyfriend/girlfriend or husband and wife, continue to keep the pimp/hoe relationship. The female can think of what she wants. But at the end of the day, it's about applying what makes the relationship work and hard cold pimping. Davonte knew he wasn't no pimp not in the least, he just wanted to keep the two he loved, and he would do that whichever way necessary.

Angie And Desiree rode together silently in the truck and although they shared in the same sadden emotions, they occupied separate thoughts, yet about the same situation. Desiree sat in the driver's seat feeling angry and sad all at the same time. She felt Davonte needed to make up his mind on what he wanted. Either he wanted her and Angie to become close and indulge in intimate sexual relations or he didn't. Truthfully, it didn't make a difference to her. Angie was *his* other woman, not *hers*. Desiree felt like the girl could possibly be cool people under other circumstances, but at this point, she wasn't feeling her. Besides, she wasn't no lesbian, so she could do without the sex shit anyway. And on top of all of that, the little cow had the nerve to get jazzy with her.

Now Angie, on the other hand, sat staring out the window on the passenger side engrossed in sadness. All that had appeared to be going well to her had suddenly been flipped up side down, but why? *"What happened?"* She wondered. Regardless of what caused things to turn around, all she knew was she had to make things up to Davonte and fast. She couldn't stand for her baby to be mad at her, not even for a second. As soon as they arrived back to the house she would start on a letter to him letting him know she was sorry and didn't mean to upset him and that whatever he wanted her to do to make things right she would. For a second, she thought of her and Desiree's little dispute. How dare she act like she had a problem because she had taken the phone to speak with her baby. Cow better be glad the officers came in there when they did. Had they not, it would have been some shit. And she better not try to put her out when they get back neither.

The only part of their thoughts that coincided was how they were unbelievingly not just sharing the same man, but actually living together with the other woman.

"Oh well," they both figured concerning the other, *"She'll be gone one day."* (Or so they hoped).

CHAPTER NINE

"GIRLFRIENDS! WHAT?"

The **F**ollowing **W**eeks that lead up to Davonte's court date were touchy. Desiree and Angie carried on around the house scarcely talking to one another, only doing so out of necessity. And the thought of becoming intimate didn't enter either of their minds, although Angie continued to prance around the house stark ass naked, Desiree paid her no mind. There were more pressing issues at hand, like the message she received on her voice mail a couple days ago about Davonte's apartment which had been totally forgotten about. The message said that they hadn't heard from him nor had they received a rental payment in awhile. An eviction of his property would be taking place and because she was put down as a reference, they figured she might still be in contact with him in order to inform him of what was about to take place. Desiree looked at it as another thing to set him off.

"This Is The situation," the lawyer Jerry Wiener said to Davonte. *"They pretty much know from cell phone taps and occasional undercover surveillance tapes that you didn't have much or anything to do with your Cousin Harry Lewis' illegal dealings. However, they know a jury would no doubt convict based on the simple fact that upon the day of arrest you had been acting as chauffeur, driving him here and there while he conducted transactions. In other words, they're not going to buy a story of ...this being your cousin and you not knowing what was going on."*
    Davonte stared at the lawyer sitting before him with his mediocre blue suit and bright red tie. Angie and Desiree were able to retain him at the last minute with a deposit of one thousand dollars and twenty five hundred owed. The

man's suit said he was able to make do, but his shoes let it be known he was far from one of the best.

"So, what is it you are suggesting?" Davonte asked, already aware from the man's opening conversation he was about to be disappointed.

"Welllll," the lawyer started to speak with a shrug of his shoulder. *"The D.A. is asking for you to tell all that you know about Mr. Lewis' illegal dealings."*

"I don't know anything about what he does," Davonte interrupted with a lie and straight faced. *"And if I did, I'm not a snitch."*

"I expected that response," the lawyer replied, *"And it's respected. However, I am obligated to tell you everything involved with the case. Now, on the other hand, if you do not wish to tell them anything or in the case of you really not knowing anything, the D.A. is going to ask the judge to sentence you to at least one year in prison for conspiracy. Which I'm positive if you don't try to fight it, I can get you six months county time."*

"And if I do decide to fight it?" Davonte asked.

The lawyer leaned back in his chair looked Davonte straight in the eye and began stroking the hair on his chin.

"It'll go to trial and if they have nothing on you – you could walk. Yet, if they have one thing to tie you in then, you could lose and get the max that conspiracy carries. And if I can be totally honest, with you, I'm almost certain they'll put you before a jury of twelve people who are not your peers and do not and are not trying to understand the life of the streets. Meaning, there will be twelve middle to upper class, middle to old age white people looking at you, a black male, thinking to themselves, "Let us do the right thing and clear the streets of this ailment." So you know, I only speak from years of experience. The final decision is yours when it comes down to what plan of action we'll take because it is your life. Take a day to think about it and give

me a call. The lawyer reached inside his blazer and pulled out a card. My office accepts one collect call a week from clients. Feel free to call and give me your response on what you want to do. In my honest and professional opinion, I don't think you should chance rocking the boat. Again, its on you," he added sliding his business card across the table to Davonte who sat on the other side in thought.

He wasn't involved in Harry's doings, yet he could remember several times being with him while he'd made moves here and there. Once, he'd even hung out with him and a few other of his baller associates.

"Okay," Davonte said, *"I'll sleep on it and give you a call."*

"Fair enough," the lawyer said extending his hand as he stood from the table. After a firm handshake, he was gone from the room and an officer escorted Davonte back to the cell.

Desiree And Angie sat on the bench beside each other in the courtroom astonished as they listened to the judge grant Davonte an agreed upon plea of six months to do on top of the three he had already done. Along with that, they were shocked that Davonte hadn't filled them in on what was to take place beforehand. Whenever they'd ask, all he would say to them was... *"Don't worry, everythings fine."*

That led them to believe he'd be coming home today. A special meal had been prepared by both of them. They'd even done a little shopping for sexy new lingerie, figuring they would come together to give him an evening of romance and treats. But here it was 'the day', and he wouldn't be coming home.

Desiree was so pissed, she wanted to scream at the top of her voice. Angie sat with tears streaming down her face. After the plea was passed down, Davonte turned to them and signaling as if he had a phone to his ear. His lips moved silently, telling them to go home, he'd be calling them in an hour.

Desiree shot him piercing eyes and just as he, her lips spoke silently, *"You better,"* she grimaced. Reaching over she grabbed Angie's wrist and stood up, *"Let's go!"* She snapped.

"Why? Why are they doing this to him?" Angie whined, sniffling and wiping her cheeks with the tips of her fingers. *"He didn't even do anything,"* she protested at the same time shooting the judge and D.A. a murderous look. They were messing with her baby and she wasn't feeling it.

Four Phone Calls and two hours after Desiree and Angie arrived home, they sat on the couch in their usual positions listening to Davonte on the speaker phone discussing the court hearing and other matters of importance.

Desiree looked over at Angie with a sarcastic smirk. *"And why not?!?"* She thought to herself.

Today, Angie didn't sit on the couch naked with her kat hanging out. Nope, today Angie sat on the couch in her bloomers and a nightgown. Today, 'Lil Ms. Angie was on her period. Desiree thought of the brief conversation they had earlier when Angie told her she had come on.

"Man, it might have been good for you that Davonte didn't come home today," she told Angie, *"You wouldn't have gotten none for a week."*

Angie had taken the comment as an insult. *"Please, you shittin me!"* She snapped, *"I would have sucked his shit dry. I mean d-r-y. Big Ben and the twins would have been e-m-p-t-y. There wouldn't have been nothing left for you to work with!"*

At the time, Desiree didn't even respond, it was comments like that made her wonder just how well Angie knew Davonte.

The young man was well equipped, truth be told, he had some garganturan type shit hanging between his legs. And his stamina was to die for. Those two elements made for a very confident man in the bedroom. She smiled remembering times of how Davonte would get undressed and stand there with that devious grin, then ask her, *"So, how you want it?"* Without even using his hand, he could make the head of his penis slide up and down the opening of her vagina. And when he entered, he didn't poke it or slide it in, he walked that mean sucker in there, literally. He had finesse to the point he could be ferocious with the pussy and Desiree loved it, every pulsating inch of it.

So, Lil Ms. Angie's comment was one sadly mistaken. Yeah, as a substitute for her being on her period, Angie would have to suck and drink him up alright. However, once he pulled it out her mouth, he would have turned to Desiree and told her... *"Turn around, bend it over, and stick it out."* He'd slap her on her ass with it like a whip and like nothing it would have rose to the occasion and to Angie's disappointment, it'a been on once again.

The evening continued on, Desiree gave Davonte the news on his apartment. It came as a disappointment, but what was he to do? He was in jail and it was unlikely that the girls would be able to swing the rent at two places with a truck note, insurance and paying the lawyer the remainder of his money. So he instructed them to go over to the apartment and salvage all his belongings by taking them to Desiree's.

Davonte's main concern continued to be the matter of keeping his two ladies with him through it all. An idea had come to him at the time he decided to take the plea. One he figured would benefit them all. Putting plenty of thought into it, he figured the best way of going about it, like all else he'd brought to them, he'd simply come straight at them being boldly honest and up front. They would either be with it or they wouldn't. Unfortunately for them, he wasn't offering the latter of the two as an option.

"Listen ladies," Davonte spoke, *"I know all this has been a bit much and I want to apologize for what has taken place. I assure you it wasn't something I expected. Also, had I known that Harry was under such a watchful eye of the police, I wouldn't have been within a hundred feet of him. However, that is what it is at this point. I just want the two of you to know I love and need you both very much."*

The words were heartfelt by both of them.

"We love you too, baby," Angie chimed.

"Yeah, and we need you just as much," Desiree added, *"And you don't have to worry, we'll be there for you. You ended up in there this year in May and it'll be over February '06. And we will be here for you okay? Do you hear me?"* Desiree questioned, *"I speak for the both of us, I'm sure."*

"That's true," Angie agreed as she slid over on the couch closer to Desiree. Placing her hand in Desiree's, she laid her head on her shoulder. *"Baby, you know we'll be here. Just be strong and keep your head up. It'll be a whole nine months that you would've been away from us, but that doesn't matter, we're yours, right Desiree?"*

"That's right!" Desiree said in agreement. *"Just let us know what ever it is you want done to make things go easier for you."*

Those were the words Davonte wanted and needed to hear. It opened the door to the next phase of his plan.

"Thank you ladies. The fact that you've said that is good, because I've been thinking, and I have a request."

"What is it baby?" Angie asked, now sitting straight up on the couch with full attention directed at the phone.

"Yeah Davonte, just let us know what's up and your wish is our command."

The two of them began to conversate back and forth with each other in a merry way, saying how he need not trip, they got him and how he should already know that much. Davonte simply held the phone listening and after a few moments, they stopped their idle chit-chat.

"So what is it baby?" Desiree asked. *"Go ahead and tell us what you want."*

Davonte remained quiet for a moment, then just as calm as one could be, he told them, *"I want y'all to be girlfriends."*

Angie responded to the request, *"Baby, is that it? I mean it's a little difficult dealing with the idea of sharing your man, but hey we're working at it for you."*

Angie was happy to respond, however, the two of them must have perceived something totally different from his words because Desiree sat there staring at the phone with one eyebrow raised.

"I mean, give it time," Angie continued, *"We'll end up being so cool of friends you won't be able to stand it!"*

"I don't mean girlfriends like buddies," Davonte said. *"I mean like the two of you in a relationship like going together girlfriends."*

"Oh," Angie said leaning her head to the side like a confused puppy. She was so caught off guard that her mind went blank, like nothing literally was in it.

The way Davonte saw it was, if they were to get into each other to the point their emotions became involved, then in a sense, they would be as one and that would make things easier for him when it came to dealing with them. What went for one would go for both. In the long run, if either of them felt for some reason they had enough and wanted to leave it would be difficult because they wouldn't just be leaving one person they cared for, but two, making it twice as hard.

"Davonte, you're causing me to become befuddled by your conversation here. Could you aah… please, make things a little clearer?!?"

Davonte **Lay In** the only too familiar position that allowed him to stare at the stained ceiling of the cell. Pondering the thought of months ahead, he had already missed the 4th of July. Now, he would miss Thanksgiving, Christmas and New Years.

"Unbelievable," he thought to himself, that and the conversation he'd just finished on the phone with Desiree and Angie had him a bit agitated and somewhat restless. He figured as long as he kept things kosher with them, he could do these few months with ease. He wondered about the way he had told the two of them to carry on and whether or not it was a little over the top?

"Hhmm, oh well, no time for regrets. What's gonna be will be and what will be is what I want, so be it."

Angie laid in bed in the room adjacent to Desiree's. It was a hot and humid night in the ATL, which made for a hot and humid Angie and being on her period only added to the misery. Not to mention the thought of Davonte's request, Angie knew good and well she would do just about anything for him, but this latest request was a bit illogical.

"Me and Desiree go together," she thought to herself, *"Y'all go together. Yeah, right, how's that suppose to take place?"*

Taking a deep breath, Angie flopped from her side to a position on her back.

"Well, Davonte baby, I love you. Oh my goodness, the Lord Almighty knows I do, but go with some chick like in a relationship? I don't think I'ma be able to do that for you. Hell, I done already slept with her, that should be enough."

With the brief thought of her and Desiree's sexual escapades Angie began to think of how horny she was.

"Damn it!" She snapped pounding her fist down on the bed beside her. *"Everytime I'm on my period I become horny enough to fuck a horse."*

Grabbing the pillow beside her, she placed it over her face. Screaming into it she kicked frantically, *"I want some fucking dick!"*

"Davonte, Davonte," Desiree mumbled to herself, *"The things you come with never cease to amaze me. Girlfriends, check that shit out,"* Desiree thought. After hanging up the phone with Davonte, Desiree only took a matter of seconds to make her decision of his bizarre request. Realizing this was only a matter of his insecurities, of which she had been subjected to over the years, although not to this extreme, she decided to go along with it. If it was what he needed for her to prove her loyalty and devotion when she spoke to him again, she would need to get some insight on just what it was he wanted them to do, how they were supposed to be. Seeing she wasn't no dike or butch, she was at a loss as to what was supposed to take place in a girl on girl relationship. Also, because she was taller and bigger, she wasn't about to be dominated by little ole Angie.

"So, I guess that would make me the man of the relationship?!?"

Ironically Desiree found that last thought to be interesting she pictured it and smiled.

"Come here bitch!" She said pretending to be talking to Angie. *"What I tell you to do?!? You want me to bop you upside your head, hunh?!?"* She laughed and placed her hand over her mouth looking side to side. *"I'm trippin,"* she thought. *"Can't nobody see me in this dark ass room."*

Desiree looked in the direction of her bedroom door, hearing the sound of slight thumping and what seemed to be a muffled scream coming from the bedroom Angie occupied. For a second, she wondered was the girl alright? Then, just as quickly as she entertained the question she let out a giggle. *"Maybe an intruder done broke in and is choking her to death. Damn, I'm terrible,"* she thought. Desiree was slightly turned on from picturing herself controlling Angie. Looking towards the bedroom door once again, she hollered out Angie's name, *"Angie! Angie if you hear me come here!"*

Moments later, the bedroom door came open, brandishing a silhouette of Angie's frame.

"And may I ask, what is it you want?" Angie questioned. *"And how bout you turning the light on so I can see?!?"*

Desiree reached over to the lamp on the nightstand and turned on the light. There she sat on top of the covers with pillows propped under her back, leaned up against the headboard of the bed. Her eyes were slits and there was a look of cunningness on her face. Her knees were bent with her feet on the bed, her nightgown revealing her long brown legs along with her bare crotch.

"Come 'er, I said."

Angie headed over to the side of the bed, studying Desiree as she did. Judging from things she could see Desiree was horny. Standing beside the bed, she looked at Desiree pretending to be uncertain as to what it was she possibly wanted.

"What?"

Desiree smacked her lips and looked at Angie with a look that said, 'You know damn well what it is'.

"Don't play," she said shooting a glance from Angie's eyes down to her own pussy and back.

Swallowing and letting out a sigh, Angie placed her hand on Desiree's leg and began rubbing up and down her inner thigh. She knew exactly what Desiree wanted for she too felt the same tingle and pulsation between her legs, only she was out of commission at the moment.

"You know the last time we did this without his permission we got in trouble?!?

"Imagine that," she mumbled under her breath, *"Grown women gotta ask to fuck. Anyway,"* Desiree said, *"What's up?"* Spreading her feet and letting her legs fall open like a butterfly's wing. She pointed to her honey pot and winked at Angie. *"Whatcha gonna do?"*

Angie slid her hand down between Desiree's legs.

"Damn!" She exclaimed once she realized how wet Desiree was. There was a smacking noise as she probed her finger in and out Desiree's vagina lips.

"I ain't getting in trouble for you," she whined with a frown on her face.

CHEATER

CHAPTER TEN

"COACHING"

It Would Make for a long Saturday with Angie and Desiree making frequent trips back and forth from Davonte's apartment so they could move his belongings. Loading the U-Haul truck with no help was strenuous and proved to be very trying, both mentally and physically.

During the course of packing up Davonte's things, they called themselves doing a little snooping and they found the cliché of 'You look, you shall find,' to be so true as they came across a purple satin robe hanging in the closet, a pair of black lace boy cut panties under the bed, that judging from the crotch must have been worn during a stimulating moment, and a leopard print bra and panty set in the hall closet, stuffed in a plastic grocery bag, that also showed signs of having been previously worn. What they found to be disturbing was none of the items belong to either one of them. Desiree was furious. Angie for some reason wasn't bothered at all by the findings, she just wanted to get things moved. It was already tension with Desiree fussing over every little thing and purposely being mean due to she still being mad – mad because Angie didn't give in and hit her off, or rather, lick her off the other night. Angie just didn't feel like getting verbally chastised by Davonte because of it. And she refused not to tell him if had they done it.

Desiree wasn't feeling her little reasoning that evening. Truthfully, Angie found it to be cute how Desiree was tripping the way she was. She wondered was it her, 'I'm the dominant one, gotta have control of the relationship act'?!? Especially after talking to Davonte on the phone earlier and him attempting to tell them how to carry on in their little female/female girlfriend relationship.

"When one of y'all returning from somewhere, work or otherwise, coming in the door I want y'all to greet each other with a kiss," is what he said. *"Angie you do this, Desiree you do that. Treat each other like such and such."*

He had a lot of shit he wanted them to do. Some of which didn't even take place in real relationships, nevertheless, one such as this. On top of all this, he wanted them to hurry home and be there by 6:30pm, because he had something planned for them to do. The instruction was supposed to arrive in a letter he wrote and mailed out.

Unbeknownst to Angie, Desiree's moodiness wasn't solely based upon the fact that she hadn't hooked her up the other night, but moreso Desiree was finding Angie's devotion and submissiveness to be a challenge. She recalled how Davonte would always say to her, *"Just do what I say, how I say."* Or, *"You need to be more obedient."* At times she would, however she had to admit to herself, the constant act of disobedience and stubbornness was something she fell prone to. Why? She was unable to answer. But she surely wasn't about to let Ms. Goody Twoshoes win her man over with some, *"Okay baby, yes baby, anything you want love."* Nah, she wasn't going for that, not one bit. From now on she was going to become his favorite, doing whatever he asked or needed.

Davonte **S**at **A**t the chipped up table reading a note from Harry telling him that taking the plea and doing county time was a smart move because no telling what they were going to try and come at him with. He also apologized for the incident and told him if he needed something or if there was anything he could do let him know. Davonte wanted to write him a note back snapping on him about the ordeal, but figured what the hell? What was done, was done. Plus, they were family. Davonte looked from the letter at the little 19-inch television screen that sat in a metal box with a clear plastic shield on the front. By checking what show was on he could gauge just about what time it was. 'M.A.S.H.' was on, so it was after five o'clock. The girls had a little over an hour to get home. He would wait patiently for them to receive his letter and begin following out his instructions. When he felt they had enough time, he would call and implement the next phase of things. Right now, he would simply work out everything in his head making sure that when he spoke to them he delivered each word perusely. Yeah, he could see it all playing out in his mind.

Angie And Desiree both occupied separate bathrooms in the house. Desiree in the master bedroom, Angie was down the hall, each preparing themselves for Davonte's call, which was to be soon.

Arriving home, they anxiously checked the mailbox. In it there was one envelope with both of their names on it. Inside was a separate letter for each of them that they gladly read. Both of them were so excited about what the letters contained they didn't even finish unloading Davonte's things from the truck. Instead, they decided to get started on the instructions they received in the letters and finish up the unloading later.

Desiree finished rubbing baby oil over her body. Feeling silky smooth, she looked through her drawer of accessories, she paused for a second then thought, *"Color? Look? Red, sexy."* And with that, she was able to finish preparing for Davonte's call.

Angie stood in the bathroom mirror brushing her hair, there was a feeling of excitement. Davonte had instructed her to take a hot bubble bath which was right on time for her just getting off her period the night before, caused a bath to be well deserved along with a refreshing douche to make things complete.

Realizing it was about time to make his call, Davonte made his way over to the phone. Picking up the receiver, he paused and thought for a moment. He figured for the girls all that was taking place with them and the relationship was just a minor part of life, however for Davonte, it was more than that. He found it to be a tad bit more complex, rather similar to a game of chess, a think before you move type situation. Dialing the number, he figured that's exactly how he would handle it.

"I Got It!" Angie yelled upon hearing the phone ring.

"Get it then!" Desiree yelled back as she headed to the kitchen to grab two drinking glasses.

Looking on the caller I.D. Angie saw it was Davonte. Snatching the receiver up, she spoke oh so happily into the phone once the recording ended.

"Hi baby," she chimed, *"How are you?"*

"I'm doing fine," Davonte told her. *"You two got things together?"*

"Yes, I believe we do," she responded, *"Just waiting for Desiree to come in here and we'll be ready to get things rolling."*

Desiree entered the room with two glasses in one hand and a bottle of Jamaican Rum in the other. The two of them gave each other the once over. Angie took notice of Desiree in her little gown that came just above her private area. If you were to look enough you could see much of her pubic hair and vagina lips. So, without a doubt, the bottom of her large butt cheeks had to be sticking out.

Desiree observed Angie's purple gown that also hung just enough to reveal the goodies. Her gown was see-thru, so the round of her nipples showed well.

"Put my baby on speaker phone," Desiree said breaking the silence away with the brief stare.

"Our baby!" Angie retorted while pushing the button for the speakerphone.

"Hey, Big Daddy," Desiree chimed placing the two glasses down alongside the bottle of rum. *"How you doing? I hope everything is okay?"*

"Yeah, sweet dick daddy," Angie added, *"Nobody better not be messing with you or else."*

"I'm fine," Davonte told them, *"Just fine. Did you two do everything you're supposed to?"*

Simultaneously they both gave a cheerful, *"Yessss daddy."*

"And you are in the bedroom?"

Again in unison they answered, *"Yes, we are."*

"Okay then," he said, *"Let's pour us a glass of rum. Make sure it's a little over a shot."*

Angie looked at the bottle and started to prepare herself mentally. She wasn't one for drinking and if and when she did it was usually sweet or mixed drinks. The idea of drinking this liquor made her stomach tighten.

"So, what's the deal?" She asked, *"No chaser?"*

"If you don't see none, there won't be none," Davonte's voice sung through the speaker. *"Now, let's get to drinking,"* he told them.

"Let's waste no time," Desiree said being sarcastic. *"Oh shoot,"* Desiree said reaching for the bottle, *"Angie why don't you go get us a couple pieces of ice?!?"*

Angie quickly jumped from the bed to her feet, *"Anything to make it go down easier,"* she said, making her way down the hall.

Finding this to be the opportune moment to speak with Davonte while Angie wasn't present, Desiree spoke what had been on her mind the last couple hours.

"Baby, we moved your stuff today."

"Thank you," Davonte said, *"I really appreciate it."*

"You're welcome babe. You know I'm your number one lady, right?!?"

Davonte knew Desiree and he knew her well. The last part of the sentence gave her away.

"Look Desiree, before you finish what you're about to say, I hope it's not something that's going to ruin the moment."

"It shouldn't," Desiree lied.

"What shouldn't?" Angie asked, returning into the room with a bowl with about 8 ice cubes in it.

"Desiree was about to ask me something," Davonte responded to her.

Angie looked to Desiree for her to finish. The look on Desiree's face was enough. Angie already knew right then she was about to bring up the things they'd found at his apartment while moving his things earlier.

"Don't start," she whispered to Desiree.

"What'd you say?" Davonte asked. *"I can barely hear you."*

"Nothing baby," Angie told him, *"We're putting ice in the glasses and pouring the drinks."*

Desiree rolled her eyes and smacked her lips.

"Y'all need to get a move on," Davonte told them, *"Let's not forget I'm on a timed phone call and no telling how many it'll take. So let's get as much done as possible in each of them."*

"Okay babe, the drinks are poured," Desiree told him, *"A little over a shot. Just like you said."*

"Good!" Davonte shot back. *"Now, let's raise our glasses, give a toast to us and turn it up, straight to the head."*

Angie pinched her nose and held her glass out. Desiree didn't pinch her nose, she simply gave Angie's glass a tap.

"To us," they both said and turned up their glasses.

After a few seconds of grumbling and scrunching up their faces, their glasses were empty.

"That ice didn't help worth a shit," Desiree gasped.

"Yeah, it was hot," Angie agreed tapping the center of her chest with the side of her fist. *"Okay baby, what's next?"*

Davonte envisioned his two ladies sitting there, looking good, feeling fresh and clean and although there was a hint of curiosity of what might take place next, they both had an idea where it was all leading to.

"Okay," Davonte spoke slowly, calmly, *"It's important that you both listen to me carefully. Now, I asked you two to partake in a relationship that may be considered one that transcends the abnormality of today's relationships. However, your love and respect for me has caused you to give it a try and I must be honest, it's this type of willingness that you two display when dealing with me, that causes me to love the two of you so very much and makes it impossible for me to ever be without either of you."*

Davonte paused for a second to let the words sink in. And sink in they did. The both of them sat there mentally and emotionally touched by his words.

"So, that's why," Davonte continued, *"I've taken it upon myself to create enjoyable moments for you to have. Also, it seems that as far as intimacy is concerned you're not coming along the way you should."*

The last part of the conversation threw both of them for a loop. What did he mean not coming along like they should? They questioned what it was he wanted? Hell, they weren't lesbos or dikes, so what was it he expected?

"The reason you're not coming along like you should be is apparent. Neither of you know what you're doing."

At that, both of their mouths fell open in shock.

"So, what I'm going to do is help you to add some spice. Now, if both of you would get on the bed facing each other, we can get started. As a matter of fact, scoot close to enough to one another that your legs are crossed. Angie, with you being the shorter one, have yours over the top."

The girls climbed on the bed, facing each other they slid into position, no longer bothered by what he had said only moments ago. Looking at each other they shared the same silly grin knowing that Davonte was about to have them go there, wherever there might be. Deep inside, they both had longed for him to turn them out in one way or another, they knew it was something he was definitely capable of doing. Although, with another woman was not and had not ever been a part of their individual fantasy, yet in a continuous effort to prove their love and loyalty they stepped into Davonte's world and allowed him to take them where his heart and creative mind lead them.

"Okay baby, we're in position and facing each other, what's next Big Daddy?" Angie asked.

"Yeah daddy, what you want me to do to Baby Girl?" Desiree asked sounding aggressive and naughty.

"Easy, easy ladies, I'ma get ya'll right," Davonte told them. *"Just kinda sit leaned back propped up on your arms. Just relax and listen to the sound of my voice while giving each other a niiice look over, if you know what I mean?!?"*

They did so and were greatly obliged.

"What the two of you already know and must keep in mind when dealing with one another," Davonte spoke to them in a deep tone with a slow drawl to it, coming off as seductive as he possibly could through the phone. He continued, *"Is that, a woman is delicate, tender. Just look at each other's eyes, lips, the neckline. Allow your eyes to travel down the neck to the breasts, look how succulent they are. Just think of how the right touch, the right caress can not only bring pleasure to them, but also send potent sensations throughout the body."*

The girls listened and followed along in their minds, thinking on what was being said to them. There was an arousal happening in them both. The things he said and the way he said them were extremely stimulating, but what really did it for them was his voice, it was always a turn on.

"Look closely at each others curves, the hips, the legs, that pleasure mound that lies between, yes ladies, let's not forget a woman's body holds many erotic zones that if approached correctly can give tremendous sensation. Continuing to listen to me, I want you both to move in closer, sit up to where you can look directly in each other's eyes. With one hand, I want you to begin gently caressing each other's nipples through the gown. With your eyes, I want you to share with each other what you want and the way you want it."

Davonte coached the girls through hours of sensual love making, guiding them through nearly an hour of 'tease and chase' erotic foreplay. The stimulating build-up was so great that they wanted to burst from anticipation, their nipples were swollen from passion and their entire love mounds pulsated and dripped soaking wet from eagerness. They were so turned on that by the time he instructed them to kiss, they savagely grabbed one another and shoved their tongues in each other's mouth. They kissed with an animal like attraction, grinding, pumping and gyrating their pussies into each other's pelvic area. They threw each other's legs in the air, rolled and turned on the bed, placing their legs in a locked scissor position with their hands on both butt cheeks and went to town.

Occasionally, Davonte would stress to them, *"Make her feel what you want to feel. Give her the desire and passion you want."*

With those words, things became more than one could imagine. Even the two of them became lost in the overwhelming passion being shared and once he instructed them to assume the sixty-nine position, there was nothing less than erotic flames of pleasure delivered. They licked, slurped, swallowed, rolled and turned in the bed. Grabbing and spreading each other's cheeks, they licked and kissed clit. They held each other's head between their legs, ate pussy and fucked one another in the mouth and face. They continued on, even after Davonte's phone time ran out and he didn't call back. Each of them blessed the other with repeated breath taking, heart-stopping orgasms. That night, they carried on until their friend 'exhaustion' took over.

NARRATION

Imagine Two Mature women in love with a younger man whose mental workings are intoxicatingly stimulating in itself, along with his sexual performance being delivered like a form of unorthodox poetry. The combination caused for him to be propitious and unmatched by any. The desire, the lust, toppled by the welcomed fear of his unquestionable pleasurable and pleasing abilities made for any woman's dreams, and would cause her to soil her panties regularly.

Simply put, what woman would deny his requests and why would you dare?

CHAPTER ELEVEN

"TRY SEXUALS"

The Ladies Began to put their individual love for
Davonte to the side and made sure it didn't get in the way
of their working with one another. Or maybe it was the fact
that they had become consumed with their new pastime.
Davonte had given them the okay to indulge in the pleasure
of each other twice a week and twice a week they did.
Sometimes at the beginning, sometimes at the end and if
they were both off on the weekends, they would save up
and do back to back days. The hot, steamy evening
Davonte had coached them through brought them to
another level of doing things. They now took a whole new
approach to their sexual dealings. They would go from
sensual lovemaking, where they catered to each other's
pleasure zones, to all out erotic aggressive sex where they
play games of teasing and 'get yours before I get mines.'
They did all they could think of from sixty-nining to orally
working each other anal to clit from the back.

Desiree learned she could get off as many times as she
wanted by laying on top of Angie and grinding her.
Whether it was her pussy or her leg in a scissor position or
she could straddle her and put her clit to her pelvic area.
She could get hers and hard too.

Yet, she continued to have Angie tongue whipped. Yeah,
Desiree was able to control Angie's sexual gratification
with the simple flick of the tongue. And Angie didn't mind
not one bit. All the kisses and foreplay was delightful. The
things they did to please each other was great, but Angie
had to admit, she looked forward to Desiree laying her on
her back spreading her legs or even getting at it from the
back in a doggy style position. Be it whatever degree of
creativeness Desiree chose, it was alright with Angie. She

gladly laid back, spread it open or bent it up because she knew Desiree was going to bring her to an explosive climax. Angie found Desiree's tongue game to be awesome. From looking at Desiree and talking to her you would have never known her tongue was as long as it was or that she could do what she did with it. You see, for Desiree it was more than just a matter of sex, it was passion and about feeling the persons energy and finding what worked for them and once discovered she'd work it, tease it, toy with it, cater to it, become emotionally involved with her work. That's how she performed each and every time with Angie.

There were times she had Angie worked up so much, Angie would beg, *"Please Dezi baby, please let me cum!"* Desiree would make her beg and scream regularly. To her, it was all a part of the moment. A moment where she was in total control of a person's action and being a Leo, that made for a moment she enjoyed.

One evening, she allowed Angie to straddle her face while she performed on her all the teasing and toying, which caused Desiree to end up with her entire face being wet, shiny and sticky from forehead to chin. Angie and Desiree had put in so much work on each other, that they encountered subtle realties such as, two females could perform all night, verses a lot of men's limited time capabilities where you knew no matter how big, small, or long they were, it was best to get yours before it was over.

However, there was no such problems with the ladies. You see, there was an unspoken overstanding that said no one stops, no one gives up until all parties are satisfied and after that, there must be the cuddling and spooning. The ladies found it to be impressive what they were able to give and receive from one another. They talked, laughed, wrestled, set traps for one another. Yeah, they shared in a variety of different approaches that lead up to many of their intimate festivities. They'd done so much and tried so many things and unbeknownst to them, they were becoming turned out. Although they may not have been aware of it, it was openly apparent to Davonte. Seeing that when he'd call and talk to either of them, they not only shared with him their private dealings, but also they both began sharing with him this sudden attraction they were having towards other females on the job, at the gas station, wherever they saw'em. They would tell him how a female had a big ass or an overall nice shape. He noticed Angie had a thing for thick thigh hippy chicks with large rumps. Desiree was showing signs of attraction towards dark complected slim chicks that would have a surprisingly big butt for their slender frames. Davonte found it to be surprising, yet delightful. It made for a hellava fantasy in his mind.

Staring **O**ut **T**he window, Desiree watched Angie pulling into the driveway. She watched closely as she stepped from the car with a bag in her hand. Angie was rather happy leaving the house for work earlier today, telling her she had a big surprise she was bringing home and telling Desiree, to make sure she was there when she got back, as if she went anywhere without Davonte telling her to do so anyway.

She'd even told Angie she'd better get her ass back before he called or she'd be in deep shit. Desiree looked at the bag in Angie's hand and giggled.

"So much for a big surprise," she mumbled to herself.

Angie shut the front door behind her, kicked off her shoes and headed happily to the couch where she spun around flopped down and called for Desiree.

"Dezi!" She called out attempting to sound flirty.

"Come here, I have a surprise for youuu."

Desiree came strolling down the hall in a pair of baby blue cotton pj's with one of Davonte's wife beaters on. Both pieces fitted snug, showing off her frame.

Angie quickly took notice to her not having on any bra or panties. Her large nipples made a very noticeable imprint in the shirt and the pajama pants fit snug, tight enough to show her vagina lips as well. Angie thought of how they hadn't done anything in four days.

As Desiree came closer, she could see the look in Angie's eyes, the look of lust. So she stood directly in front of her with her legs spread seductively, knowing Angie had a thing for her hips. She stood, allowing her to take it all in.

Angie swallowed, then licked her lips, she was always ready for a roll in the hay with Desiree.

"So, are we dating tonight?" She asked staring directly between Desiree's legs. Desiree returned the same silent naughty stare Angie was giving her, then held out her hand.

"Come here baby girl," she said pulling Angie up towards her, grabbing Angie around the waist. She looked directly in her eyes and in a whispered voice, she repeated the question while leaning in to kiss her.

"You want to know if we are dating tonight?" As she planted a soft kiss on her lips.

Angie shook her head yes.

"Why you feeling frisky?" Desiree whispered.

Once again Angie shook her head yes, this time with a smile on her face that said to Desiree 'you know what it is'.

Desiree smiled back, *"I don't think so,"* she said quickly pushing Angie back on the couch. *"Now where is this big surprise you're supposed to have for me?"*

"Ahhh, you played me," Angie said smacking her lips, *"You'd better be glad you my girl, or I wouldn't even give you the surprise for playing me like that."*

Desiree shrugged her shoulders as to say 'so what'.

"It's on you," she told Angie, *"But whatever you gonna do, you need to hurry up because there's a good movie on the Lifetime Channel."*

"Okay, I hear you Lifetime Channel," Angie said rolling her eyes, *"Don't try to play like you don't want to know what I got you."*

"Sike, you right," Desiree said flopping on her knees on the couch beside Angie, *"Let me see what you got!"*

Angie slid her hand in the little colorful bag she held in her hand.

"I shouldn't show you," she told Desiree.

"Aahh, come on," Desiree whined, then reaching over she teasingly rubbed on Angie's breast, *"You know you want to show me."*

"Stop playing!" Angie snapped.

"Well, show me," Desiree whined again, this time bouncing up and down on the couch like a big kid.

"Okay, okay," Angie said looking Desiree in the eye, *"You ready? BAMM!"* She yelled pulling out the surprise before Desiree could say anything else.

For a second, Desiree sat speechless staring at the object in Angie's hand. Her eyes roamed down to what looked to be a price tag with numbers on it. Her eyes bucked along with her mouth falling wide open as she saw the number 14 and the inches beside it. Looking at the big black 14inch dildo, she shot Angie a glance, then back at the dildo.

"So, what you think?" Angie asked, rubbing her middle finger over the head of the object. *"You think its something we can work with?"* Angie asked right before opening her mouth and sliding the head of the dildo in and out.

"Here," she said, releasing the dildo from her mouth with a loud suction noise, *"You try it."*

Desiree sat back on the couch and took the dildo from Angie's hand as she smiled.

"You trippin'," Desiree said squeezing the dildo as though she was checking it for firmness. Angie's smile faded.

"Why you say I'm trippin'?" She inquired, figuring she just about knew the answer.

"Davonte? That." Desiree said offering no more as she slid her finger along the makeshift veins of the dildo.

"That and what else?" Angie asked with a bit of an attitude coming on.

"Look," Desiree said taking a deep breath, *"I know exactly where you're coming from, trust me, I do. A sister miss her some penetration too, but damn girl a 14 inch strap on dildo?!? And how thick is the damn thing?"*

"I don't know why you trippin'," Angie said standing up and stepping out of her skirt. *"Davonte's big too,"* she told Desiree while taking the dildo from her hand strapping it on, *"So now what?!?"* She said standing there with the dildo on like a man pumping back and forth.

"Yeah, he is," Desiree said in agreement, *"He's ten inches easy and I must say a mean ass ferocious ten inches. Still its not 14 inches, and if it was, I wouldn't fuck him. I be having a time with the ten. If we do it two days in a row, I be wore out. If we do it twice in one day I need 3 days to recoup. And I know your ass be getting handled by him, you smaller than me!"* Desiree went on to talk while Angie thought of how true the last few words were. Davonte would put it to her in a fashion that would have her spazing out sometimes.

"Yeah, and when he be wanting to get at him some ass and I let him hit it afterwards my spine feel like its sore. Not to mention my asshole and on top of that when I use the bathroom for about 3 days, girlll let me tell you my shit just falls out my ass."

Angie looked at Desiree with a stunned look.

"Wait, wait wait, wait one second. Back up a little, when you say you let him hit some ass, you mean hitting pussy from the back don't you?!"

"Hel-lo!" Desiree said tapping her finger on her own forehead, *"Anybody home?"* She mimicked, *"Didn't I just say my shiiit would just fall out?!? What that sound like to you?"*

Angie was shocked at what Desiree just shared with her, she was appalled. Angie looked on as Desiree continued to talk.

"Honestly, I had ass and hips when I met Davonte, but I have to say, since letting him come with the anal sex, my shit done definitely spread. I know it has, ass and all. And let me add, as much as I like to be in control in the bed, as you already know," she told Angie with a wink of the eye. *"That's the one time he is most definitely in total control."*

Angie stood there holding in her emotions. Here Davonte was doing a sexual act with Desiree he had never even brought to her. Even though she'd always said that would be the one thing she undoubtedly saved for her husband. She felt he could have at least asked her or tried. She loved him enough to where she felt he would have one day been her husband, until then, she may have been willing to bend the rules.

"Another thing," Desiree continued, *"When we first started doing it, I was like man this shit hurt and I wasn't really feeling it all like that, now his butt be stroking and doing some shit to my ass got me enjoying it to the point I sometime be feeling like I'm about to cum."*

"Oh, you do?" Angie said not really meaning to ask the question.

"Hell yeah!" Desiree exclaimed, *"A few times I went down on him, then when he would get nice and hard I would turn around, spread my butt cheeks open, talking about, "Come on baby get you some ass." Knowing damn well I'm trippin'!"*

"Yeah, you trippin'," Angie told her.

"Trippin' and kinda liking the shit," Desiree retorted partially smiling surprised at her own words. She talked on unaware of little ole Angie being pissed.

Finishing His Tenth set of push-ups, Davonte glanced at the television. Because of many of the other inmates still sleeping, it was turned down low to where he couldn't hear it. Judging from the screen, the morning news was on, so it wasn't nine o'clock yet. He decided on doing a quick set of a hundred sit-ups then he'd hit the shower and call his ladies. It was Sunday and they were both off, so he knew he could expect a visit from them today. He purposely hadn't called since Friday evening. He laughed to himself thinking of the phone call. Angie calling herself coming clean about a dildo she'd bought. Desiree in the background yelling, *"It's 14 inches too babe!"* They must have thought he was going to be upset, however it was quite the contrary. The fact that she'd done it let him know her sexual perversion could be taken to another level. It most surely brought ideas, but he would deal with that at another time.

What he couldn't believe is how she actually had a problem with the fact he'd never attempted anal sex with her. She was really upset over it, to the point she made him make her a promise – a promise that they would have repeated anal sex when he got home, without a doubt, he promised her they would. She was flipping out on how she didn't think that was fair how he had done it to Desiree and not her. She felt if they were both his ladies, one shouldn't get more than the other. They should be dealt with equally in all areas. She asked him why he hadn't done it to her, and truthfully he should have left the question alone. But no, he responded with some mess about how he didn't think she'd like it. Angie really flipped her lid then.

"Bullshit!" She snapped into the phone, *"Desiree up here saying some shit about how you got some technique to where not only do it hurt so good, she be wanting to cum from it! Oh, and let's not leave out how it done made her hips and ass spread more."*

All the while Desiree's butt in the background hollering, *"Go head babe give it to her. Hook her up with it. I wanna see this shit! Lube her up and drop anchor on her ass, or better yet, do like they do in the pornos, just spit on her butt hole and slide it in."*

Desiree was clowning, she knew Angie was a lot smaller than her, especially in the rear end department. She just wanted to see Angie taking the width and length of "Big Ben" so she could tease her knowing the initial entry could be something else if the female didn't relax and Angie was a squirmer.

Davonte smiled to himself as he reminisced on the thought of the technique that had allowed him entrance and repeated access to the rumps of several lovely women. It was all a matter of creating a mental comfort zone for the female first, then with very patient and intense foreplay, get them to a point that cause them to crave being penetrated. From there, he'd simply rubbed the rim of the bootyhole, a little lube is welcomed. With his pinky finger he would slowly, gently enter the bootyhole. He would do that several times, stroking it in and out as he did. This was done because it was painless and gave them somewhat of an idea of how something going in and out of the rectum may feel, because there was no major discomfort it caused them to be willing to take things a step further. From there, he would kinda slightly stretch the bootyhole by turning his finger in circles and applying pressure as he did. That step led to the using of the thumb, which was larger, yet tolerable. Only when entering with the thumb, you press down as you went in. The same steps taken with the pinky

135

finger is applied here. However, while stroking in and out and striking, he would massage the inner and outer areas of the bootyhole to create a pleasurable sensation.

From there, much lube is needed now, because the insertion of the main vein is to take place. This is where he'd caress the lady's body and ask her was she okay, and fine with things. Upon sliding the head in, whether she'd be missionary or doggy style, press down and forward, not hard, in one smooth motion, but it must be remembered, patience is key. Be even more patient than she. As he'd press down and forward, before she could even get a good feel for it, he'd pull back. This was done repeatedly, sliding in deeper each time, but pulling out before she got a good feel for it. This would seem to come across in a teasing fashion and caused a craving within the female to be penetrated.

Once he noticed this happening from her response, he would caress her body again, legs, breast stomach, then he'd tell her, *"I'm about to give it to you. All of it."* That would warrant a gaspy, *"Okay,"* from the lady. At this point, the head was slid in slowly, but steadily until he would feel a 'pop' that would cause a moan from the female, but ahh! Not trying to give too much too soon, he'd pull back and repeat the slow steady process of sliding it in again. After the 'pop' honestly you were all good. Stroke in circles as you penetrate deeper, pulling back if she moaned from discomfort. Yet, no sooner than she relaxed, give it to her again. This technique could be used for three or four sessions until you were just all out sexing them in the booty. From there, it was a matter of positions and strokes that were applied. At this point, one could trust the female would discover what way she liked it best and let it be known. Stroking with a massaging like penetration was the key and he was definitely willing to hook Angie up.

Many would say, if a man's woman wanted or preferred anal sex more than vaginal, he might not be packing much. For some, that may have been true, but for Davonte, he knew better than that. He was holding and was simply good at what he did. With Desiree being sprung, and down for however he wanted to bring it, that in itself was bragging rights along with being his badge of honor.

CHAPTER TWELVE

"SECRETS"

Putting The Finishing touches on a mouth watering broiled lobster dish, Angie let out a sigh, as a question she'd answered several times already ran through her mind once more.

"Why? Why are you here in Atlanta?" Figuring the answer was simple, she answered to herself each time she asked it, *"Davonte, that's the reason."* However, the fact that it continued to be a surfacing question she wondered how simple it really was.

"Lobster up!" She yelled, turning to prepare her next dish. As she oiled up a medium sized skillet, she gave thought to her present job and how much she liked it. Cooking was something she always enjoyed, although she initially started college to become a pastry chef. The fact that she'd taken it farther and became a Sous chef didn't bother her nonetheless. She saw it as broadening her skills in the kitchen, which would allow for more opportunity down the road. But for some reason at this very point in her life, there was a feeling of emotional discomfort. A feeling of whether or not she could be doing better and she wasn't quite sure what had brought about this feeling of discontent. Whether it was her missing Davonte or Desiree's funky attitude, not to mention, was the reason for her working the overtime she had been lately. Yet and still, she wasn't sure what it was. All she was sure of was how she wanted that feeling of happiness back that had over the last couple of days attempted to elude her.

"Well, hi there," a cheerful voice said, bringing Angie out of her gloomy thoughts. Turning to see who it was, a smile came across her face. It was Antonio. Antonio Serengeti, the owner's son. He was a tall slender guy, 27

years of age, part white, part Jewish, part Italian features along with the fact he either stayed in the sun or at the tanning booth, made it difficult to determine his nationality or even what he might supposed to have been. Strangely enough, he was an attractive guy at least all the waitress's thought so. Seeing how whenever he came into the restaurant, they'd do everything from whistling to cat meows and hissing to actually pinching him on the butt. Angie had to admit, there was a coolness about him. However, for her, it wasn't in the normal boy meets girl kinda way. He had jet-black hair and wore it in a goofy style that he thought was the-e-e shit! Him having the confidence to wear it was what made her see a coolness in him. It was probably safe to call it the dare to be different persona. Along with, like Davonte, he had a unique taste for nice smelling cologne and like Davonte he always had some on.

"Hi to you too, Mr. Serengeti," Angie chimed with a slight wave of the hand.

"Antonio," he corrected as he threw an arm across his stomach and bowed.

It was at that moment Angie thought of another reason for his coolness. He had a sense of humor about himself. His jokes were dry, but caused her to laugh from time to time.

"Okay, Antonio if that's what you prefer," she told him.

"What I'd prefer, I don't think you'd give," he responded pausing for a second then quickly adding, *"So, Antonio will have to do for now."*

Angie didn't feed into his comment. He had been a little flirtatious the last few days. She figured he would stop once he saw she wasn't responding to it.

"How can I help you, Antonio? It's busy around here today, I can't talk much. Plus I'm sure the girls up front could use your presence if nothing else." She shot him a quick glance, one that said, did you catch the brush?

"Hey, Angie did I tell you the one about the guy at the bar with the frog?"

"No, you didn't," Angie told him not caring if he did or didn't. She had work to do and didn't care to be disturbed.

Antonio, on the other hand, went on to tell his joke about a frog and two patrons at a bar, male and female. The joke took about 20 minutes to tell and ended with some crap about the man talking to the frog and the frog giving oral sex to the woman. Angie hadn't really listened to what he was saying, she faded in and out of listening in between what she was doing. Antonio studied her for a second then placed his hand gently on her shoulder. Softly he spoke to her.

"When you take interest in someone, you tend to notice things about them."

Angie stopped stirring the sauce for her cream of mushroom. The hand on her shoulder along with the words that followed caused her to wonder what he would possibly say next. I mean, how much could he have noticed. She'd just been working there close to two and a half months. And what did he mean by, when you take interest in someone? Turning to look at the hand on her shoulder in disapproval Angie cleared her throat.

"Excuse me. Just what are you talking about?" She asked.

Noticing the look on her face, Antonio quickly removed his hand.

"I'm sorry," he said, *"Placing my hand on you wasn't a wise decision. I assure you I meant no harm."*

Seeing his sincerity, Angie trusted his words.

"No harm done," she told him.

"Good." Antonio responded with a sigh of relief. *"That's good. I would have hated to offend you when my only intention is to let you know I see a change in you. I mean, I could be wrong, but it just seems like you're not as*

happy as you once were. Now again, I could be wrong. If so, forgive me. However, with the unfortunate chance that I'm not, please feel free to talk to me if you need to."

Angie thought to herself, *"There's no way it's that noticeable, lucky guess."*

"So what makes you think there's something wrong?" She asked the question, but turned to finish preparing her next dish, or at least that's what she pretended to be doing. Honestly, it was done to break the eye contact before he was able to see just how right his assumption really was.

"Well, I have a mother and three sisters, each older than myself. I'm not an expert on women, but because of my mother and sisters, I have come to learn certain things about them."

"Is that so?" Angie questioned hoping that he didn't think he knew her because he grew up around women. (Because of course, all women are different, aren't they?)

Antonio noticed she was becoming agitated and decided it was best to say what he was going to say and be on his way.

"Angie, a woman's face is a window for other people to look in on and when it becomes pale or flush, its saying she's done something that her moral conscience told her she should not have, or something has taken place to cause her unhappiness. I'm leaning towards the latter of the two. With that being said, I'm going to take off. But by all means if you ever need to talk, vent or whatever, feel free to let me know. And don't worry, I know this isn't the place for that, so if need be, we can go somewhere nice and quiet. Just let me know."

Angie listened and his words caused her to think something her grandmother once told her, she said...

"When you reach a point in life where there's a question of your happiness, its wise to go over past events to see what has led to this, as well as, its okay to talk to someone.

People tend to hold things in and that usually makes matters worst."

It was Davonte Angie talked to when she needed. However, with his present situation, that was now difficult and when he did call the house, she was unable to talk to him the way she would have liked to because of Desiree being present and she didn't want to cause any unnecessary waves. Antonio saw Angie pondering on what he'd just said to her and wondered had he made a mistake.

"Listen," he began speaking, *"If I have said anything to offend you, I apologize. As well as, out of all that I've spoke on and suggested by all means it's totally up to you. If you feel like it let me know something, if not, I'll respect that. Okay, you hear me?"*

"Yes," Angie responded softly, *"I hear you."*

"There it is then. I'll talk to you later."

Angie watched as Antonio walked away.

"What the hell just happened?" She asked herself.

One of the waitresses came briskly walking by with a tray of dirty dishes, *"Hey, Nettavon. I see you were talking to Antonio. Better be careful girl. They say he's like a philter."*

With that being said, she was off.

"A what?" Angie wondered.

Young Marcus, the dishwasher, stood observing Angie and Antonio's conversation. Marcus had a crush on Angie and was now jealous. He also had a mental disability. Walking over to her, he handed her a wilted flower from one of the dirty trays.

"W...W...What bout us Angie?" He asked looking teary-eyed.

A Lot **Of** small petty things were occurring over the last few days. Things Desiree didn't really care for. Gossiping at work, the surgery doctor getting on her nerves behind scheduling pre-ops, Devonte not calling but every other day. Not that she really mind, because it helped the phone bill, but when he did call, he was fussing and complaining about her and Angie falling out last weekend.

Angie had caught her at a bad time. After she had told her the night before she was cramping real bad. Waking up the next morning, she wasn't doing any better. In fact, because of the cramping, she hadn't gotten much sleep. Angie comes busting in the room at 6 in the morning talking about she was on her way to work and wanted the five dollars Desiree owed her.

Desiree asked her, *"You need it or you want it?"* Not really wanting to get up.

Angie flipped out, *"What difference it make!? It's mine and you owe it to me!"*

From there they went into a heated argument that ended up with them calling each other bitches and threatening to hurt the other. It should have been over once Angie left out for work, however, when she returned in the late evening for whatever reason it started back up again. They were even having words when Davonte called causing him to become upset and go off on them. Sharing your man was some heavy shit to do. Desiree had heard a lot of women say they would rather their man just be honest and let it be known there was another woman.

"Shiiit," she thought, *"If they knew what I know, they'd leave well enough alone. Because the saying 'What you don't know won't hurt you' has some truth in it. Cuz what you do know will make you want to kill somebody!"*

Turning on the shower, Desiree headed over to the bed and sat down. Work was a mess along with all that has been taking place.

"When will it all end?" She wondered.

Staring at her purse, she shook her head in disbelief. Reaching in it, she pulled out a card that read, "Nubian

Clothing, men and women ethnic apparel and accessories."
There was a number and under it was a name, Taalib. She
would not have even taken the card had the guy not been so
persistent, in between him trying to sell her a pair of jeans
with a blouse that had an Egiptian print on it that she liked,
by the way. Along with the continuous compliments, that
she felt was overkill, being that she was in scrubs and
didn't feel as sexy as he claimed she was. What she
overlooked was, her shape was noticeable regardless of
what she wore and brother Taalib let that be known. He
even offered to pump her gas for her and she accepted.
Seeing how much she liked the blouse, he used it to his
advantage and made her an offer she couldn't refuse,
although she should have.

He offered Desiree the blouse if she would have one
drink with him and she quickly said yes. Not because she
really was going to do it, but because it was a free shirt. To
her, it was worth the little white lie. Holding the card in
one hand, the blouse in the other, she had to admit he said
some very charming things and although he was no
Davonte, he was an attractive guy. Yet there was a point
where he had turned her off. It seemed he had the concept
of a thug and being just straight ghetto mixed up.

"Oh well, my brother Taalib," she thought out loud,
*"Hopefully, you don't use your clothes as a ploy to pull all
the sisters you find attractive because if you do, you'zz
gonna be one broke brotha."*

With that and a giggle she headed to the bathroom to
shower. Desiree had never cheated or stepped out on
Davonte before and had no intentions of doing it now.

NARRATION

As It's Said, Black women enjoy being desired and told that they're beautiful to the point that they are always open for a line and a chance to be hit on. The giving of attention with persistence, spiced with a small occasional gift will persuade the majority of them to indulge in a meaningless intimate frolic. But hey, what can one expect? This is the same person who in the book of Genesis spoke with the serpent in the Garden of Eden, listened to him, ate from the fruit and never once asked the serpent who he was or why he would dare have her go against God.

Davonte **H**ad **B**een having a heck of a time with the ladies the last week or so. Things just didn't seem right. The conversation with each of them had begun to be short and seeming with less enthusiasm. And although they both assured him the love and loyalty was just as strong as before, he questioned it. Call it intuition, to him things just didn't seem right. But in retrospect, neither of them had ever violated the relationship even after knowing of each other. So that led him to believe all was possibly well and whatever was taking place and causing them to act out of the norm had to be a female thing between the two of them.
   "Oh well, they're rational thinking females and adults at that." So, he figured they'd work it out. Although, it may take a minute, seeing they both admitted to wanting to stay out of each other's way for a while. They meant it too, as they both were putting in overtime this Saturday, which was alright with him. He had a little sum sum he needed to look into himself. You see, for him jail was only a momentary hindrance.

Angie **D**rove **H**ome feeling a little out of place, she'd been attempting to call her grandmother yesterday evening only to find out from her uncle Vincent, she left earlier in the week with her best friend on a trip to Germany. That depressed her, seeing her grandmother had been leaving messages for her to call back all week, plus she was in need of those supportive and encouraging words that only a grandma could give.
   "Oh well," she sighed reaching to turn the radio up. Traffic was smooth, yet a little congested, but moving. She'd be home in a minute and a hot bath would be the answer to her problems, for now anyway.
   Hanging up the phone, Desiree walked over to her dresser and took a last minute look at herself. It was a chilly

November day, so her plaid wrap a round skirt with matching blouse would do the job.

"I look descent," she told herself as she squirted on some perfume. And with a deep breath, she spun around grabbed her purse along with a piece of paper from the nightstand and hurriedly, she made her way out of the door and down the hallway.

"So Tell Me Mr. *Davonte, why is it that you have summoned little ole me after all this time?"*

"Well, you know me. I like to keep in touch with close friends."

Melissa sat there looking through the glass that separated her from a gentleman whose very presence turned her on. She and Davonte had been special friends for some time now. They would indulge in each other's delicacies when time allowed in between their personal lives and relationships. They had agreed early on, that a commitment wouldn't work, so they decided to just keep in touch and assist one another when the need called for it. Their moto was… "A friend in need was a friend indeed."

"You look to have put on a little weight," Davonte told her.

"Yeah," she smiled, pushing her breast up being flirty. *"I haven't had any in awhile."*

"Oh, you haven't?!?" Davonte exclaimed, smiling ear to ear. *"So, we're going to have to do something about that aren't we?"*

"Yeah, I would say we do. But when that's going to be?" She asked rolling her eyes and sticking out her tongue. *"When you getting out of here?"*

"February," Davonte responded.

"Aah, excuse me it's November. So, I have to wait 3 more months for some of Big Ben and the twins?"

"Yep, but it'll be worth it." Davonte gave her an assuring look.

"And what about your not one, but two women at home?"

"Don't worry, I'll work that out. I'll tell them I get out a day later than I really do and hope they don't check into it. That way I can have a whole day to get that back straight, ya know what I mean?"

They both laughed.

"I hear you," Melissa said, *"Let's not forget you dealing with two women, Black women at that, and you think they ain't gonna check into the release date of their man, shiiit sho you right."*

"I'll handle it," he smiled.

"You better!" She snapped jokingly. *"I haven't been able to get hit off right since you been dealing with those two. Another thing, Mr. Davonte you know I chill out on Saturdays, but here you done got me down here visiting you at some freaking county jail."*

Davonte paid her words no mind, instead he began blowing kisses and sticking out his tongue.

"I got something you can do with that," she laughed. *"I like it when you're impish."*

Putting **T**he **T**oilet seat down and placing the phone on top of it. Angie climbed into the tub of hot water.

"Oweee, this feels sooo good," she moaned as she sat down and the water embraced her naked body. She couldn't help to let out a slight laugh as she thought about how upon turning on the street to the house she passed Desiree. She blew the horn at her, but she acted as though she didn't see her.

"Silly cow, you wasn't in no hurry so no need to act like it, ha! Where you got to go?"

After 30 minutes in the tub, Angie turned on the hot water to bring back the heat that was trying to escape. She waved her hand around to help with the circulation of the hot water. The bath was wonderful and seemed to suit its purpose.

"Who you fooling?" Angie questioned out loud and grabbed the receiver from the phone. Listening to the phone ring, she massaged her temples with her finger and thumb, her expression said, *"What am I doing?"*

"Hello," the voice said on the other end.

"Antonio, is that you?"

"This Has Got to be the spot," Desiree said to herself, putting the car in park and looking down at the piece of paper with the directions on it. Stepping from the car, she headed up the walkway. *"I knew he was lying, I could hear it in his voice. This ain't no dang café."*

Approaching the door, she asked herself what it was she was doing? Without allowing herself a chance to answer, she knocked.

As if her arrival was anticipated, the door came open no sooner than she knocked.

"Well hello," the gentleman said.

Desiree smiled, *"How are you, Taalib?"*

CHAPTER THIRTEEN

"CONFESSIONS"

"Hold Up A minute! What do you mean you want to quit your job at the restaurant you're at now and find another one?"

Angie thought about the past weekend and how things were at work before Saturday.

"I'm waiting for a response!" Davonte snapped, *"What reason do you have for wanting to leave a job you've only been at a couple months?!"*

"I just do," Angie said flatly, *"I don't know why I just want to work somewhere else. What's wrong with that?"*

"Desiree do you hear this mess?"

"Yeah, Davonte, I hear it."

Angie cut her eyes at Desiree and smacked her lips.

"And what do you think about this?"

Before Desiree could answer, Angie went off.

"What you asking her what she thinks about it for?!"

Davonte held the phone in disbelief. Inside he felt something wasn't right, but he couldn't quite put his finger on what could have taken place for her to want to quit her job. Just this weekend she was trying to put in overtime, now she want to quit.

"The reason I asked Desiree what she thinks about it is because we are all in this relationship together. Now you may choose to forget that, but I haven't. Now, like I asked before, Desiree what do you think of that?"

"I don't know Davonte, I'm just as surprised as you are, whatever you allow her to do," Desiree said being sarcastic, *"I hope she's still able to pay her bills."*

"Psss, ain't that bout it," Angie smirked.

"Yeah, that is bout it," Desiree returned.

"Y'all stop fucking bickering!" Davonte's voice rang
through the speakerphone. *"All y'all do lately is be at each
other's throat. That's not what I want so cut that shit out
or you know what, I can do without both of you!"*

The words caused both their mouths to fall open.

*"How you gonna get mad over her wanting to quit her
little piece of job and say something like that?"* Desiree
questioned becoming angry.

"Whatever," Davonte roared through the phone, *"It's
about y'all falling out all the time that has me pissed, not
her wanting to quit her job which she won't be doing. You
hear me Angie? Until you can give me a good reason for
quitting, you'll be working there."*

"Oh," Desiree snapped, *"Now all she has to do is give
you a good reason?!?"*

"Shut the fuck up!" Davonte yelled. *"I'm about to get
off this phone. I will call you a little later and when I call
back y'all need to have your minds together both
figuratively and literally! Do y'all hear me!?"*

The girls didn't answer right away which made Davonte
even madder. To him, it was sign of disrespect, which
would possibly mean he was losing control, something he
couldn't dare let happen.

"Oh, so I take it I have to repeat myself?"

At that, they jumped to answer him.

"Okay, Davonte we hear you, loud and clear."

"Good!" He snapped, then without as much as a
goodbye, he hung up.

The girls sat there staring at the phone for a moment.
Breaking the silence, Desiree looked over at Angie.

*"So, what has somebody or should I say, what have you
and somebody done to each other at work?"* Making a face
as if she was just too disgusted.

Angie jumped up to walk out of the room.

"What you talking about, you crazy?" She told Desiree.

Desiree watched Angie walk towards the bedroom door and then with perfect timing she asked, *"Who is Antonio?"*

Angie stopped dead in her tracks, as if she were on a rotating floor, she turned around slowly.

"What did you say?" She asked Desiree shrugging her shoulders as if she had no earthly idea of what or whom she was talking about.

"Let's do it like this," Desiree said, *"Because I really don't have time to play. Your little friend Antonio called here late Saturday night or maybe you could say early Sunday Morning seeing it was about 1:30 am. I take it you must have called him from the house and forgot to block the number due to the fact he started his message with an apology for calling the number. However, he just wanted to see if you made it home okay seeing how you were a little exhausted when you left his place."*

Angie stood there frozen, her face gave it all away. *"Damn,"* she thought, *"How the fuck did I slip up like that?"*

"Now, if you're worried about whether or not I'm going to tell Davonte?!? Don't worry bout that right now. However, I would like for you to explain to me how the fuck you go out there fucking with some stranger knowing how Davonte be having us get down and niggas be out there having shit! Tell me that Angie!"

Desiree had her ass and knew it. She gave Angie a look that said, *"Yeah, bitch I got one up on you, now what?"*

Angie stood looking at Desiree gloating in her thoughts.

"First, let me say I'm far from worried about you telling Davonte shit, seeing how I ain't the only one around here slipping."

Desiree looked at Angie like, *"Yeah right cow, you ain't got shit on me."*

"Anyway, Angie don't try to play like you got nothing on me, because you and me both know better. Oh, and by the

*way, Antonio wouldn't happen to be the bosses' little son would he? You know, the one you told me about when you first started working there. The cute little boy with the silly hair cut. That wouldn't happen to be **that** Antonio would it?!?*

Angie couldn't believe Desiree was sitting here running off out the mouth as if she really hadn't done anything.

"Like I said!" Angie snapped looking Desiree directly in the eye, *"I wasn't the only one slipping around here. It's the little things you over look that get you caught up. Wouldn't you say so?*

Desiree looked on at Angie still convinced she had nothing on her.

"You see, Saturday Davonte called expecting to speak to you, but I answered the phone. He was concerned about why you was working overtime and thought maybe it was because you was trying to get the lawyer paid off. He had me click over on the three way to call your job. He wanted to tell you not to put yourself through any unnecessary heartache. But guess what!?" Angie said with her eyes bucked, being mimicky, *"You wasn't there and the damn voice machine said the office was closed until Monday 8am. Now, how you gonna work overtime when the office you work at was closed altogether. That, along with the fact your room reeked with perfume when I came in the house kinda made thing suspicious, along with you being in such a hurry, you didn't even notice me blowing at you when we passed at the stop sign."*

Desiree heard everything Angie said, but not as much as the part where she had called with Davonte on the three way and the answering service said the office was closed til Monday. And just think, this trick didn't even have the decency to tell me. Suddenly, Desiree didn't want to play the little game of having something over on some one. She needed to find out where Davonte's head was because she knew if he even felt or thought for a second she had been with some guy, two things were coming from that, the Ike Turner shit, then he was gone and there was no looking back. Angie stood there hands on hip, she didn't quite know what Desiree had done, but knew she'd done something all the same.

"Look, we need to talk," Desiree said.

"I would say we do," Angie agreed. *"You might want to start by telling me what took place with you this weekend,"* she told Desiree trying to get her to spill the beans first.

"Excuse me, you the one got some guy from your job calling here, the job you oddly enough want to quit all of a sudden, so you need to be telling me what happened."

Before Desiree had gotten the last words out, Angie started whimpering, *"I...I d... didn't even mean to call him or go over there, it kinda just happened. Then I get over there he on some other shit when I just wanted to talk and..."* Angie paused as she replayed that evening in her head.

"And what?" Desiree asked, thinking this fool done really went and got fucked by her boss' son. *"I'm listening Angie, what happened?"*

Angie continued on explaining to Desiree what had happened, even telling her about the brief conversation they had at work and how she just needed someone to talk to because things seemed to have been crazy around the house with them. Desiree overstood that because she too shared in the same thoughts and feelings concerning how things were going between them. The two of them spent the next hour and a half telling each other what had taken place during their sacred outings. Both claiming to have only needed someone to talk to and didn't intend for the evening to end up the way it did.

They talked until Davonte called back. Both had changed their attitude while talking to him, knowing it was best.

They talked until the phones at the jail were cut off. They even slept together in Desiree's bed, but neither of them went to sleep until after thinking about what the other had told them. Each listened attentively to the other, picturing step by step in minute detail what they were being told. Desiree pictured Angie pulling up in the upper class suburban neighborhood where Antonio's bachelor condo resided.

"Check this shit out," Desiree thought to herself.

Angie sat talking to Antonio about work for a while, then in the process of this conversation she felt comfortable enough to tell him things weren't quite the way she wanted things to be at home. She didn't let on about Davonte being in jail or her and Desiree's dealings.

In the midst of this conversation, Antonio expressed to her she seemed tense and suggested a cold fruity drink. She accepted being she was thirsty. When Antonio returned, to her surprise, in his hand was a bottle of Arbor Mist wine and two glasses. She really wasn't expecting alcohol. But since it was wine and cheap wine at that, she went along. They talked and talked. When she looked up, they were into a second bottle of wine. Half way through it, she remembered she hadn't eaten anything and could feel the affects of the wine pretty well. Before she knew it, she was still talking even more than before and Antonio was sitting close up behind her on the couch massaging her shoulders. She thought nothing of it, only that it was a kind gesture.

That's all he needed was for her to overlook his actions and allow him into her personal space. From there, the massage turned into a caress. Someone must have told him about what she likes, because before she knew it, without warning, he had pulled her back into his arms and began kissing her. The touch, a kiss, from a man she did want, because she knew that the man she wanted was Davonte.

The wine told her it was just a kiss and that it was okay. Her conscious, which hadn't been taken over by the alcohol, told her this wasn't right. The two opposing thoughts caused her to become caught up in the moment, like a deer stuck in headlights. Angie said she unintentionally returned the kiss. That's when Antonio became creative. He moved fast, but smoothly, keeping his tongue darting around in her mouth. Angie found herself going back on the couch. Before she could say anything, he had the two top buttons of her shirt undone and was caressing the nipple of one of her breasts.

Before she could object, he moved his hand and began kissing with more passion and aggression. He moved himself around and smoothly placed himself between her legs. He stopped kissing for a tenth of a second, only to utter the words to her, *"It'll be alright."* From there he placed his penis directly at her clit. She could feel the erectness through both of their pants.

Antonio rolled his hips around in perfect circles, occasionally jerking up and down from her clit to just above the opening of her vagina. First it was slow, easy rotations.

Angie pulled her mouth away, *"Antonio listen,"* she said.
"Hold on, I got you," he quickly responded.

Why she let him continue she'll never know. After he said that, he began working overtime. It was like he was a type of snake between her legs going to town. Angie had thought to tell him to stop, but right before she did she felt it. The swell and pulsation of her clit, before she knew it Angie had thrown her legs up and back, spread eagle. What'd she do that for? From there, Antonio grinded with precision, so good not only did Angie grab his ass as he worked. You could hear the wetness of her pussy through her black dress slacks. As he grinded and rolled his hips, Angie's legs and body moved with his motion as if on a boat. Angie's foot curled and a strap came off the back heel of her foot.

"Mother fuck!" She yelled out, *"Aaaah! Shit!"*

Angie came and felt pleasure and disappointment at the same time. As her heart rate subsided, she placed her hand on her forehead.

"Damn, damn, damn," she mumbled, *"I done fucked up."*

However, Antonio wasn't hearing her or didn't care, cause he jumped up pulled his shirt off and quickly slipped out his pants.

"Come on, lets' go to the bedroom."

Angie moved her hand from her head and looked up at him who stood there looking as happy as one could be.

"This three inch mutherfucker," she thought.

He stood there, dick sticking out. She couldn't even call it a dick, it was a pecker and he was skinny and childish looking. Closing her legs, she sat up and slid the strap of her shoe back on.

"I gotta go," she told him with tears in her eyes. On the way home, she fought with the thought of what had taken place. The traces of wine still in her system had her going through changes. Her body told her it was okay. Her mind, well, that was something altogether different. She kept telling herself she didn't have sex, so she hadn't cheated. Angie was lying to herself and knew it. She regretted it and felt guilty, at least that's what she told Desiree.

Angie felt bad telling Desiree about what happened and even worse when Desiree went into telling what happened with her and started with, *"Well, unlike you, all that didn't happen with me. Grinding and cumming and whatever else took place with you."* She'd said it in such a nasty way, it caused Angie to feel small, real small. However, Angie sat holding her composure, listening to Desiree tell her how she had arrived at the front door of "Gas station Taalib's" the clothes salesman.

Desiree claimed she didn't know the directions he had given her was to his house until she arrived there. He had led her to believe they would be meeting at a café. What struck Angie was Desiree knew she would be going to have a drink with the guy, something about a trade off for an Egiptian blouse. Yet, she says she too needed to just talk to someone. Not even a two-way conversation, just someone to listen, she said.

"And he seemed to be a worthy participant, available if nothing else."

When Taalib opened the door, Desiree knew he had more than a drink on his mind because he was in some type of two-piece pajama set, black satin. It was evening, but not that late in the evening, and to be receiving first-time company in such style and manner was a bit much. So he didn't get the wrong impression and think she was with whatever he had planned, she used a little reverse psychology. Looking him up and down with a slight unpleasant look upon her face, she asked him, *"Is it safe to come in?"*

"Yeah, yeah, of course," he told her, *"I was just chilling. If it's any consolation to you, I can put on a robe."*

"You do that," Desiree told him, not that he was revealing anything, but still.

Upon entering his house, he had the incense burning, Sade was playing on the CD player. Surprisingly it was well lit. The lights weren't dimmed to imply anything. Desiree sat down and observed Taalib's place, while singing to the words of, "Smooth operator."

"Coast to coast, LA to Chicago..."

Minutes later, Taalib returned.

"So, now that you're here, what will we be having to drink?" He asked, rubbing his hands together causing himself to look eager.

Desiree spoke with sarcasm, *"Let's get drunk and jump right in, why don't we?!?"*

"I'm sorry," Taalib told her, *"I don't mean to sound rushed, its just that you've already made it clear you'll be having a drink, brief conversation and that was it. So, I figured you wouldn't be staying long. That's all, I meant no harm."*

Desiree looked at him with a raised eyebrow, *"I hear you mister, what is it we will have to drink?"*

Taalib smiled, *"I make a pretty decent strawberry daiquiri."*

"Daiquiris it is then," Desiree told him.

Just as quickly as she'd said it, he was off and the sound of ice in the blender was heard from the kitchen. Taalib returned to Desiree in the living room with two fairly large glasses.

"Here you go my lovely lady friend," he said to her with a wink.

"Why thank you sir."

Taking a sip of the drink, she scrunched up her face. It was strong and rightfully so. Where he should have used one part Vodka, he used two and a half. Stirring the drink and taking another sip, she placed her drink on the coffee table.

"Do you think the glass is big enough?" She mimicked.

"Yeeaa, it is a pretty big glass," Taalib grinned. *"I figured if it's going to be one drink, might as well do it right."*

There were a few moments of silence and Desiree took notice that Taalib was a young guy who just happened to have some size on him.

"So, what other music do you have?" Desiree asked, noticing the Sade CD had stopped.

"Why of course," he responded with a bit of excitement, *"I have just the thing for you."* Taalib strolled over to the stereo, fumbled around a little, found the CD he was looking for, dropped it in and pushed play. Desiree asked him what he put in? And he presented her with the CD case.

"Okay," she said, *"I guess I can work with this."*

As she handed him the case back, Jodeci came through the speakers. Grabbing their glasses, they both began sipping away. They talked and laughed. For Desiree it was a brief get away, a break from the norm, and always good, that is until she had gotten half way through her second drink and decided she needed to use the bathroom. That's when she took notice of two things. One just how tipsy she really was and two, just how dirty Taalib was.

Squatting, instead of sitting on the toilet to take a pee, she couldn't help but to slide the shower curtain back and peep over into the tub. Boy what'd she do that for? She overstood having to wash your clothes out in the tub. No doubt she had been there before and surely wasn't above it. As a matter of fact, to this day, she may wash a pair of panties out in the sink, but to leave a tub full of socks and underwear in the tub wet and dirty was too much. And there was a ring around the tub that made her question if he even used it for cleaning his body. After that had disgusted her, she looked around to see no toilet paper.

"That's a damn shame," she thought, then looking up drunkenly at a face rag hanging in front of her, *"Fuck it,"* she said, leaning forward to grab it. Making her way back into the living room where Taalib was, she decided it was time to go, but she wanted to give herself a little time to sober up.

"Well, Mr. Taalib," she started to say.

"I know, I know," he interrupted, *"You're about to be on your way."*

"Yeah, that's about the size of it," she said taking notice of him pretending to be pouting. *"Cut it out!"* She said, *"That doesn't become you."*

"No?" He questioned jumping up from his seat and standing in front of her before she could sit back in her spot on the couch. *"Then what does?"* He asked looking her directly in her eyes. Before she could answer, Taalib decided to try his luck.

"Look, I know you have to go and so you know I enjoyed myself. The talking and all was great. But, before you leave how about a dance?!?"

Desiree leaned her head back, not out of surprise, but because he was so close up in her grill, their noses were about to touch.

"A dance?" She repeated looking at him like, "Are you serious?"

"Yeah, a dance," he said as he placed his hands on her waist and began swaying side to side, *"You know a dance?!? An action based on rhythmic body motion."*

"Ha, ha!" She returned, *"I know how and what dancing consists of. I was just caught off guard that you asked that."*

Desiree went ahead with Taalib's little antics. For her, it was all a matter of buying enough time to sober up, in which from the way she felt would probably be a minute. Desiree thought for a second what it was she was doing, *"Why am I over this stranger's house?"* She questioned herself and how has a drink and conversation come to this she wondered. Her eyes closed for a second, taking notice of Jodeci coming through the speakers louder than when she left to go to the bathroom.

"Every freakin' day and every freakin' night, I wanna freak your body cause it's so freakin' tight..."

Along with that, Taalib went from a subtle swaying to
actually attempting to grind on her and his hands had begun
moving up and down her waist and hip. The movement
was causing her to feel even more intoxicated. Mr. Taalib
must have noticed, seeing how he was now actually pawing
her butt.

"Fuck this!" She told herself, *"I'll just go out to the
truck and sleep it off."*

Before she was finished with the thought, she could feel
herself going backwards. It didn't feel like she was falling
though, unless the spinning in her head from the alcohol
caused her not to be aware of it. She figured, *"Oh well, I'll
find out soon enough when I bust my butt."* Strangely
enough that never happened, but what did happen was the
feeling of Taalib's tongue trying to dart in and out her
mouth. Opening her eyes, she saw he had laid her on the
couch and kissed her on her breast. She couldn't help but
laugh because he was kissing them through her shirt.

"Damn bro, is you desperate or what?"

Desiree figured the insult would cause him to stop long
enough for her to sit up and gain her composure. Instead he
kept on working his way down, kissing her stomach
through her shirt.

"Unbelievable," she thought, *"Now, I got to get rude."*
Desiree took a deep breath, her intentions was to say, *"Get
off me mutherfucker!"*

But, by the time she'd finished inhaling, he had stopped
trying to kiss all over her. Now he was just staring down at
her. There he was just staring down between her legs.

"What the hell's wrong with you?" Desiree asked
propping herself up on her elbows looking down at herself
to see what he was looking at. She rolled her eyes in
disappointment. Taalib had undone the tuck of her wrap
and exposed her underlings.

Looking at him, she could tell he was truly overwhelmed by what he saw. She had on red lace panties that were see-thru in the front.

She remembered Davonte would tell her, *"You have very sexual looking hips and the way your pussy sits when you're laying down, it looks like its sitting on top of your ass being its so big."* He'd even had her go a year and a half without shaving, it was a jungle. He'd say, *"I want it to look like a pussy when I get at it, not some damn coochie."*

Taalib's eyes traced her shape, he was truly blown away by what he saw. The thought of Davonte made Desiree regret being there.

"Let me get my ass up," she thought, *"Things done gone too far."*

Taalib reached forward and she figured he was going to fix her wrap back, which was the least he could do. But no, he dove in face first, pulling the leg of her panties to the side, he buried his face between her legs and started working his tongue overtime.

"Boy!" Desiree yelled. *"W...W...What the hell you doing?"* Is what was supposed to come out of her mouth, but the length of his tongue inside her honey pot interrupted her train of thought. Taalib actually had his tongue in her pussy licking directly on her G-spot. He started pulling it out licking up and from the lips to the clit. Flicking the clit with the tip of his tongue and then back to the G-spot.

"Damn, damn, damn," she thought. She wanted him to stop, it wasn't right she told herself. She hadn't come there for that.

Taalib didn't seem to even notice Desiree anymore, he was consumed in the task at hand. Desiree felt her legs being put up in the spread eagle position.

"Aw come on with this shit! Ow," she moaned as he took both hands and spread her open and began licking her from

asshole to pussy. Desiree's pussy was wet. Her clit
throbbing and her asshole was tweeking. Desiree placed
one hand over her eyes in frustration, the other on the back
of his head for controlling the rotation.

"Ssssss, yeah go head," she mumbled, *"Go head and eat
my pussy, ole weak ass nigga."*

Whether or not Taalib heard wasn't clear. But once she
put her hand on the back of his head and pushed down, he
went slap off on the pussy licking, sucking, swallowing, it
tickled and felt good at the same time when he would shove
his tongue in her bootyhole, she could tell he enjoyed eating
ass. He did it a bit too good and would moan or mutter,
yea, yea in between slurps or licks. It made her wonder
what he was really into. Desiree squeezed down hard on
his head. Her bootyhole tighten, toes curled and her clit
became swollen and hard. She could feel it pulsating.

"Right there, right there little nigga," she spoke in a
blissful whisper.

Taalib felt her body responding to his performance. He
had her right where he wanted her. Desiree moaned one
good time as she felt the floodgates attempting to open.
The river was rising and about to overflow and cum forth.
Out of nowhere, Taalib jumped to his feet and slid out his
pants. There he stood naked from the waist down.

"What's up?" He said, *"Let's get it."*

Desiree laid there on her back, legs up spread wide open.
"What the fuck," she thought.

Sitting up she looked down between her legs, her panties
was soaked along with the crack of her ass, clit and pussy
sticking out the side of her panties.

"What's up?" Taalib said, *"We can continue."*

Desiree's head was still spinning. Placing her hand on
her stomach, *"I feel hot,"* she told him.

"That's because you still want to cum," he said walking
towards her with his meat hanging stiff. *"Why don't you*

hook me up like I did you," he said standing in front of her, his meat damn near in her face. *"Here,"* he said reaching for her hand, *"Why don't you touch it and guide it in?"*

Desiree looked at his pipe, it was somewhat long, but it was so skinny. She wondered if it ever touched the insides of any woman. It wasn't attractive at all.

"Here you go," he said placing her hand on it and taking a step forward so it was practically at her mouth.

"That's when I threw up all on him and his skinny little dick!" She told Angie.

Angie sat thinking on the shit Desiree just told her. *"Nigga probably pushed his shit to the back of your throat,"* she thought. *"Oh well,"* she said, *"What'll we do now?"*

They sat there in thought until the phone rang. It was Davonte and they knew it was almost ten, the phones at the jail would be cutting off soon. They looked at each other and Desiree pushed the speaker button, then 3 to accept the call.

"What's up ladies?"

"Hey babe," they both chimed.

"So, I take it you two have pull things together?"

"Yes," Desiree said, *"Everything's fine."*

"Hey, let me ask you two something. I kinda dosed off for a minute waiting to call ya'll back and like I had a short dream. It was about a snake crawling around in a bedroom. You know I'm not on all that superstition stuff, but I remember my mom telling me that meant your partner was cheating on you. What y'all think about that?"

For a minute, both the girls were silent.

"Helllloo," Davonte sang into the phone.

"We here baby," Angie spoke up, *"I don't know about reading dreams."*

"You know how your mind will play tricks on you?!?" Desiree said hoping he left well enough alone.

Davonte was good for piecing things together. The thought of that made her start silently crying. Angie saw what was taking place and began to share in the emotions. They had both messed up, bad and knew it.

"Yeah, you right," he agreed with her, *"But you know me, I don't be having dreams for no reason. I don't know, maybe I'm tripping. Because y'all ain't been no where or nothing to play me like that. Y'all have been pretty much normal with the exception of all the overtime last week. Desiree, yours was really unexpected. But hey, get the money baby. But don't over work yourself doing it ya know?!?"*

"Yeah, I hear you baby." Desiree responded making sure her voice was clear and showed no signs of how she was really feeling.

"Let me ask you two something."

Desiree was hoping he didn't ask about her working last weekend. Little did she know, Angie had already covered for her by telling him when she clicked back over that she was too busy to come to the phone.

"Two things," Davonte continued, *"I'm just curious, would either of you ever cheat on me? And what would make you do it if you did?"*

This was too close and too much for the both of them. They knew if they didn't answer right, he would continue.

"You have one minute," the voice on the recording chimed.

"Oh well," Davonte said, *"Guess we'll have to finish up tomorrow."*

"Okay baby," they cried out, *"We love youuu."*

"I love y'all too, and y'all better make sure you keep it together. Things seemed out of place around there lately and I ain't..." the phone clicked off.

Desiree and Angie both were sweating bullets.

"That was some shit there," Desiree said.

"You think he knows something?" Angie asked.

"How?" Desiree responded, *"A dream?!? I don't think so. Any way we got until tomorrow to sort things out."*

Desiree looked at Angie who had a strange look on her face.

"What!? What is it?" Desiree asked.

"Well, I don't know about you," Angie said, *"But, I'm not about to lie to him about nothing."*

Desiree couldn't believe her ears, *"What'd you say?"*

CHAPTER FOURTEEN

"SELECTIVE HONESTY"

Davonte **R**olled **O**ver out of his sleep. He felt drained and his mouth was dry. The heat must have been turned up in the jail, occasionally they would do that. The times they didn't, it would be too cold to move. November 24th, he thought to himself. Today was Thanksgiving and he wondered what the girls would be doing and whether or not they would be preparing a feast of gratitude. He figured he'd give them a call once he got up.

"Well, well, well, what do we have here?" A forgotten, yet familiar sounding voice sang out. Davonte rubbed his eyes and looked towards the table area.

"That's a damn shame," he mumbled while shaking his head.

At the table sat Mr. Wonderful and another guy. They must have been brought in late last night seeing that you sit in a holding cell for damn near nine hours before they move you to one of the tanks.

"Now that you've awaken from the dead, why don't you come join us?!?" Mr. Wonderful called out while gesturing with his hand for Davonte to come over.

Davonte held up one finger, then pointed to his mouth letting it be known he was going to brush his teeth first.

"Yeah, by all means," Mr. Wonderful told him, *"Get at that dragon."*

Davonte stood up with toothbrush and paste in hand. He let out a slight chuckle. Not at what had been said, but at how he remembered Mr. Wonderful telling him jail was a revolving door for him, especially in the line of work he did. After Davonte brushed his teeth and washed his face, he straightened up his little spot on the floor. He made his way over to Mr. Wonderful and the other guy whom he noticed was probably several years younger than himself.

After a brief greeting and taps of balled up fists, Mr. Wonderful turned back to the gentleman who sat across from him and resumed talking.

"So you telling me, you went to re-up on your goods so you could get your hustle on and walked into a police raid that wasn't even for you?!?"

"Exactly," the guy told him, *"I had been going there regularly to get my stuff, but I would always go on off days like Monday or Tuesday, mid morning. I never went at night or the end of the week.*

Coming in at the middle of the conversation, Davonte didn't know what they were talking about. Probably some fabulous story of how the guy got busted doing what he do. Everybody had one and everybody was a super hustler with money and plenty women, at least that's how it went in the county jail.

"So, tell me something player, how is it you be doing your thing the same way all this time and its working, then suddenly you change up?"

"Naa, naa," the guy protested, *"It wasn't that I changed up, I had a little situation jump off that messed with my schedule and had me miss my usual day I picked up. I was cool doe cause I was gonna go ahead and wait til next week. But when I called my peeps to let them know and to see what was what, they told me I'd best come out then, cuz they were gonna move and be out of business for a minute and what little they had was going fast. Now, when they told me this, it should have raised a red flag. But naa, I grabbed my gym bags and headed out. I wasn't there ten minutes looking through stuff before the police ran up in there."*

Davonte was still at a loss, but he sat listening anyway, not that he had anything else to do.

"Damn playa that's a bum rap. But if you don't mind me asking what did you do that was so important that you missed you regular pick up time? I mean, because with me, ain't nothing coming in between me and my hustle and definitely I ain't changing up my routine, not when it's working. I mean, your hustle is how you feed yourself."

"Yeah, I know," the guy said, *"And my reason is the weakest one in the book. I messed around and met this older broad at the gas station and trying to play Big Willie style and get at her, I done gave her ass this tight ass Egiptian blouse. So, to get even, I had her come to the crib for a drink that was the trade off. So, the day I would have normally been doing my business and picking up clothes, I'm up in the crib with her drinking and trying to hit skin.*

"Damn player," Mr. Wonderful said smiling, *"A piece of 'worth nothing' got you in jail."*

"What you mean a piece of worth nothing?" The guy asked.

"A piece of worth nothing!" Mr. Wonderful snapped. *"A piece of pussy! How many broads you done met on the first night and they gave you a piece of pussy just because or y'all have a couple drinks and next thing you know you up in a hotel, back of the car, wherever, dickin'em down like the shit been yours?! All for nothing, half of them don't care if you use a condom or not. Ain't I telling the truth?"*

Davonte and the other gentleman both shook their heads in agreement.

"You right about that," Davonte said.

"I know I'm right, cause it ain't worth nothing. Hell, you got a broad to bring hers over behind a damn shirt."

At that they all laughed. After a good laugh Mr. Wonderful asked the guy, *"What'd you say your name was again?"*

"Taalib," the guy answered, *"Taalib or you can call me T."*

"Okay, Taalib, now that you're in jail, did you at least hit the pussy, get you some head, something? I mean, at least for the shirt?

"Man, let me tell you what happened..."

"All I'm Saying is you don't quite know Davonte the way I *do."* Angie replied in between bites of her food,

"W...What, do ,y...you, mean?" She asked not feeling Desiree's comment.

"Angie, I know we are both with Davonte and have been for sometime, but I've been with him a while longer than you."
Angie felt slighted, once again, by Desiree's choice of words, she felt Desiree was trying to say she and Davonte were closer or something, but she wasn't to be outdone.

"Oh, I see, so you think since you've been with him longer you've got a better feel for how he is?"

"Right!" Desiree said.
Angie continued, *"And because of that you have a better knowledge of him?"*

"Exactly," Desiree smiled.

"I see," Angie said calmly, *"So, because of that, fuck it, just lie to him, he don't deserve the truth, hunh? Is that right, is that what you're saying Desiree?"*

Desiree knew Angie had a point and it would be wrong to lie to Davonte. She also knew to tell him about the foolishness they had done would lead to some painful consequences, with Davonte doing the afflicting.

"Look, all I'm saying is, unless you're willing to deal with his reaction, it might be best if we were selective about the truth. I'm saying, if we tell but don't tell all, we didn't lie. We weren't totally truthful, but we didn't lie."
Angie sat looking at Desiree with disbelief.

171

"You know, that sounds just as crazy as you having me sitting here eating Curried chicken with red beans and rice and these plantains on Thanksgiving, instead of fried turkey with dressing, cranberry sauce, mac and cheese and the rest of the fixings."

"Yeah, yeah," Desiree said. *"There was nothing stopping you from cooking, now hand me a piece of that coco bread. You need to be thinking about how we're going to handle this situation instead of your stomach."*

Angie was thinking about things more than Desiree could see. She hadn't eaten more than three or four bites of her food.

"When Davonte calls to wish us a Happy Thanksgiving, which, it's not, I'm telling him what I did, you can do whatever."

"Well damn," Desiree exclaimed putting her food down, *"I suddenly just lost my appetite."*

"You Say She *had on a plaid wrap around skirt?"*

"Yeah man," Taalib said excitedly, *"And her hips were like WHOA!"*

Mr. Wonderful sat listening to the younger fellows, he knew from Davonte's line of questioning that something was up. He figured maybe he knew the chick Taalib was talking about, but whatever the case, it was on them. The way he saw it was, if Taalib would trade a blouse he was supposed to be selling for money to a chick to come over and have a drink with no guarantee of sex, then he would definitely buy some and that's where he came in.

Davonte was still questioning him, Mr. Wonderful wondered why? He thought, he probably didn't believe the guy and he could just about see why, Taalib's story changed up here and there when it came to what he was supposed to have done.

"Niggas," he thought, *"They need to learn how to be selective about the lies they tell."*

"Hey hmm, Taalib!" Mr. Wonderful called out interrupting Davonte's interrogation. *"I think once you're out of here, we should keep in touch, I figure we can benefit each other seeing that we're both in sales."*

"Yeah, yeah, that's cool." Taalib said, *"I can hook you up with some clothes.*

"Sho nuff," Mr. Wonderful chuckled, *"Some clothes? You got to have tight threads for Mr. Wonderful to buy something. I mean tight, tight baby, like something never before seen.*

Davonte Laid Back on his mat on the floor. Although he appeared calm, he was rather pissed off. He had questioned and listened to all that Taalib had to say. What was supposed to have happened, where and when. Although Taalib seemed to be one of those young cats that fabricated things for the purpose of notoriety, it was clear to Davonte that there was some truth in what he spoke. For how would he have known of Desiree, her name, detailed description, it was all too similar. And the day and time he'd given was supposed to be the day Desiree worked overtime. Thinking about it, Davonte realized Desiree had never worked overtime on the weekends and very seldom the weekdays, unless she went in an hour or two early. So, not only does that mean she was somewhere she should not have been, but also Angie was in on it too, seeing she had lied about clicking over and calling on the three-way.

Suddenly, Davonte's anger subsided as he thought over the years, the things he'd done in the relationship from stepping out, to getting Desiree to accept the presence of Angie. Yeah, those thoughts calmed him, yet, he was still a man and within all men, ego and pride had their place and until a man became seasoned enough to control those two ends of the paradox, he would continue to be eaten away by their consistent nagging and desire to prove their existence through one's emotions. And Davonte was not an exception at this point. He surely had intentions to call the girls and get to the bottom of things and although ego and pride would be the driving force for this action, he did have intentions of remaining cool and calm knowing at least until he found out what he wanted. This would bring about better results.

The Ladies Stared at the phone ringing.

"Go ahead and answer it," Desiree told Angie as she took a deep breath. *"No need to clam up now, since it's all about telling him the truth. Might as well get it over with."*

"You right about that," Angie said, pushing the button for the speakerphone. As soon as she pushed the number three on the dial pad to accept the call, she chimed right in.

"Hey baby! Happy Turkey day!"

"Happy feast of gratitude to you too baby. Where's Desiree?"

"She's right here."

"Yeah, I'm right here, babe. How you doing?"

"I'm good," Davonte responded, sounding as pleasant as possible. *"And how was you two's dinner?"*

"Welllll, it was good," Desiree said, *"But it wasn't the traditional meal."*

"No?!? So what did y'all have?" Davonte questioned.

Davonte used the first thirty-minute phone call just talking about their Jamaican Thanksgiving dinner and not anything important. Once, he took out the time to pay attention and put an attentive ear to how the girls were talking and responding, he could tell that something wasn't right. The two of them weren't in their usual rambling mode where they both would talk so much at the same time, you didn't know what was being said. No, today they spoke as though they had something bothering them, only speaking if spoken to or asked a question.

"Pick up the receiver and cut off the speakerphone, Desiree."

Davonte was tired of waiting. It was time to see what the truth was. When he told Desiree to pick up, it was done so he could question her and Angie not hear, so they were unable to lie together.

"Yes babe, what's up?!" Desiree asked, knowing if he had her pick up the phone, causing Angie to be exempt from the immediate conversation, something was up.

"How you been feeling, baby?" Davonte asked sounding flirtatious.

"I've been feeling fine," Desiree responded. *"What you want me to do, Big Daddy? Play with this thang for you?"*

At that she and Davonte chuckled causing Desiree to feel at ease and giggle too. His laugh abruptly stopped.

"Nah baby, what I want is for you to tell me about you and Taalib."

Desiree's heart fell to her shoe. It was as if she'd practically died, no heartbeat, no air going in and out of her lungs. She knew she had to respond. Her mind was racing, her mouth wouldn't open, *"How did he know?"*

Davonte made the pressure even greater by not saying a word. No, he just held the phone in silence, waiting. After a few moments and realizing she was stuck, he made a noise as if clearing his throat.

"I'm still here," he told her.

However, she still hadn't gotten her thoughts together. Looking over at Angie, she managed to speak.

"T...T...Taalib? W...W...Who, w...what are you talking about?"

At the sound of those words, Angie's eyes became as big as a hoot owl.

"Look," Davonte spoke remaining only too calm for Desiree, *"I already know what's supposed to have happened. I just want to hear it from you. So, why don't you tell me how you spent your Saturday being worked over. I mean, working overtime."*

The words shattered her. At that point, she was only too through. How he knew was beyond her. It was only one of a few ways he could have known. Lil Ms. Angie told, Taalib's scrub ass done ended up in there with Davonte, or somehow Taalib done spoke of her to someone who knew someone, that knew someone. Her mind flashed to a time she and Davonte had a hot steamy night and afterwards, they were talking, he asked her would she ever cheat on him? He'd told her, *"Nevermind, don't answer that. If you do, just allow me the decency to tell me and don't let someone in the streets tell me. At least save me that embarrassment. Even if I go off and want to physically harm you, just tell me."*

Now, here she sat done actually lived out what she said she would never do. Her mind came back and she began to reason and think logically.

"I fucked up," she told herself. *"I...I...Fucked up,"* she mumbled, not knowing if Davonte heard her and not really wanting him to.

"I would say you did!" He snapped, but not in a loud tone. *"So, why don't you let it be known just how this happened?"*

Desiree knew Davonte, how he and his mind operated because she began telling him what took place and how it came about as the tears ran down her face. She told him the detail on what she now realized was an act of foolishness that wasn't worth the consequence.

Angie sat nearby tears also streaming down her face. Neither did she know how Davonte found out, but without a doubt knew, she was next in line. She listened, comparing what Desiree told her before, to what she was now saying.

After Desiree finished, Davonte only held the phone. It was all a matter of weighing her version of what happened against Taalib's. That's what allowed him to determine what really took place.

"So, now what?" Desiree asked.

It took her by surprise that he wasn't going off on her probably because of where he was and the fact that he couldn't reach her. Davonte knew he should take time to think things out to make sure he hadn't over looked anything that was said by either of them.

"Sleep on it," something told him. And that he would. *"So now nothing,"* he said surprising Desiree once more. He thought of how Angie had apparently lied about calling Desiree's job that day and her being busy. Now, that it was all out, he was eager to hear what she would say. *"So, I take it Angie has something to say too?!?"*

Looking for a chance to get out the hot seat, Desiree quickly said, *"Yes, I think Angie does have something to tell you."* It was spoken in a deliberate tone, so Angie knew it was her turn to fess up about what Davonte somehow already knew.

"Here you go," Desiree said practically pushing the receiver into Angie's hand. She couldn't wait to hear her tell Davonte what *she* had done since she was so game for being honest about everything. Silly girl is under the impression that Davonte won't go off on her.

"Hey Davonte," Angie said with a gloomy sounding voice.

"Save the sad act," Davonte said, *"I'm the only one who should be sad here. My lady cheats and the other one lies for her. That could only mean neither of them loves me."*

"That's not true," Angie said, *"We both love you so much."*

177

"If that's the case," Davonte said, *"Then why did she do what she did? Would you do that?"*

Angie felt like the dog Scooby Doo when asked the question. What did he mean, would she do that? She wondered if he even knew about what took place with her? Why of course he had to, especially after Desiree just told him she too had something to tell him.

"And you need to be saying something to me, don't you?!?" Davonte snapped.

Angie always pushed herself off as the do gooder. Now, here she was in some silliness. Davonte held the phone in silence, waiting for Angie to apologize for lying to him and to explain her actions.

"Fuck it," Angie said to herself, *"I'ma put it out there and be done with it."* She was still unsure of things, but at this point what was she to do. Desiree looked on wondering when Angie was going to go into the details of her frolicking.

"Well baby, it's like this," Angie said dropping her head as she spoke.

"Bout time," Desiree thought, *"Got me up here in this shit by myself."* Knowing Davonte was going to go off on her when he came home, she wasn't trying to go through it alone. She messed up and she had to face what was to come, but so did Angie. Desiree watched and listened closely as Angie continued.

"I know you going to be pissed and I know this destroys the trust and hopefully one day you'll forgive me, but... I quit my job and got another one."

Desiree literally fell off the chair to the floor.

"You did what?" Davonte asked.

<u>NARRATION</u>

They say that men and women alike tell lies in order to hide a truth that may surface one day anyway. Men are said to lie about little things, he may be asked where have you been? And he'll say, "Helping so and so move furniture," when in all honestly he was out having a drink. Or, he'll be asked, "Are you going to cut the grass today?" He'll say yes, knowing he's going to spend the day watching football.

In short, they say men tell little unnecessary lies, ones that when he gets caught, it's like, 'What was the purpose?'

However, they say women tell big dangerous lies, ones that could cause someone to be hurt. She sticks to her lie to the point of death before confessing up to it, living with it for years. It's even been said throughout history, the heart of the woman is one that holds the deepest darkest secrets. Yes, she's a very unique creature. So much so, that in the beginning the devil chose to talk to her instead of man himself. Picture that.

OR

DAMN FOOL

CHAPTER FIFTEEN

"HE'S MINE"

*"**D**amn **Y**oung **B**lood, I wondered why you were looking a little disassociated lately, now I know."*

Davonte waited until Taalib had made bond and was released before he let Mr. Wonderful in on what had taken place. He didn't want to give Taalib the satisfaction of knowing Desiree had a man.

Rubbing his goat-tee, Mr. Wonderful gave Davonte a curious look.

"So, you asked your ole lady about it, hunh?"

"Yeah, of course," Davonte responded.

"And what do you think based on both their stories?"

"It's hard to say," Davonte told him while taking a deep breath. *"Honestly, I'm sure someone lied a little and the other lied a lot."*

"Check that out," Mr. Wonderful said. He watched Davonte closely. Over the years he's turned out plenty women, some single, some with would be boyfriends, others married. He'd also seen many fellows old and young flip out from what Davonte was now experiencing. Many could not even handle the thought of their lady laid up with someone else. Yet, here Davonte sat cool as a fan and although it may have bothered him mentally or even emotionally, you couldn't tell for he remained calm.

"You know for me," Davonte said, *"It's not the fact of what may have happened when she got there. Nah, for me, it's about how my game wasn't tight enough to keep her from even talking to the guy which is what led to her going over there, ya know?"*

Mr. Wonderful smiled, *"Yeah, I hear you young blood."*

He couldn't help but to recognize the potential player in the young brother. He thought to himself, *'Once I sprinkle him with a little insight on things, he'll be fine, just fine.'*

"Ya know young blood, there's only a couple things you need and you'll be okay?"

"What's that?" Davonte asked.

"All you need in dealing with these women is to make sure that nothing they do affect you. Control your emotions baby. That's what you must do."

Davonte thought about what was said to him and wondered what Mr. Wonderful meant. *"Then again,"* he thought, *"Maybe my emotions do need to be controlled. How do you suggest I do that M Dub?"*

Mr. Wonderful smiled, *"Hey, you know what? You just tagged me. I'll always be Mr. Wonderful to the ladies, however from now on when I talk to my fellow man, I'll instruct them to call me M Dub."*

"Glad you like it," Davonte said with a partial smile.

*"Now, in response to your question on how to have total control of your emotions when dealing with the ladies, it's simple. In order to make sure nothing they do affect you, all you **must** do and I put emphasize on the word must. Subtract your feelings from the equation from the very start, that way whatever they come with doesn't affect you and you're able to see clearly what it is they're coming with. Hell, sometimes you'll catch it before they even do. What they gon do? You catch it while the thought is still formulating in their minds. And that's where you wanna be baby, ahead of everything and everybody, you overstand?"*

Davonte heard Mr. Wonderful and overstood exactly where he was coming from and he couldn't have agreed more. Although at the moment his emotions were attempting to get the best of him, the question he was trying to answer was, how does he go about dealing with things now? Although, what was done had already been done. It wasn't over for him.

As Davonte thought deeper on what happened, his mind raced with many thoughts of malice. Three weeks had passed with him only calling the girls once or twice a week and he had denied them the privilege of coming to visit him. However, that wasn't enough, not even the slaps were enough, which he was sure they didn't really lay into it.

"Get back in control," he told himself, *"Take them even deeper, further. Remove their world and place them in mine. They must now eat, sleep and shit Davonte. Yeah, that's what it will be."* He thought, *"Davonte's world."*

Tension **B**etween **A**ngie and Desiree was thick enough to cut with a knife. Desiree didn't know how to take Angie. She felt betrayed by Angie's failure to admit to Davonte that she too had been involved in an unlikely affair where she claimed to have cum but really didn't want to. Every time Desiree replayed that evening in her mind, her blood would boil. Angie got on the phone and played liked the only thing she had to tell Davonte was that she'd quit her job after all the talk about being honest and not keeping anything from him. Davonte flipped things on both of them by seeming to be calm through the entire phone call. Then, right before getting off the line, he had them put the phone on speaker. He told them to stand directly in front of each other, gave them a lecture about loyalty and how he was disappointed in them both and how lucky they were that he wasn't there. But, since he wasn't, *they* had to carry out what he would have.

For a moment they were stuck as to what it was he was talking about. That was until he filled them in by telling Angie to slap Desiree, which seemed to have been done with no hesitation. However, the first one apparently wasn't to his satisfaction, because Desiree was subjected to being slapped not once, not twice, but three times by Angie. Right before she released the third one Davonte told her, *"Stop playing and slap the shit out of her!"* So, she did. It brought tears to Desiree's eyes, not just from the sting of being slapped, but the shame and disbelief that Davonte had pulled such a stunt to have not only somebody else, but his other woman put hands on her face.

He spared neither of them though, no sooner than Angie had slapped Desiree for the third time, he told her to slap Angie's ass too.

Angie attempted to protest and ask, *"What did I do?"*

But before she could get the word "did" out, Desiree had smacked stars out of her. A couple more smacks followed without Davonte having to tell her to do it. Hearing the sound of smacks Desiree riddled Angie with, Davonte told her that was enough. Lucky for Angie, because it seemed Desiree was just starting to get warmed up. Angie had just barely regained her senses from the first one, had Desiree continued, she would have dropped her.

After that, Davonte hung up the phone, no goodbye, nothing, just 'click' and left them to deal with whatever feelings they had behind it.

Out of anger, Desiree called Angie a bitch around bout the second slap and Angie later had the nerve to tell Desiree, *"I smacked you because he told me to, but I didn't call you no bitch."*

At the time, Desiree wasn't trying to hear shit from Angie and quickly dismissed her and her conversation by telling her, *"Bitch! Get out of my face before I slap you again."*

And to add fuel to the fire, as if this wasn't enough, when Desiree returned to work with a puffy looking cheek, mind you, instead of going out to get something to eat for lunch with the rest of the nurses like she normally would, she decided to grab something from the hospital cafeteria to avoid questions about her swollen face. And guess who

was working there? Yep, Ms. Angie. Desiree thought she
was going to throw up and probably would have, but she
hadn't eaten anything yet so there was nothing to come up.
So she stood there trying to control the dry heaves. Work
was her escape from Angie and now this. The whole ordeal
was more than could be imagined, but despite it all, Angie
hoped and prayed Desiree didn't tell about her ill dealings
and Desiree couldn't wait until the moment was right to do
just that. Meanwhile, her mind explored the thought of
how she was going to deal with all this, feeling that whether
she was right or wrong, she wasn't letting things go down
this way. Something had to give.

Once again, Davonte witnessed the release of the man he
nick named, "M Dub" and once again he left him with a
mind full of tactics to deal with his present situation
concerning the two women he loved. And without a doubt,
it would play a pivotal rule in how he would now deal with
them. Some of the things M Dub shared with him, he could
do without, all the little sayings and catch phrases. Davonte
felt they were a bit over the top, all his pimp hoopla.

*"That's me Daddy Supreme, a rich chicks cream, poor
whores dream. Some say I'm the best pimp they've ever
seen."*

Or the one, *"You forgot the quote the Christians wrote
about honesty and fair play, for you can't live sweet not
knowing how to cheat. The game don't play that way."*

Or the one Davonte did seem to take a liking to, *"Why
there wasn't a time the sun set when her cunt wasn't wet,
and it released its honey gold and many a trick with a
weekend dick, got took for all his roll."*

"Cute," Davonte thought, however, he would be coming
live and direct at Desiree and Angie, so catchy phrases were
last on his list of things to come at them with.

It was mid December and he had just about two months
to him being released. In that time, he had plans of taking

185

the two of them on mental and emotional roller coasters. He knew he was about to go there. He felt it himself, but so be it. The nice guy roll had gotten him cheated on and that hurt bad! And although he felt the steps he was about to take would eventually cause him to feel vindicated, he overlooked the fact of him being a man which caused him to be born with ego and pride so honestly, he would never be totally over it.

Davonte **W**aited **P**atiently for another inmate to get off the phone. The more he thought about things, the more he felt tried and anger kept attempting to get the best of him, causing him to enter a don't care state of mind. Which could cause things to be taken to an extreme. With Davonte being the creative thinker he was, he was able to go left or right with things and his vivid imagination allowed for him to see the details and outcome of the most bizarre situations while others may not even be able to begin visualizing what he was clearly able to see. His ability to conjure up things in his mind and bring them to reality gave him a strange power that caused many to be willing to do whatever it was he wanted, even at their own risk. As soon as the other inmate was off the phone, Davonte had the receiver in his hand wiping it off with the shirt he wore. Davonte dialed the number while thinking to himself, *"If I've ever been a puzzle to them, I will surely be one now."*

Reaching **U**p **A**nd pushing the button on the garage door opener that was clipped to the sun visor of the truck, Desiree whipped into the driveway. Her day had been stressful. The majority of the day had been spent on her feet running back and forth between three surgical doctors. And when she'd finally gotten a break, her co-worker

Leslie came to her asking, *"Is the new chef in the kitchen your roommate?"*

"Unfortunately," she responded.

What did she do that for? It caused Leslie to go into a talkative frenzy.

"Why do you say that?" She'd ask, *"She seems cool."*

Desiree didn't want or need personal business on the job, so she quickly cleared that up by telling Leslie she was only kidding and that Angie was cool.

Stepping from the car, all she could think of was some food, a hot bath, and rest. Angie had arrived home before her and once again, her car was parked all crazy in the garage, causing Desiree to hit her door with the truck door. That made her even more bothered. She opened the door that led from the garage into the house, quickly she headed towards her bedroom.

"The faster I get in my room and shut the door, the better off I'll be," she thought.

Angie was in the other bedroom where she slept. Passing the room, Desiree took noticed of the door being cracked and the loud music being played. It was loud enough to where if the door was shut, it wouldn't have made a difference. Reaching her bedroom, she could hear Angie singing along to the words of the song.

"You need to give it up, I've had about enough, the, boy, is mine..." the words rang out.

Desiree shut her bedroom door and began peeling off her clothes. Folding the front of her panties down, she stood in the mirror scratching the imprint on her lower belly where the elastic had been. Why it felt so good to scratch this area, she didn't know, but she scratched and rubbed away. She turned and made her way to the tub grabbing her honeysuckle bath beads on the way. Running water in the bathtub, she found herself mimicking the words she'd just heard, *"You need to give it up, I've had about enough, the, boy, is mine."* Pausing to think for a second, she questioned, *"Who made that song? Oh yeah, Monica and Brandy,"* she answered. *"During a time they were supposed to be feuding or something."*

"Hold up a hot second," she thought as she stood from beside the bathtub, spun and marched out the bathroom headed toward the room where Angie was. Desiree had a disturbingly angry look on her face. Without even such as a knock or an "I'm coming in", Desiree stormed into the bedroom where Angie sat on the bed stark naked looking at her toes dry.

"Damn!" She snapped, *"You could've knocked."*

"Anyway!" Desiree said, ignoring Angie's statement. *"What's the deal with the music?"*

"What!?" Angie questioned mouth hanging open, eyes bucked. *"I'm listening to it, that's what's up with it."*

"That's not what I'm talking about," Desiree told her, *"What's up with the words?"*

For a second, Angie thought Desiree was losing it. Then she thought of the words to the hook. Although she was playing the song because she liked it and it made her think of Davonte, there was no pun intended. Yet here Desiree stood ready to get as jazzy as all get back.

"Oooh, I see," Angie said, *"You think I'm playing the song to be spiteful or something. I can assure you that wasn't the case here, Ms. Desiree.*

"Good thing it wasn't," Desiree said turning to exit the door.

"Phhh, and if it was?" Angie retorted feeling very much tried by Desiree's statement.

"Like I said," Desiree told her turning around with one hand on her hip and a pointed finger at Angie, *"Good thing it wasn't."*

"P...Please, what? Angie said, *"He's mine, now what?"*

"Bitch! What?! You're sadly mistaken!"

Desiree snapped as she headed towards Angie who had jumped to her feet. *"You got things all screwed up. Ain't no he's yours, especially when I done **let** you in this relationship!"*

"Yeah right!" Angie barked, *"You ain't let shit in. Apparently he needed more if I'm here."*

The two of them exchanged verbal insults, while slowly easing towards each other. Angie balled up her fists and Desiree prepared to pull Angie's hair and scratch her eyes out. Before they got in good reach of one another, the phone began ringing.

And as if they weren't about to squabble, Angie turned and headed to the phone.

"That's probably my baby there," she said rolling her eyes at Desiree as she picked up the receiver. Without even listening to the recording, she pushed three.

"Hey there Angie baby," assuming he asked Angie what was up or going on, seeing that she spoke into the phone telling him, *"I was about to fuck your girl up."*

Which set Desiree off again, *"You wasn't about to do nothing 'cept get your feelings hurt and bad too."*

"Hey, hey, hey!" Davonte yelled through the receiver. *"Put the phone on speaker phone now!"* He ordered Angie.

Once Angie pushed the button for speakerphone as they continued to argue.

"Both of y'all need to shut the hell up!" Davonte said becoming angry himself. *"I can't believe two grown ass women are up here arguing and threatening to fight one another and I just can't wait to hear what it's all over."*

The two of them looked back and forth from the phone to their would be opponent.

"So, who's going to speak first and tell me what's going on?"

At that, they both began speaking loudly at the same time.

"Whoa, whoa!" Davonte yelled into the phone. *"I guess I have to have y'all speak one at a time like children?!?"*

Davonte listened to both stories on what had taken place, in which he realized it was nothing more than tension from things that had been happening. After they'd finished, he simply told them to get over it. From there, he went into explaining how they needed to be coming together and getting back close. He let them know some things would be taking place, however, he would be filling them in on just what it was through instructional letters that they were to be followed to the T.

"Remember," he told them, *"All things taking place with the three of us is because the two of you say you love me. Let's not forget it and let's not question anything I ask of you."*

Before he'd hung up, Angie assured him she would do whatever he requested. Desiree on the other hand remained quiet, because she knew two things. One, whatever Davonte was about to have them do was all a matter of him getting back at them for what had happened with her and Taalib. Two, she knew Davonte had the ability to go there, and no doubt it would start out subtle, then escalate to them doing something extremely and possibly immoral.

Davonte figured that from talking to them everything was okay. The only thing that continued to ring in his mind was something Desiree said during the phone call. Something about how she didn't appreciate Angie acting like she didn't have something to tell him. It sounded kinda twisted or as if she were fumbling her words. All in all, he was at a lost as to what she meant by it.

CHAPTER SIXTEEN

"CHRISTMAS/NEW YEAR'S EVE"

Unlike **D**esiree, **A**ngie had to work Christmas Eve. So, she was sort of running behind. Once she'd gotten home, she quickly opened up the first part of the instructional letter Davonte sent her. It seemed to by pretty reasonable to her, with the exception of a thing or two. So, she hurried up and got dressed and made her way out the door. As she headed to the nearest bank to withdraw the money, she was instructed to get, she couldn't help to think how overwhelming things had been for her. From the very start of her triad relationship with Davonte and Desiree until now, she had to admit it was a trip, particularly, the last few weeks. The cheating, the arguments, it was all a lot to deal with and what had her thrown off the most was how she and Desiree was in each other's face about to literally fight until Davonte called. He calmed things down, said what he needed to say and was off the phone.

From there, Desiree walked out of the room and moments later called Angie into the bathroom where she was apparently going to take a bath. However, the bathtub had run over. Desiree reached into the tub to let the water out, then turned and walked over to Angie who was on the defense and ready to fight if Desiree tried some shit. But she didn't, instead she looked into Angie's eyes and said, *"Baby girl, I'm sorry,"* then, wrapped her arms around Angie pulled her in close and laid a lip locking kiss on her that was passionate, so sensual it caused Angie to forget all that took place only moments earlier.

"Do you forgive me?" Desiree asked, once she released Angie's lips.

Angie just shook her head yes, thinking to herself, *"What the hell is going on?"*

191

But that wasn't the end of it. After getting the bathroom straightened up from the water, Desiree had Angie take a bath and shower with her. The stopper was in the tub while the shower ran. For Angie, it was definitely a bathing to remember. First, it started with another one of Desiree's mind blowing kisses where she put tongue and lips to work in such a way, to have seen it would have turned on the most sanctifying onlookers. So one could only imagine what it had done to Angie. This was done all the while she scrubbed and sudzed up Angie's whole body. This added to the eroticness of it and made for an eerie romanticness. With all the caressing, romancing and foreplay, all the tenderness, not once would Desiree allow Angie to touch her back, not in the least. She kept Angie receiving pleasure but giving none. It had Angie so turned on as the suds ran down her body and between her legs. So did the nectar from her throbbing pussy. Desiree kissed her from head to toe. She even subjected Angie to a little roughness as she turned her around smacked her on the ass and ordered her to hold on to the towel rack as she had her spread her legs and bend over forward.

First, she held Angie by the waist as she grinded her from the back as if she was getting it doggy style. Occasionally, she would smack Angie on the ass and jerk at her waist making her grind back. Then by her hair, she pulled Angie up towards her and began kissing the back of her neck. She slid her right hand around and began caressing Angie's breast as she slid her left hand down between her legs from the back.

Then she whispered in her ear, *"I know you saving a little something special for Davonte and that's cool baby girl. But if its okay with you, I would like to put you on to a little something, is that okay baby?"*

As she let the words sink in, she kissed and sucked on the back and sides of Angie's neck aggressively as she wiggled her middle finger around in between the opening of her vagina lips. Angie was so consumed by the passion of the ordeal she shook her head and let out a submissive, *"Yes,"* without even really knowing what was to come.

The moves Desiree came with after that was the moves of an exotic sexual demon. Reaching around with her right hand, she took hold of Angie's right nipple between her thumb and index finger and pinched it. It was just enough to send a painful pleasure throughout her body and cause her to suck her teeth and moan.

"Sssss, ooohh."

"Bend over bitch," Desiree told her.

Angie didn't care, she was in a moment of ecstasy, so she delightfully did as she was commanded. It didn't even matter that Desiree had called her a bitch. Actually, it added to the whole persona of the situation.

Once Angie bent over, Desiree again started rubbing up and down between her soapy coochie lips and butt cheeks. Once she created a sensation from that, she smoothly slid her middle finger in Angie's honey pot and began massaging the walls of her kitty kat, while at the same time sliding the thumb of the same hand in her butt hole. Angie was so turned on and it was done so skillfully it was as if she wanted it. Desiree sent Angie climbing the walls as she stroked both thumb and finger in and out of her. First slow and deep, then in circles, stretching both orifices, then fast and hard. She even had her bend over and hold her ankles while she worked her over. Suds and bubbles splashed everywhere as Angie screamed and moaned and Desiree made sure she knew who was in charge.

"Who's working this ass and pussy?" Desiree would ask while slapping her on the butt cheeks. *"Who got you loving it when they get at this pussy?!"*

Each question resulted in Angie screaming out, *"You! Desiree you, Desiree o my God, you Desiree!"*

It didn't even matter that they used up all the hot water and the tub filled up with just barely lukewarm water. Nah, it didn't matter at all, not with the hot steamy tactics Desiree was performing.

A car horn blew, bringing Angie out of her stimulating daydream. She put her little Honda in first gear and moved up to the ATM machine.

"Oh well," she figured, Desiree didn't perform like that for nothing, all must be forgotten as well as forgiven.

"What Time You got Dep?" One of the guys yelled out to a passing officer.

"12:45," he hollered back. Davonte laid there in his usual position staring at the ceiling.

"That's cool," he said, hearing the time the officer had given. He told Angie and Desiree to meet up between one and one thirty to handle business. He also told them, to be done and back at home by three o'clock, seeing that he had time, he decided to take a little nap, when he woke up, he'd call and analyze things, see what's what.

The Mall Was noisy and crowded as expected on Christmas Eve. Desiree had purchased Angie's gift just as Davonte had told her to. A black after five mini dress with the back out and a low cut front. Desiree had to stop herself from looking at it. If not, she would have decided to keep it for herself and get Angie something else. Making her way to the food court, she glanced at the watch on her wrist. Angie should be showing up soon so they could read the second part to their letter and carry out the remaining instructions. Which Desiree already had a pretty good idea of what was supposed to take place just from what he had her bring. If things were about to go down the way she expected, then that was all to the good for her.

"Most definitely would be," she told herself.

Then out of nowhere, she let out a devilish laugh, *"Yeah, Davonte you got so much trust and love for her, and she so much in love with you or so she claims. I'ma turn her ass out. Yeah, sure nuff. Literally freak her mind and body every time we get down. That's right Davonte, you got us two women kissing, hugging, licking, and sucking each other and that's cool,"* she mumbled to herself. *"Yo bitch gone choose me."*

"Desiree!" An only too familiar voice called out.

Looking up from her thoughts, it was Angie sitting at a table looking happy and full of cheer. Desiree made her way over. She sat down and they stared at each other's shopping bags wondering what was inside. Davonte told them not to exchange gifts until they got home.

"Well, you ready to read the next step?" Angie asked smiling ear to ear.

"Yeah, that's what we're here for," Desiree responded, reaching into their purses. They pulled out the envelopes and read the second part to the charade.

Two Ladies Stood at the restroom sink in front of the mirrors looking over their shoulders as another walked by quickly pulling her daughter along. They all seemed to stare at the same stall. It may have been because of the sounds coming from it, or it could be because of the sight they saw when looking under the bottom. Just beneath the stall door, was the sight of what looked to be a woman's pair of black slacks with a pair of red lace panties down around the ankle of someone in a pair of black leather boots. In front of that person was someone else with a pair of heels and without a doubt those calves belong to a female. Now, from the outside view of the stall, you'd be very confused about what you were seeing and the sounds coming from within surely wouldn't have helped to figure out what was going on. However, if you were on the inside

of the stall you would be able to see Desiree standing there
with her pants and panties down to her ankles with her shirt
and bra up exposing her breast, with Angie bent over in
front of her with her skirt hiked up on her back and Desiree
drilling into her with the same 14 inch strap on dildo Angie
had bought months earlier.

Desiree had Angie by the waist bent all the way over
trying to really put the 14 inches up in her. It was long and
thick and Desiree knew Angie was having a hell of a time
taking it. But her being a woman too, she knew how to
push and pull to make it hurt and feel good at the same
time, which is why Angie moaned and groaned all in the
same breath.

Davonte instructed them to go into the ladies restroom at
the mall food court and get at it. He had Angie go in and
kiss Desiree and suck her breast, while she strapped up.
And Desiree was to work Angie's pink love glove from the
back and they were not to stop until Angie came.

"Bend over and take it," Desiree hissed at Angie while
pulling her back by the waist and thrusting forward.

"I'm bent over as far as I can go," Angie said with sound
of strain in her voice. The fact that she had hold of the
handrails on both sides of the stall, which was the only
thing keeping them from falling forward.

"Well, spread your legs further," she told her, just
messing with her truthfully.

She was surprised Angie was taking it as well as she was.
Desiree watched as every time she stroked the dildo
forward, both Angie's hairy vagina lips got pulled in with
it. Angie continued to moan with each penetrating stroke.

"Why don't you lube it up or something?!?" She told
Desiree.

Desiree backed the dildo out of her pussy. As it released
the dildo, it let out a loud suction noise. Desiree gripped it
like a man would who was sure of himself, tilted it up, bent

her mouth down toward it, spit on the head of it and told Angie, *"That's the best I can do for you,"* and slid it back in.

"That's a little better," Angie said as she braced herself to take it some more. They bumped, turned and grinded in the stall for about twenty minutes with Desiree occasionally spitting on the head of the dildo and by all means she kept Angie bent over, legs spread.

"Ass and elbows," she would say from time to time while slapping sparks out of Angie's butt cheeks. However, with some mean stroking and the help of Angie's finger, she finally came and surprisingly, hard. Desiree pulled the dildo out. The pink of Angie's coochie hole showed like never before and the lips were spread enough to make one wonder if they would ever go back in place.

"Mmh, mmh, mmmh, damn," Desiree said.

"What?" Angie questioned standing up straight with her hand on her stomach.

"Nothing," Desiree responded unstrapping the dildo and pulling her pants up along with popping her tits back into her bra.

Angie straightened out her clothes and placing her hand over her private area, she looked at Desiree and told her, *"My shit is sore."*

"I bet it is," Desiree said, *"Now, are you ready to go?"*

"Yeah," Angie answered.

"Good," Desiree responded quickly. *"Hold this,"* she said handing the sex-covered dildo to Angie who accepted it without a second thought.

From there, Desiree snatched the stall door open and stepped out, Angie followed slowly. They were met with the eyes of other women who appeared to be stunned. Two oriental ladies stood looking at them talking in Chinese. Desiree turned to head out the door, Angie paused to look in the mirror. Desiree grabbed her arm and mumbled under her breath.

"Bitch, you better come on."

As she turned and headed with Angie to the door, the large dildo was visible in Angie's hand. The two oriental ladies saw it. One gasped.

"That's a damn shame," the other one said.

Stepping out the restroom, they made their way across the food court with bags in hand trying to look normal. Desiree's hair was sweated out. One of her breasts wasn't in the bra right, causing it to look much larger than the other. One side of her lace panties rode up her butt. She twitched and threw her hips a couple times to get it out, but to no avail. Angie's skirt looked very wrinkled and she kept messing with her hair. She didn't wear any panties or bra so she looked loose. And although she tried not to, she couldn't help but to walk gapped legged, sorta up on her toes. They both shared in facial expressions that said the same thing and they couldn't hide it. It was clearly obvious they'd been fucking.

"My damn hair wet," Angie said, sliding her hand down the back of her head and squeezing water from the tips of her hair.

"Why would your hair be wet?" Desiree asked puzzled at Angie's comment.

"I don't know," Angie said, *"I think my hair was in the toilet."*

"Damn," Desiree smiled.

The New Year of 2006, had come in with Davonte in the county jail. It was a big disappointment for him, yet, he manned up and accepted it.

"Never again," he told himself, *"Never again."*

The guys who he shared the tank with tried to make the best of a funky situation. They had a spade tournament and attempted to discuss happier times. But in all honesty, they knew not only was there nothing worst than being away from your family during the holidays regardless of what they did. There was nothing going to fill that void. It was the worst, especially for those who had children.

Davonte didn't engage in any of their pastime activities. His mind was too consumed with the thought of whether or not the girls were carrying out his instructions the way he'd told them. Inside, he was questioning himself on why? He knew he was angry with them, but how was what he had them doing now going to ease that? He didn't even have an answer, as well as, he truthfully didn't care. It was how he was. Doing what he was doing was his way of getting back at them mentally. And until he figured out another way of doing just that, he would keep this up. With that final thought, he pulled the raggedy blanket over his head and tried to get some sleep.

Desiree Was Staring out the front window of the truck, when Angie climbed back in. She looked over at her wondering how it was she had no problem whatsoever with Davonte's illogically perverse orders time after time.

"You know," Desiree said, becoming serious, *"When we get back, I got some words for him."*

"I hear ya," Angie said, continuing to prepare herself for the task at hand. *"When we get back, you can talk to him about whatever you want. However, right now, you need to be getting it together so we can get this party on the road.* Desiree looked over at Angie and smacked her lips, *"You act like this shit is normal!"*

"No!" Angie said holding up her hand letting Desiree know to say no more, *"For your information what it is, I act like I'm going to do what he told me he wanted me to do. If I wasn't or felt as though I had a problem with it, I*

would have let it be known the very moment he said what he wanted done."

"Bitch right," Desiree thought, *"You wouldn't have told him shit. You ain't been telling him nothing."*

"Now, are you telling me you ain't gonna do it?" Angie asked, knowing good and well what the answer would be.

Desiree thought for a second and figured if she turned back now, it would just cause problems later.

"No, that's not what I'm saying," she answered, hating it all the same.

"Alrighty then," Angie chimed, *"Let's get it. He's counting on us!"*

"Yeah, he's counting on us alright," Desiree mimicked, wondering how the hell it was that Angie was so happy. *"Let's get this preposterous shit over with,"* she snapped. *"Oh, and just so you know, I am a bit perturbed."*

"Yeah, yeah," Angie said reaching to hit the button for the sunroof.

As it slid open, the cold night air came through. Turning the radio up loud, she clapped her hands so Desiree could get with the program. They both let the passenger and driver's seats back as far as they would go. Angie made room for Desiree so she was able to straddle the armrest of the truck with her legs spread and a knee in each seat. She leaned her body forward and placed her hands on the backseat that had been laid down flat. Angie got behind her, straddling the armrest, only instead of leaning forward, her head stuck out the sunroof. They both wore sexy black after five dresses. Angie threw Desiree's dress up on her back and smacked her on the ass.

"You ready?" She questioned gleefully, looking down at Desiree's large rump.

Angie pulled her own dress up and tucked it so it wouldn't fall down. Underneath, she too wore no panties. Instead, in place of panties, she wore the strap on dildo.

"Just come on," Desiree said sounding disgusted.

With one hand Angie grabbed hold of the dildo, with the other, she grabbed a handful of Desiree's butt cheek and spread it open to prepare for entry.

"Here we come," she said as she spit on the head of the dildo and pushed forward to enter Desiree's awaiting love glove. *"Catch this,"* she said thrusting into her.

"Shit," Desiree cringed.

"At, aat," Angie said smacking her on the ass, *"Hold that head up."*

It Was Sunday, 4 am. January 1st, 2006 and Desiree sat soaking in a tub of hot water replaying over and over the events that took place only hours earlier. Not that she would ever forget the uncanny events. At the moment her vagina surely wouldn't allow that, seeing how it was sore inside and out in the worst way. She just shook her head. At first, all the little sexual escapades were doable, it allowed her to get off on Angie and open her up just the way she wanted. However, Davonte was on to something else and no doubt was taking it there. Christmas Eve was one thing at the mall in the restroom of the food court. Yet, his latest ventures he had them on, let Desiree know he was on some get back type shit. Sending them to the movies early New Years Eve and having them lay across the seats and 69 in a theater full of people until they both came. That caused an adrenaline rush brought on by excitement and fear. Then, they say whatever you are doing at 12 midnight New Year's, is what you'll be doing all year long.

"Check that shit out," Desiree thought, *"I was in Davonte's truck with a hundred and fifty dollar evening dress on thinking we about to party. Instead I'm bent over with my dress hiked up, ass out, getting boned doggy style by another female with a 14 inch strap on dick. Not to mention, in the parking lot of one of Atlanta's hottest*

nightclubs during a major celebrity bash with everything from limo's to Rolls Royce's pulling in. With a camcorder in the back of the truck on record filming everything. Even the people walking by were pointing at us in the truck. It may not have been so noticeable if Angie wasn't trying to dog fuck the shit out of me with her head stuck out of the sunroof. Oh, and let us not forget the blaring sound of Missy Elliott's voice saying, 'Pussy don't fail me now' coming through the speakers."

It was all beginning to be more than she cared to be doing. It was as if Davonte was trying to turn them into stone cold lesbians. Something they weren't and didn't care to be. Sure she was going to turn Angie's ass o-u-t, out, but that would be done in her own way. Desiree realized it was time to have a heart to heart with the man she loved.

"Yeah," she told herself, *"I've got to fix things between us."*

Turning on the hot water and spreading her legs, she mumbled under her breath, *"That's a damn shame,"* as she thought of how after freaking in the truck, they still slid up in the party to get a peek at the entertainers that attended the event. They wiped with napkins and sprayed a little perfume to kill the smell of sex, but she stepped up in there with a stretched out sore coochie and all.

CHAPTER SEVENTEEN

"ALWAYS SOMETHING"

Desiree **L**aid **O**n the couch naked with her back propped up on the arm of the couch with three pillows. Angie lay between her legs on her stomach occasionally kissing and caressing her breast.

"No, Davonte, I'm not asking you to forget what I've done. We both know that'll never happen. However, I do want you to forgive me. That's possible, if you're willing. Trust me, I am very aware it was wrong and God knows that if I could take it back I would. And as I told you before, I did not fuck the guy. Yesss, he did go down on me and I could have done a better job of preventing that."

"Like not taking your ass over there," Davonte interrupted, *"Or, better yet, by not even stopping to talk to him in the first place."*

Refusing to let his emotions get the best of him, Davonte took a deep breath and proceeded to talk calmly.

"How many times have I told you, if a guy stops you 9 times out of 10 its to get at you because of what he sees physically?!? And unless you have intentions of letting him hit you off, you need to keep on moving."

Desiree held the phone to her ear, listening to the words she'd heard on more than one occasion. She couldn't argue, nor in anyway dispute what he said, she knew better.

"I know Davonte," she pleaded, *"It was just that a lot was going on, and my mind and emotions were in the wrong place. I was looking for an outlet, a form of release. But in no way was it supposed to end up like this."*

"Bet it wasn't," Davonte commented.

"Davonte, I know you. Sometimes I feel I even know you better than you know yourself."

"Don't trust that feeling," Davonte told her.

"Okay, maybe I don't, but I do know that because of all this you've changed. And you've changed in a way that's not you at all, at least not the wonderful man I know. And if you would please, become your old self again. The things you have me and Angie doing aren't doing anything for you. So, again, please take into consideration what I'm saying and know I will never mess up like this again. I promise you."

Angie made a slurping sound as she sucked the nipple of one of Desiree's breast. Desiree popped her on the back of the head. When she looked up, Desiree placed a finger to her lips motioning for her to be quiet.

"I hear you," Davonte told her, *"And your words are noted. We'll have to finish this conversation a little later, they're bringing the trays with the food so, I'll call back."*

"Okay babe," Desiree said, *"Keep in mind, you come home next month and I want things to be okay when you get here."*

"Yeah, talk to you later," he said flatly.

"I love you," she told him.

"I love you too!" Angie yelled, taking notice that they were about to get off the phone.

Hanging up the receiver, Davonte took a second to think. He had told Desiree he heard her and that her words were noted. He did and they were and honestly, he knew where she was coming from. He knew her well or at least he thought so. The latest incident made him question just how well. Surprisingly, she didn't bring up all his incidents with countless females. When he thought about things, he realized he was even upset with Angie. He couldn't quite place the reason why, but he was.

"Anyway," he told himself, *"I'm not through with them yet."*

Angie didn't even ask to speak to him during that phone call, although Desiree said she needed to discuss matters, Angie usually still would ask to speak to him.

Davonte had a moment where he could hear the voice of his mother.

"Don't rush to be in love son," she'd told him.

"Why?" He'd ask, figuring she was just being mom and talking.

"Love can hurt son. Just when you think it's all good and safe to hand your heart over, here comes the pain."

"How true that is Mama," he mumbled under his breath, *"How true that is."*

There was a hard lump in his throat and his eyes tried to tear up. Yeah, he had a little more to put them through.

Desiree Pushed The button on the cordless phone to hang it up. Dropping the phone on the floor, she slid down to become more comfortable on the couch. While she went into thinking over things, Angie made herself comfy and began kissing and sucking on Desiree's neck and collarbone. Desiree thought of how things had taken place as well as how she and Angie both were guilty of the same wrongdoing, yet, she was the one in the hot seat. She wasn't completely mad at Angie for it, because by all means she had gotten straight up busted. However, Angie talked all that smack about admitting up to Davonte about what she'd done, but when the chance to do so arised, she turned into a Mexican talking to the police, "Me no speak no English." Desiree felt that amongst women, there should be a bond of overstanding, an unspoken trust. She knew everything wasn't going to always be peachy between them. But, damn, she had opened up her home to her, behind a man at that. She wondered if Angie had what it took to be the woman she thought she would be or was she expecting too much from her. Whatever the case, she had allowed the stress of her presence to cause her to take steps she normally wouldn't have and now, there was friction between her and the man she loved. There was no doubt she was willing to make up for what she'd done and with the man she loved. For sure, she was gonna do that much and she still had plans to cause Angie to have a desire and passion so great for her, only to break her little heart.

"Hey you, are we good to go?" Angie asked. *"Plus, it looks like it's all good."*

Desiree looked down at Angie who was rubbing and pulling at the hairs of her vagina. Angie leaned forward and kissed Desiree on the lips, then propping herself up with both hands on the sides of Desiree yelled out, *"Bamm, bamm!"* Then a loud, *"Meow!"* As she first pumped up and down at Desiree's hairy snatch like a man would if having sex. Then slowly, girating her hips grinding clit to clit.

"What's up?" Angie said in a whisper attempting to sound seductive.

Desiree forgot, earlier, she had Angie dye her pussy hairs a light hazel brown and shaved the sides and told her once it dried and took, she would hook her up.

"Come here," Desiree ordered her.

Angie leaned forward again.

Desiree kissed and sucked her tongue aggressively, the way she knew Lil Ms. Angie liked and spread her legs up and out.

She asked Angie, *"You want this?"*

Angie looked down at Desiree holding the fat hairy lips of her brown melon open exposing the tender pink.

"Yeessss," Angie said sounding like a baby. *"And this too,"* she said placing a finger on Desiree's lips, then sliding it in her mouth.

"Show me how much you want it." Desiree told her.

Angie didn't hesitate as she slid down between Desiree's legs and buried her mouth in the opening of her snatch. After a few seconds of loud slurping and moaning, she lifted her head up and with shiny lips asked Desiree, *"How's that for show? Or should I say starters?"*

Desiree smiled. *"Lay back and let me see just how ready you are,"* she told her with a look of devilishment in her eyes. Angie laid back on the other end of the couch and spread her legs. Desiree held back from laughing when she saw just how turned on Angie was. The child was wet from her kitty cat to the crease between her butt cheeks. Desiree looked at the silly grin Angie had on her face.

"Well, maybe later," she told Angie as she stood up and headed towards the kitchen.

"What?" Angie snapped, *"Don't play!"*

"I'm not," Desiree said looking over her shoulder with a smile. *"Trust me, I'm about to fix me something to eat and watch T.V."*

Angie slowly put her legs down, hearing the fridge door open, she knew Desiree was seriously about to get something to eat and they wouldn't be getting frisky. Putting her finger between her legs and sliding it in her coochie, Angie yelled into the kitchen, *"You trippin!"*

"Ain't no more Kool Aid?" Desiree asked.

Angie pulled her finger out from between her legs and placed it in her mouth, after sucking the sex off, she got up and stomped to her room.

"I'm horney as fuck and she playing, on some rationing it out shit."

Hearing the bedroom door close, Desiree giggled to herself.

"Oh, don't worry baby girl, a bitch gone break you off, and when I do, you'll know.

Davonte Just Shook his head as he read the note he'd received from his cousin Harry. Unfortunately, they had pictures of him transacting and dealing drugs that was going to be used in court. As well as, there was supposed to be some small time dude that he'd dealt with occasionally who'd gotten himself knocked that was going to testify against him to save his own ass.

Harry said the D.A. offered a deal of 10 serve 3 with seven on parole probation. If he didn't want the deal and he went to trial and lost, they were going to give him a straight ten. His lawyer told him to hold tight on making a decision.

Harry stated he didn't know what he wanted to do. He ended the letter by saying all the money, fun and glamour wasn't worth what they were talking.

Davonte felt for his cousin, but had problems of his own to deal with, problems that may not have occurred had he not been in jail behind Harry's crap. He made another mark on the wall to count down another day.

Davonte laid down his thoughts, which carried him to the time he and Desiree first met. It was a church function they were both attending, he had seen her on several other occasions, but didn't approach her. However, this day he was unable to help himself. Her chocolate beauty had gotten the best of him, as she strolled in the grass wearing a soft pink sundress that only hinted at what it concealed. When he'd finally got up the nerve to grab her attention, he was pleased she'd stopped and upon her face she wore a lovely warm smile. Her eyes were seductive looking yet just as warm. They hit it off well that evening and agreed to meet again the next day. They spent the entire following day together, laughing, partaking in the different activities and talking, well she did most of the talking. And talked she did, all night until 2 am in the morning. But Davonte didn't mind, it allowed him to get to know her and realize she had nothing to hide. From there, their relationship blossomed; they were on the phone all hours of the night, even though they had to work the next morning. It was as if they were teenagers all over again. And once the dating and intimacy started, it was nothing but pure fireworks. The thought caused an unconscious smile to come across Davonte's face, as he remembered the many times he'd sent Desiree climbing the walls and introduced her to many a new positions and techniques that started with her yelling out his name and ended with her snoring and slobbering on herself.

"How sweet and wonderful the times," Davonte thought.

It was obvious that he and his mind were sharing in a moment of quality time as the thoughts and visions carried on to how he'd first met Angie and went along with it. There was Sonya, an ex he just happened to keep in touch with after the relationship had ended. One day, she asked him to meet her over her grandmother's house to move something out the basement. When they finished, he was sitting on the couch while Sonya was in the other room talking with grandma. The front door comes open, and in walks Angie. She strolled into the living room, flopped down on the couch across from Davonte. For a second, they just stared at one another. Then, Angie raised an eyebrow and said, *"You must be Davonte?"*

After answering her, she told him, *"I'm Angie, Sonya's cousin and you're cute."*

It was all innocent at first, from time to time they would by chance bump into each other at a restaurant or the movies, they even came across each other at the park on the nature trail several times. Davonte had found Angie to be a good conversationalist, as she was willing and open to talk about any and everything. He was honest about Desiree early on. Angie was about her being single but not by choice. Her luck with finding someone compatible wasn't going too well. Truthfully, it was all good, they overstood each others situations and respected it.

However, Angie had what seemed to be a little car trouble one day, so she called Davonte and asked him would he do her front brakes and she would pay him. At a chance to make a few tax-free dollars, he jumped on it. He'd put the brakes on in the driveway of her mother's house, although at the time, he didn't feel she needed them. But hey, it was her car. Once he finished, he knocked on the screen door, she yelled for him to come on in.

"I'm in the kitchen," she said.

When he entered, she handed him his money and told him to have a seat she had cooked.

Money, free food?!? He was with it. She fixed him a plate of fried chicken, real mashed potatoes, macaroni and cheese, green beans and sweet yellow cornbread.

Davonte was grubbing back on the plate of food, paying Angie no mind. When halfway through, she suddenly had a bold and somewhat desperate outburst.

"Davonte," she called out to him from across the table and as soon as he looked up from his plate of food at her, she told him, *"I can't take it anymore, I want to fuck you."*

"Hey, who got the fucking roll of toilet paper?!" A voice yelled out immediately snapping Davonte out of his daydreaming. Looking up, it was old man Tyreik.

"Man," Davonte said to himself, *"I was hoping to be sleep by the time he took his nightly dump."*

He covered his nose and threw the blanket over his head in an attempt to block the smell. He tried returning to his thoughts, but unfortunately he was unable. He was too tired, sleep was a pressing issue now, however, he was able to briefly recall just how lovely things were at one time, and it seemed it could have always been. That is, until just recently, with Desiree, Angie, and some scheming nigga named Taalib.

"That's okay," he thought, *"I don't have long now. Nope, not long at all and when I get home, I'll straighten their asses, both of them."*

Flipping **A**nd **F**lopping her head on the pillow, Angie tried to figure out what Desiree's problem was tonight. One minute it's all good, she had her in between warm embraces, caressing cuddling, to being on her back, legs spread wide delivering unspeakable jolts of pleasure to not caring to be bothered at all.

"Who you fooling?" A voice in her head asked. *"You know what it is. She's feeling you and all that, that's why she doesn't mind pleasing you the way she does. However, she hasn't gotten over that night... that night of confession."*

Angie thought on it for a minute, *"Maybe I could have told him,"* she thought. But the fear of how he would react had gotten the best of her. Thinking on it some more, she questioned what it was she could do to make things better?

"Come clean, tell him. It'll kill two birds with one stone. Desiree will feel as though y'all was equal, both sharing the hot seat and you'll be honest with Davonte and that's what's important," the voice told her.

"Alright then, that's what I'll do. He'll be home in a matter of weeks. I'll sit face to face with him and let him know what took place. Yeah, that's what I'll do. And for now," she said flopping her legs open and sliding her hand down to her throbbing clit.

"I don't want you playing with yourself," she heard Davonte's voice say, *"I'll be there soon, so no finger play!"*

"Damn it!" She exclaimed.

Then closing her legs tightly, she rolled onto her side and fought to go to sleep.

"Can't believe you've done what you did," she heard a voice say in her head. That evening with Antonio came to her head. *"And for what?"* She questioned herself angrily as she clinched her teeth tightly together and tears streamed down her face.

"That was plain stupid of you Angie!" She cried out loud to herself. *"Plain fucking stupid!"*

Desiree Laid Across the bed letting herself air dry from the hot shower. Weighing the pros and cons of everything, she looked at the present situation from all angles and each point of view. For Davonte, she had let him down by doing something silly. A move a simple-minded little girl would have done. If Davonte was able to get past it, she would do all she could to make it up to him and never again would she dare allow herself to make such a foolish mistake, that she would promise him. Now, looking at Angie, truthfully Desiree wasn't totally upset with her. Had she just said from the start she wasn't going to tell anything Desiree could respect that better than the talk not matching the walk B.S. So, therefore, Desiree felt a lesson was in store for Ms. Thang and being that Angie was a chef by trade she would re-enforce what she already knew, that some dishes are best served cold!

In Retrospect, It would seem Davonte was being torn between his emotions and his ego. Not surprising in this particular situation, seeing that it has been said, in death the last thing to leave a man was his pride and Davonte was very much alive. So, he not only felt the need for what he was doing, but also the need for his pain to be felt.

Now, Desiree was in a survival tactic mode, and in order for her to achieve the desired outcome she was looking for, it was necessary to play two ends from the middle.

Now Angie, well Angie was in an emotional stupor, only aware of the fact she was happy to be sharing her life with two others.

CHAPTER EIGHTEEN

"DADDY'S HOME"

The Clock Was ticking and it was now a matter of days before Davonte was released and returned home to his ladies. He hadn't had them do anything outlandish lately, figuring he would continue subjecting them to his mental mayhem when he got there. Although he had instructed them to get rid of the dildo, telling them there was no more need for it. He would do the penetrating when he got there. The fact that he made such a comment, caused Desiree to feel as though things may be alright and not totally messed up, she kept that in her mental notes. Meanwhile, she and Angie shopped for clothes for Davonte. His daily push up routine caused his arms and chest to be a size larger. They also picked up little things for the house, so it would seem brighter and homely when he got there, and without a second thought, they made sure he'd be able to enjoy his favorite pastime and purchased four DVD's of the latest movies he'd missed while in the county. Also, for the celebration, they grabbed a bottle of Hennessy XO and Moet champagne.

In between getting things for Davonte, Desiree had stepped things up a bit when it came to her intimate dealings with Angie. Like a termite on a fresh piece of wood, Angie was being worn out regularly. She wanted Angie's mind and emotions to be at a certain point by the time their man got home. Angie's poor self didn't know what was going on. To her, it was like living an orgasmic dream. Desiree had her sent and why wouldn't she be?!? She was getting hit off before work, after work. Desiree made sure she said all the right things to Angie she also delivered the most hypnotic and tantalizing performances one could imagine.

One morning she cursed her out over leaving the iron on two days prior, then she called at work the same day and told her she would be bringing her lunch and to meet her outside in the truck. As soon as Angie climbed in and shut the door, Desiree smashed strawberries in her face and mouth and began kissing and licking it off while sliding her hand underneath her clothes. Rubbing strawberries on her breasts, in her panties, between her legs, on her coochie lips, at mid afternoon, in the front seat of the truck in the hospital employee parking lot, Desiree turned Angie into a one fruit, fruit basket and ate it up she did. When she finished with her, Angie was a strawberry mess. Wearing a Kool-Aid smile, glassy eyed and smelling like a mixture of sex and strawberries, adorned with not one, but two strawberry passion marks on both sides of her neck and no panties on, she returned to work.

You see, Desiree being a woman herself and knew it was all a matter of maintaining mental and emotional control over Angie all the while creating an imbalancement within her. What started out as an act of sexual experimentation between the two for Davonte, was now Desiree's all out war tactic. And the rules of engagement were set by her and her only.

Davonte Made Sure he spoke clearly to Angie about certain business he wanted taken care of when he returned home in the next two weeks. There were things to be paid and he already knew they hadn't done basic things to the truck, like an oil change or a tune up. So, he let her know it was necessary for him to know what was what with the finances.

Angie lay sideways on the couch with her back against the arm of it. She had the phone tightly pressed against her right ear listening carefully to what Davonte was saying, or at least trying to. In between the flinching and twitching

215

being caused by pulsating sensations being given by Desiree who was beside the couch on her knees vigorously sucking Angie's titties while rubbing her clit and probing her two fingers in and out of her vaginal opening.

Keeping her finger inside her love canal, Desiree released Angie's nipple from her lips and slid her mouth up to her ear quick and softly, she flicked her tongue in and out her ear. Chill bumps covered Angie's body as she bit down on her bottom lip.

Whispering in her ear, Desiree asked Angie, *"Do I make you feel good?"*

Angie gleefully shook her head yes. Then with her two fingers, Desiree rubbed Angie's clit around in quick little circles, whispering once again, *"Can I get at this whenever I want, anytime, anyplace?"*

Angie flapped her legs open like a butterfly, then closed them tightly with Desiree's hand clamped between them. She turned her head so they were face to face, then flicked her tongue out and licked Desiree's lips. Then, without any sound coming out, she formed her lips to say the words, *"Hell, fucking yeah."*

"Good," Desiree told her in the same whispering tone, *"I just want to make sure you happy and feeling good. It's all about a bitch giving you what you want and need, seeing that this is what you really and truly wanted its good that as a woman you made the intelligent decision to open up to me."*

These words were not only spoken in Angie's ear to caress her ego with the words intelligent and woman, but also to give her the impression that she was in control with the word 'decision'. With these words spoken, directly to her brain, they lodged themselves as a permanent fixture in the part of the brain where emotions were often built.

Continuing on, Desiree pressed her mouth closer, her lips were practically in Angie's ear.

"With that being said, I want you to be honest and tell me will you and can you be in love with a bitch like me?"

Angie's legs remained clamped on Desiree's hand as the words penetrated her mind. Desiree could feel the pounding of Angie's heart from the pulsation between her legs.

"Are you listening to me!?" Davonte barked into the phone, causing Angie to jump slightly.

"Yes, baby," she responded, *"I hear you, everything you saying."*

No sooner than she'd said that, she removed the phone from her ear, turned to face Desiree and with her free hand grabbed the back of her head and plunged her tongue in her mouth. The kiss was pure passion. When she finally let go, she looked Desiree in her eyes and said nothing. Not that she had to, her eyes said it all. Placing the phone back to her ear, she caught the ass end of a sentence Davonte was finishing.

"And with that, I'm out. I'll call y'all back in a couple hours. Tell Desiree I'll talk to her then."

"Okay baby," Angie said, *"Love you."*

"Love you too!" Desiree shouted.

"Mmmhhmm, same here," Davonte said hanging up the phone.

Desiree took the cordless phone from Angie and threw it on the floor. Then climbing on the couch, she got between her legs and laid on top of her. Hitting her off with the same passionate kiss that was given to her moments earlier, she gently rolled her hips. As soon as Angie began rolling hers to grind back, Desiree suddenly stopped, pulled her tongue out her mouth and whispered in Angie's ear.

"Hey you, you didn't answer me."

Angie knew exactly what she was talking about. It was the question that made her heart thump and fireworks go off. It was the question that made her feel the same way

217

that Davonte did that day in the kitchen at her mother's house.

He had her drop her pants and panties, bend over and hold her ankles, while he long-dicked her standing up from the back, in a way so vicious you'd thought she stole something from his mother. And although to this day, she could still feel how his balls smacked up against her clit and how the head of his tool slammed so deep into the depths of her tender pussy that for days, she could feel the soreness inside of her from the top of her ass to the middle of her back. Very memorable it was. However, it was the words he spoke to her that put the icing on the cake or rather the cunt, so to speak. When he'd pulled out of her, she remained stuck in that position with legs trembling and slobber running up her cheek into her eye. He slapped her firmly on the rump, pulled her up surprisingly by her hair and told her, *"Hey, I ain't fucking just for kicks, no this here shit is crucial, from now on you rolling with me. You and all that is you belongs to me."*

With that being said, he gave her another firm slap on the rump, spun and walked off. She was so blown away, it took her a moment to pull it together. Once she did, she'd taken the bottom of her shirt and began wiping the drool from her face. Anyone witnessing this would have asked, "What's the use?" What's the use of wiping drool from your face and you standing in the middle of your mother's kitchen floor, pants and panties down around your ankles and piss running down both legs.

The incident was so overwhelming for Angie, she had a talk with her mother about it and told every detail. You would have thought her mother would have at least asked, *"Ain't that your cousin Sonya's ex man?"*

But instead she gave wise words to her one and only daughter, being a freak herself. She told her, *"It's not often a man can rock your tender spot and your brain at the same time, you better keep him."*

Those thoughts, along with what Desiree asked her, made her feel so good she wrapped both legs around Desiree's back and squeezed tightly.

"Ooh, Desiree baby, its nothing for me to love you, trust me."

Desiree noticed Angie was in a brief daze, thinking about something. She would get to what that was later.

"So, this is what you want, right?" She asked looking Angie directly in the eye.

"Yes, yes, yes," Angie chimed reaching up to suck on Desiree's ear lobe.

"Good, baby girl that's what time it is," Desiree said pulling her ear out Angie's mouth and raising up from between her legs.

"Now then," Desiree spoke in a take charge way, *"First, you're gonna hook me up and then we're going to talk."*

"Talk about what?" Angie inquired as she watched Desiree grab a little teddy bear shaped bottle of honey from an end table. *"And what's that for?"*

"We're going to talk about you and whatever you feel the need to tell me. And don't worry about what this is for, you just get in position," she ordered Angie as she positioned herself facing the back of the couch on her knees, legs spread wide, back arched, ass out.

Angie got up and positioned herself on her knees directly behind Desiree on the floor. The way Desiree had her back arched with her butt tooted out, caused Angie once again to be taken over by the shape and curves her hips and ass made. There was a bizarre sexual attraction Angie had for Desiree's shape. Placing a hand on both her butt cheeks, Angie rubbed the two smooth brown lumps as she stared between them at Desiree's pleasure cavern. Slowly, she took her hands and parted her cheeks. Leaning forward she hadn't even reached her target and her tongue was out. She was going to devour something. The first lick was for her.

"Hold up," Desiree said as she took the bottle of honey and squeezed a couple drops on her finger.

"Mannn, what's up?" Angie asked, not appreciating being interrupted.

"Patience, patience," Desiree sang out, *"It's just that I need you to do me right,"* she said placing her honey dipped finger on her clit. *"And to do that, you need to start riiiight here,"* she said as her finger slid slowly from her clit up the middle to the bottom of her coochie lips, then up between her butt cheeks and rested smack dab at the center of her booty hole.

"You got me?" Desiree asked looking over her shoulder at Angie.

"Yeesss, I do," Angie responded.

"You sure?" Desiree asked as she let the tip of her finger slide inside her anus.

"I said yes!" Angie exclaimed.

"Good!" Desiree snapped quickly pulling her finger out and putting it in the face of Angie, who as if on queue stuck her tongue out seductively. Desiree wiped her finger down the middle of her tongue, then turned back around arched her back and stuck it out.

Angie grabbed her butt cheeks, spread them open again and in a chipper voice, told Desiree, *"That's all you had to say, crazy."* Then like a Cambodian with a smorgasbord in front of her, she went face first and put in work.

"Oweee, yeah baby girl," Desiree moaned, *"Work something for me biiitch. Eat that chocolate donut hole."*

"L...L...Look," Melissa said as she laid on her stomach panting for air. *"The part were you putting it down marathon style is no doubt all good. But the part where you beatin' my pum pum up, baby we can do without that.*

Now, I know a brother done been locked down for nine months and he got to make up. I overstand that and that's why yesterday I let you do your thang, now here it is today a sister still sore. I had to pull out the KY to ease it up. But naah, you wanna still get at it like it done did something to you. Believe me baby, I know what you capable of, you ain't got to carve your name in the back wall of my shit! Please believe, I know what you packing."

Davonte stared at her for a minute, then reaching over smacking her on the ass, he told her, *"Shut up! You know you like rough sex."*

"Aggressive, Davonte, aggressive," she told him, *"There is a difference. Plus, you have to keep in mind what you working with. Some guys are long and skinny, others are fat and average in length, or thick and short. Here you are surprisingly long and overwhelmingly thick! Why do you think I refer to that muthersucker as "Kong"?!? Look at the girth of this bad boy,"* Melissa told him reaching over and grabbing the shaft of his meat. *"On soft, it's a handful, when it's erect, it's scary."*

Whether intentionally or unintentionally, Melissa laid there talking and stroking Davonte's manhood. All the while, Davonte paid her words very little attention, however, the fondling of his love pipe caused immediate arousal.

"Yeah, yeah," he said. *"Lift up,"* he instructed her once again. He fixed the pillow under her lower stomach causing her rump to be elevated. Straddling over her, he positioned himself for re-entry into her. Melissa continued to talk, that is, until she felt the helmet of his pleasure muscle touch the lips of her catch all. Her abrupt silence was noticed by Davonte, *"So, I take it that means you wouldn't mind some more?!?"*

"Yeah, Davonte I want some more. But I would appreciate it if you would go easy this time. You know I

got a man and you already got me having to put him on hold for a week. If I have to go two weeks, how am I gonna explain that?"

Davonte lined his manhood up, grabbed hold of her hips and began walking his pipe forward. He smiled as he watched Melissa grip the sheets in both hands and bite down on the pillow as she buried her face in it. You see, to Melissa, Davonte was a man who made it hurt so good.

It Was A happy and joyful Friday for Desiree and Angie as they rushed home from work together. They talked, laughed, and shared what they had gotten for Davonte, not only for his return home, but Valentine's Day as well. Once they were in, it was all about getting things prepared and then the fun could begin.

Davonte Had Gotten showered, dressed and made his way out of Melissa's apartment. He didn't bother to wake her. He simply gave her a kiss on the forehead along with a gentle pat on the rump. From there, he let himself out with the key they agreed he'd use only on special occasions of his coming and going. At no point was it to be used just because or on pop ups. There were rules to their dealings and apparently all was respected seeing that he'd had a key to each of her apartments for the past four years.

Davonte drove to the house in silence. He'd been dealing with Melissa for a minute, but he still couldn't help to wonder about her. She was a fine chocolate sister with an all out body. The thighs, hips, small waist, with a big round ass, full lips with a nice nose, along with chinky eyes. Her hair was short and even shorter in the back. It was probably her ghetto mouth and the fact that she smoked like a chimney and drank like a nigga, that made it difficult for her to keep a man. She didn't seem to care though, and if she did, it never showed. The first two times she and

Davonte had messed around, she told him, *"Oh yeah, me and you gone always have special relations and handle business, even if I get married,"* she told him. Davonte figured she was wild and just talking, however, still to this day, they managed to keep up there occasional frolicking. When Davonte asked her why she continued to fool around with him? She explained how he was able to have good stimulating conversations, he had a rough sexy look about him, and the fact that he was a gentleman that was rough around the edges made him so cool. And in finishing the answer to his question, she told him, *"And that, is a must have!"* As she pointed her finger at his private section. *"That's right,"* she said with a serious look on her face. *"I'm a damsel in distress. You and "Kong" there must save me from time to time. Let's just say, when you break a sister off, she straight for a while."*

Davonte just shook his head and allowed his thoughts to change. He had been out since Wednesday. The last two days the girls had been told he was looking for a job, since that's what his probation called for, 'Employment Upon Release'. However, he had been going round for round with Melissa for the past two days.

Now, it's more than likely that wouldn't have taken place, but oddly enough, both Angie and Desiree were on their monthly cycles. They told him with them both living together like that, it was only a matter of time before their bodies synchronized and they would come on at the same time. They let him know they only had two days left on and all would be good. Davonte wasn't tripping, it only sat his plans back a little.

"Ta dah!" Angie sang out as she pranced into the bedroom twirling around like a model on a runway. *"So, how do I look?"* She asked Desiree who sat there rubbing baby oil under her breasts. Desiree observed her closely, the two-piece lace lingerie set she bought for Angie looked

good on her. It was a deep red color, the top came mid stomach. It allowed you to see through and get a peek at her firm breasts. The paisley pattern on it only blocked enough to make you desire to see more. The bottoms resembled a boy cut style but different, because instead of the waistband around the front going straight across, it dipped down into sort of a V-shape accentuating the crotch area. Angie's kitty kat hairs stuck out the sides in abundance. To a woman that was tacky, but to Davonte, that was sexy and the only way to go.

"Don't come to me with all the hair shaved off from in between your legs. Damn thing looking like some young virgin coochie," he would say. *"Hell nah, bring it to me when it ain't been shaved in a year and when you open your legs up to me I want it to say p-u-s-s-y, pussy!"*

"Yeah," Desiree thought to herself, *"Davonte liked it raunchy, raunchy all the way around the board. If the room don't stank when we done, we ain't do it right!"*

"Hello," Angie said, still standing in her little pose, *"How do I look?"*

"Turn around," Desiree told her.

The panties had the same V dip in the back, causing the crack of her butt cheeks to be exposed at the top.

"You look good," Desiree told her, *"Now, come here."*

Angie walked happily over and stood between Desiree's legs. Desiree slid her hands up the side of Angie's body raising her top up and exposing her breast. She asked her, *"You like the outfit I got you?"*

Angie shook her head yes, and Desiree took one of her breast in her mouth.

"Hey!" Angie protested. *"We gotta save all that for Davonte."*

Desiree pulled her head back and slid Angie's top back down over her breast.

"Yeah, you right," she agreed with Angie, then she slid a finger inside the crotch area of her panties, then pulling it out, she told her, *"Yeah, we gonna save it for Davonte, but it feel like you ready to give it up now."*

Angie just smiled.

Desiree stood up, threw an arm around Angie and with Davonte's signature move, kissed her on the forehead, tip of the nose, then softly on the lips.

"I want you to make sure you do everything the way I told you, you hear me?"

"I hear you," Angie said, *"We've been over it."*

"Good," Desiree told her becoming serious. *"So, I shouldn't have no problem with you sucking and fucking the way I showed you?!?"*

"No, I got it," Angie said feeling kinda strange for answering the question seeing she had been sexing Davonte for some time now with no complaints.

"Alright," Desiree said, slapping her hard on the butt, then with authority told her, *"Go put the heels on I got you and make sure everything is okay. He'll be home in a minute."*

Angie spun and hurried off rubbing her butt as she did.

CHAPTER NINETEEN

"LET US RECAP"

Laying **A**cross **T**he table with her skirt hiked up, Desiree cringed and moaned, *"This Davonte must be one hellava guy,"* Thomas said to the girls.

"He is," Angie said standing in front of a mirror. *"I like it,"* she chimed, *"I think it looks nice."* She said referring to the tattoo she'd just gotten on her right butt cheek. It was the face of a purple kitten with sexy red lips drawn on it. Its features were to emulate that of a black female, sexy, juicy, and seductive. Over top of it in fancy lettering it read, *"Davonte's Thunder Cat Pussy."*

"Glad you like it," Thomas the tattoo guy told her.

Angie walked over to the table to see how Desiree's tat was coming along. Hers was of a female lion bent over with large hips and rump. Over it read, *"Davonte's Lioness Forever."*

"That looks real good. You're doing a wonderful job." Angie told Thomas.

He didn't respond, just continued to do his job.

"You okay, Desiree?" Angie asked.

Desiree just shook her head yes while gritting her teeth.

Davonte told her, *"Since you have such a large butt, I want the tattoo to be 41/2 inches by 41/2 square inches and placed directly in the center of your left cheek."*

Once again, Desiree found herself trying to put things together in order to get an overstanding to the method of Davonte's madness. He had only been home a little over two weeks and things were a bit crazy. She figured he would return home and there would undoubtedly be some uneasiness from what had taken place with her and Taalib. However, she'd thought for the most part, when they'd discussed things it was to be a matter of moving forward and closing the wound.

But Mr. Davonte was on something else. If he was trying to close that wound he sure had a hellava way of going about it. It all started the day he came home. True enough, the girls couldn't get into no "on their back, legs in the air, huck-a-buck, froggy style sex", because they were both on their monthly. However, they had cooked his favorite meal, jumbo shrimp with fresh spinach and pasta, along with a thin crispy crust extra cheese, cheese pizza. Now, they figured just because they were momentarily inoperative, didn't mean they couldn't straighten him out. Hell, the man had been locked up for nine months, so they both agreed to take turns drinking from the honey dripper until he was on 'E'. They were both going to share their oral abilities on Big Ben and the twins. Ha! Or so they thought. Once they fed him, they suggested he take a nice hot bath and they'd give him a full body massage and they would take things from there. They let him know they both had two days left on their cycle but not to worry, it was still his day. Oh, but contrary to what they had in mind, Davonte took a pass on the offer, took a hot bath and spent the evening watching television. He told them he'd wait out the two days. Now, they felt that was cool but he didn't even sleep in the bed with them for those two nights, and as soon as morning came, he was out the door on the job hunt, figuring that was his move to be responsible and start out on the right track. They rolled with it and prepared for when their cycle was off.

Now, this is when things became interesting. The girls had shopped for some sexy little pieces to wear for Davonte, prepared a nice meal and put together a plan for a hot, steamy, raunchy gang bang session they knew he'd enjoy. They figured since they'd done nothing for Valentine's Day, this would be a hellafied make up session.

Let us see what took place…

"Alright," Desiree said slapping Angie hard on the butt, then with authority told her, *"Go put on the heels I got you, and make sure everything's okay. He'll be home any minute now."*

Angie spun and walked off rubbing her butt as she did. While she slid her feet into the heels and laced them up around her ankle and calves, she heard the sound of the garage door going up.

"You hear what I hear!?" She yelled back while sliding into a black fishnet bodysuit. The girls rushed to get into position as Davonte made his way into the house through the door that led from the garage into the kitchen. No sooner than Davonte entered the house and around the corner to the living room, there they both stood in what appeared to be granny dresses with big buttons down the front.

"Hey Daddy!" They sang out.

"Listen," Desiree started in, *"Today is your day. No ifs, ands or buts about it. So you need be heading in that direction."*

"That way," Angie said clapping her hands twice and pointing in the same direction as Desiree.

"Everything is already set up and laid out for you, so let's get it!" Desiree told him with an obvious sneaky look on her face.

Davonte said nothing, just headed in the direction they were pointing. He didn't say anything about the heels they wore with the corny dresses, which was a dead give away to their would be secret plan.

All seemed to be going well. Davonte bathed in a hot bubbly tub, which was fine with him. It kinda gave him a chance to wash and soak his private area and get rid of any evidence that may have led to what he'd done with Melissa.

While doing that, the girls set the mood by placing large pillows with silk coverings all around the living room floor along with silk sheets and rose petals. On the floor beside the sheets and pillows sat a three-inch stand, on it rested a bowl full of assorted cut fruit. Once, Davonte finished his bath, he dried and stepped to the bed where there laid a red and black pin-stripped silk robe, beside it was a note that read, *"For you Big Daddy."*

Davonte slid on the robe, then took a look in the mirror. He had to admit, it looked damn good on him.

"Hey Big Daddy!" The girls yelled from the living room, *"We're waiting on you!"*

Davonte grabbed a little surprise he had himself out of the closet and headed for the living room. It was time to rendezvous and all parties were ready. As soon as he entered, the living room, he took notice of the candles burning, the sweet mellow smell of incense. If nothing else, when it came to romantic, it made for a picture perfect scene. The girls stood side by side both brandishing the same seductive smiles.

"Hey baby, glad you could join us," Angie said.

"It's definitely a treat," added Desiree.

Davonte stood looking at them with his hands behind his back. The words, *"Freak me baby!"* came from the stereo speakers and as they did, the girls began undoing the buttons on their dresses. Once they'd finished unbuttoning, they allowed for the dresses to slide slowly and seductively down their bodies. There they stood as the dresses hit the floor, legs spread wide, breast out enticingly, invitingly, Davonte looking back and forth between the two of them. They were both hot and ready for action. Angie's breast showed a very noticeable print in her top. The nipples of Desiree's breast poked through the holes of the bodysuit. Their legs and hips called out to Davonte, *"Come have your way with us,"* is what they told him.

The holes of the fishnet bodysuit did nothing to stop the hairs on Desiree's vagina from donning its fierce V-shaped afro that she'd dyed a light hazel color that blended well with her skin to create a sexual spectacle. Angie was already a hairy woman and to not cut her vagina hairs caused the area between her legs to look like two healthy muffins.

Davonte nodded his head in approval. They had done well. So, he decided to play along, reaching to the front of the robe, he pulled at its matching belt. As the robe came opened he shifted his shoulders to assist in its downward journey to the floor. It stopped short, because of being hung on the one arm that he kept behind his back. However, the unveiling of his body wasn't halted by this. Both Desiree's and Angie's eyes became wide as they looked on at him.

Davonte stood there looking immaculate, his broad shoulders and arms showed strength, his chest looked wonderful. It called for you to lay your head on it. It said, "Here you will be safe and protected". Although his stomach didn't show lines of a creased six-pack, it was relatively flat. His legs looked strong and sexy. His body screamed stamina! There was a stimulating, seducing, cockiness that radiated from him. One that would cause a virgin to surrender herself to him knowing he would never be hers, or that would cause a married woman to step out at 2 am in the morning only to return 4 hours later with her panties wet, pussy still pulsating and look her husband straight in the face and tell him, *"I just needed a walk to clear my head."* He was one you would want to have a one-night stand with, just to say you did it.

"Cause tonight baby I wanna get freaky with you…" the words of the song added to the girls desire, as they stared at Davonte standing there looking marvelous with his manhood protruding from the middle of his body like a

"Louisville Slugger". For those who don't know, that's a baseball bat. There was a healthy vibrant look to it. His balls hung with dignity appearing as two golf balls in separate sacks. A woman could only surrender to the behest of Davonte and his undeniable shlong.

Desiree swallowed as her mouth watered and her heart rate quickened. Her legs began to wiggle as she did an unconscious frisky little dance in her mind. She heard the words, *"Horse dick muther fucker,"* running rampant in her head. She felt anticipation oozing from the lips of her pussy.

Angie was already foolishly amorous when it came to Davonte and this moment, this scene only heightened her every thought, desire and lust for him. She too felt the quickening of her heart rate as her arms hung to her sides and her hands tapped unconsciously on her thighs. Out of nowhere, she closed her legs together, she squeezed them tightly as her eyes began to tear up. The thought of what Davonte was able to do to her consumed her. She was never able to fit the entire length of Davonte inside her, no matter how hard or how deep they worked and pushed to cram it in. There were always several visual inches that couldn't be buried within her sex dungeon. But that was okay, he had taught her how to get down with it and how to work its large size to her advantage. Davonte wore a mental smile, as he took note of the effect he had on these two fine older sisters. He took his finger and motioned for them to come forward.

Desiree's breast rose as she took a deep breath and stepped forward. The thought of how much she missed Davonte flooded her mind and she was about to make up for it and more. Angie hesitated for a second, causing Davonte to wonder why. That was, until she took that first step. It was then he saw just how excited and overwhelmed she was, as the pee ran down the inside of her thighs. He

231

couldn't help from becoming egotistically engrossed behind the powerful effect he had on them.

Stepping to him, they both began kissing him on the neck and ear, then together working their way down. Once they got to their knees and below his waist, the two of them caressed and kissed the head and shaft of his large vein covered meat. They gave him top-notch fellatio and although performed in a very aggressive and savage way, they worked in unison taking turns going from head to balls. To see it would have led one to believe they were drinking from the well of eternal life!

Davonte watched for a few moments, he found it to be very interesting. Desiree gave head with pure passion and devotion as if she were driven by a hidden force that demanded her and the dick to become one. She licked, sucked, slurped and moaned as she reunited with her old friend.

Now Angie, was simply an unadulterated freak and she performed as such, refusing to let a well-hung penis be in front of her face and she not formally introduce herself. She would bob her head back and forth taking as much as she could straight to the back of her throat.

Yes, Davonte saw it to be an enjoyable site. He even found it to be cute when they both flicked their tongues out and simultaneously licked the head of his manhood, then kissed each other. It was a sure sign of their coming together. However, enough was enough. It sure felt good, but it was now time for him to share with them his surprise.

"Hey ladies," he said grabbing hold of his pipe and pulling it from them.

Desiree jumped and jerked as if she was being taken off life support. Angie's head followed with her mouth still making sucking motions like a puppy. Davonte looked down at them.

"Stand up and bend over the couch," he told them. Looking down at Angie, he wondered if she had some weird sexual fetish with pissing. There was a small wet spot on the carpet and the crotch of her panties was soaked.

"I can't help it," she told him as she stood up, realizing what he was looking at.

Davonte didn't respond. He just pointed over to the couch. The two of them made their way over, being as frisky as they possibly could be, ass cheeks wiggling as they walked, tits bouncing. As they bent over and placed their hands on the couch, they spread their legs wide and arched their backs while swaying their butts from side to side.

The fishnet body suit Desiree wore had an opening at the crotch, however, her entire vagina area was covered with the glistening of her juices. She was very much ready to get down and she let it be known as she contracted her butt muscles, which caused her cheeks to jump up and down like a stripper.

Angie couldn't make her cheeks jump, but she refused to be out done. So she quickly slid her pee soaked panties off, bent over, spread her legs, placed two fingers on her vagina lips and spread them to expose the inner pink part of her hairy muffin. Looking in each other's direction, they shared a glance, Angie saw Desiree's lips move and silently form the words, *"Do you love me?"*

"Yes baby," she responded back in a whisper.

"Okay," Davonte said suddenly, *"Let's get this party on the road."*

The girls couldn't wait. They were more than ready and well overdue. Although they both shared in the same thought of which one he would penetrate first, it didn't really matter as long as they got a piece. Davonte peeped the vibe between them.

"I know y'all wondering who I'ma hit first. Don't worry, I got that all worked out."

As he walked closer to Angie she smiled then arched her back and stuck her ass out as far as she could. The visual gave you the impression of a cat stretching. The thought of what Davonte was about to do to her made her clit throb. Nine months of pent up sexual pleasure was about to be released into her and she was with it.

"I want to thank you both for the little surprise," he told them. *"I guess we all had surprises in mind.*

"That's right," Desiree thought as she envisioned how she was going to work Angie while Davonte put it on her. Desiree was going to turn Angie all the way out, even more than she already was. She looked back and gave Davonte a devilish seductive look that revealed the presence of a sexual demon within. That's when she noticed Davonte's dick wasn't hard and the hand he'd finally pulled from behind his back had a belt wrapped around it and the look he had on his face didn't say sex. It said, *"I'm about to beat y'alls asses!*

That evening he did just that. The first caught Angie off guard and sent her crawling up the back of the couch.

"Naah, don't run!" He yelled at Angie who was in shock. *"Bring that pretty little ass here!"*

It was then Desiree realized what was taking place. Davonte's ego and emotions had been tampered with while he was locked up and although she'd talked to him and apologized. Davonte hadn't forgiven a damn thing.

"W...w... what'd I do?!" Angie cried out.

Desiree knew there wasn't any escaping it, Davonte was going to put that belt on their asses. She could see it in his eyes, he had been waiting for this moment. The moment of payback for the pain he endured. She felt sorry for Angie who was now running around the coffee table to nowhere as Davonte simply stepped over it and caught her with the belt on her right butt cheek as she turned to try and run. The lick dropped her to the floor where she kicked and threw her arm and hands out to block the belt. Davonte beat her ass then turned to Desiree.

"And your ass!" He snapped.

Desiree was already crying. Angie was screaming some shit about she was telling her dad.

"Go ahead!" Davonte yelled to her as he raised the belt to hit Desiree with it. *"I'll beat his ass too."* Desiree didn't even move that is, until the belt made contact. The first lick caught her on the thigh tearing the bodysuit as it did. The sting was too much, she tried to run, but to no avail, Desiree got what was coming to her that night too.

When he was done with Desiree, he threw the belt down and walked over to Angie who laid there still on the floor whimpering, *"Why you do that Davonte!?"* She cried out, *"I didn't do nothing to you!"*

"Quiet!" He told her as he bent down and turned her over on her stomach.

"What you doing?" She whimpered as Davonte got on his knees behind her and lined his manhood up for entry.

Desiree watched as he doggy styled Angie's ass into submission. When he finished, she just fell to her stomach and lay there breathing hard. He stood, turned and walked to Desiree and put her in the same position, then delivered the exact same long head to the back of the pussy treatment. He went back and forth between them for three hours until he finally came, then he left both of them stretched and worn out on the floor, and that's where they slept until morning, no cover, no pillows, only their sexed up, welted up bodies on the bare carpet.

Desiree didn't know what to think about that night. She questioned whether she was going crazy. Why? Because it seemed that each time Davonte stroked into her, it made the sting of the welts he'd just put on her go away. And oddly enough, mad, sad, or in pain, she and Angie both had heart-stopping orgasms that night, several at that.

"Hold still," Thomas the tattoo guy told Desiree. *"I have a couple more letters to go and you're all done."*

Desiree truthfully wasn't listening to him and had no idea she'd moved. Her thoughts continued to be preoccupied with Davonte and the things he'd been putting them through. The surprise beating was not only a bit much, but it was surely an attention grabber, if that's what he wanted, he got it. And there was a message being sent, it was well sent. All in all, that night would never be forgotten. Yet, he didn't stop there, days later he had sexed both of them in an interesting kind of way. Having them take turns riding him while each watched, then when he'd climax, he'd have them get up, the other go down and suck the sexual juices of the other off and until he became erect again. He had them do this repeatedly, causing him to release four nuts.

But that wasn't it, once he'd had his fill, he sent Angie to run some bath water. The thought of a hot bath sounded cool and could possibly have led to more acts of satisfaction. Not so, because Davonte climbed into the tub by himself and began bathing. Yet, all wasn't lost, as they stood by the tub wondering if they were going to get to climb in too, Davonte told them he'd seen a bottle of champagne in the frig and sent Desiree to get it and bring two glasses with it.

"That's what I'm talking bout," Angie said happily.

When Desiree returned with the bottle of champagne and glasses, she handed them to Davonte who placed them on the side of the tub.

"Desiree," Angie chimed, *"I think we need to make a toast to our baby being home. What you think?"*

"I'm with it," Desiree said wearing a smile. She figured things could only get better. After fumbling with the top on

the bottle for a moment, Davonte motioned for her to hand him the bottle. With ease he popped the top.

"Heyyy!" The girls yelled out with cheer. Angie did a little happy dance and Desiree rubbed her hands together in a greedily fashion, ready to drink up the Moet she'd paid thirty dollars for.

In one hand, Davonte grabbed the champagne glasses from the side of the tub. In the other hand, he held the bottle of Moet looking up at the girls he smiled and said, *"To us,"* then he dipped both of the champagne glasses into the tub filling them up with his bath water.

"To us," he said holding the glasses up so the girls could each take one.

"Okayyyy," Angie said softly while reaching out and taking one of the glasses as she looked at Davonte with a bewildering smile, she asked, *"So now, you want us toooo liiike do what?"*

Extending the other glass in Desiree's direction, he said, *"Take a drink, of course. Remember it's a toast to me being home."*

Desiree looked at the glass of grayish soapy water, then at Davonte, then back to the glass. *"You want us to drink your bath water? Dirty bath water at that?"*

"Here," he said pushing the glass into her hand, *"It's the least you could do."* He told them, *"I mean, that's if you love me."*

Desiree's mouth opened in an attempt to protest, but before she could, Angie turned her glass up and downed the glass of bath water.

"Baby," she said gasping for air, *"You know I love you."*

With those words being said, Davonte looked over at Desiree with a look in his eyes that said, *"Well, your turn."*

As Desiree slowly raised the glass to her lips, she swore to herself that she'd get Angie for this shit! True indeed,

Davonte was still upset over what took place while he was in jail. But damn! How far would he take it?

"Alrighty," Thomas chirped giving Desiree's butt cheek one last good wipe. *"You're ready to go,"* he said taking a stand from his stool and pulling off the latex gloves.

"So, how much we owe you?" Angie asked grabbing her purse.

"Well, I gave you two a $15 discount since you both brought artwork. So, it's a hundred eighty-five a piece, making it a total of three hundred seventy dollars."

"Damn!" Desiree exclaimed. All she could think of was why Davonte would want this, his name permanently tattooed on their asses.

After They'd Paid for the tattoos, they headed for the parking lot and climbed in the truck. Desiree was still set on turning Angie out which wasn't far from reach seeing that at this point she had her wide open. Turning the ignition to start the truck, Desiree looked over at Angie.

"Let me ask you something."

"I'm listening," Angie told her.

"Lately does it seem to you that Davonte is acting crazy?"

Angie let out an uncomfortable giggle. *"Why?"* She asked. But before Desiree could answer, she continued, *"Because he beat us and shit?!?"*

"Yeah," Desiree said paying close attention to Angie's actions.

"Nah," she said in a nonchalant way, *"We deserved that shit. Look at what we did. Besides, I think it was just a matter of him sharing his ability to be a voluptuary."*

It was at that point, Desiree realized Angie was the daughter of the one who flew over the cuckoo's nest.

"Let the seat back and pull your skirt up," she instructed Angie who gladly obliged.

"What you trying to do?" She asked Desiree in a whining voice.

"Put your feet up on dash," she told her ignoring the question. Angie did as she was told, Desiree put the truck in drive and reached over, slid her hand in Angie's panties and began rubbing her clit, stopping before exiting the parking lot into traffic. She started working Angie's love button with soft circles and quick side-to-side motions.

"You like that?" She asked feeling Angie becoming wet.

"Yes," Angie cooed. *"But don't wreck this truck playing with my pum pum."*

Desiree decided to try Angie.

"What!?" She snapped, causing Angie to look up in surprise.

"You want me to stop!?!"

"No, Desiree," Angie said softly. *"I just want you to be careful,"* she replied placing her hand on top of Desiree's she grinded a little. *"Just be careful, you know what I mean? You can do what you want to me."*

Desiree held back the devilish grin that tried to appear on her face while she probed in and out of Angie's wet muffin.

Desiree pulled the truck out into traffic, thinking to herself, *"This bitch crazy and all she got is sex on the brain, sex on the brain!!"*

Stepping on the gas and weaving in and out of traffic, she pulled her finger from the lips of Angie's vagina and placed them in her mouth.

Once again a devilish grin attempted to appear on Desiree's face, only this time, she didn't hold it back. She glanced out of the corner of her eye at Angie who was sucking sex juice covered fingers like a baby doe nursing on its mother.

NARRATION

*To The Thinking person, it would seem that karma had
taken a part in this relationship of three. Davonte having
Desiree and occasionally doing what men are said to do at
times, that is, stepping out. Some would argue that it is in
the nature of men to do this or whether the man was simply
a cheater. Now, because Davonte at some point stepped
out and ended up with Angie does that make him a cheater?
After all, he did finally tell the truth about seeing them both
and from there brought Angie home so that she and Desiree
could be friends. Does this cancel the idea of him being a
cheater and certify him as a player? Whatever the case,
when Angie gets on the scene, she is occasionally rude to
Desiree in her own house only to cause Desiree to wise up
and flip the script, now using Angie's carnal desires
against her. She has Lil Ms. Angie literally eating from her
fingertips amongst other places. (Pun intended)*

*Davonte's idea of bringing them together however,
initially was a bit more than they were able to handle
causing them to both step out and end up in desirable,
although they would lead you to believe undesirable
situations, where somehow unwanted climaxing took place.
Image that? Would that be a matter of the cheater being
cheated, or the player being played? They say, what goes
around comes around. Could this be so? That's a hellava
question, seeing that some people are said to never get
caught doing the dirt. But, that wasn't the case with
Desiree whose in the dark secret came to light just as soon
as it happened, making her have to get back right with
Davonte, which at the time doesn't seem to be working.
Meanwhile, her plans to turn Angie out and cause her to
think of Desiree as her panacea was in full effect. Or, was
Angie playing along so Desiree wouldn't expose her little
dark secret?!? At this point, we would have to ask, would*

that ever come out? Would karma pay Lil Ms. Angie a visit?

CHAPTER TWENTY

"THE THREE OF US"

Davonte **H**ad **A**ppeared to be coming around and stopped
putting the girls through the emotional torment of his alter
ego. As it was, he wasn't totally affected by Desiree
supposing to have fooled around with someone else.
Seeing that at the tender young age of fifteen, his Uncle Ed
on his mother side had told him, *"Nephew, don't even
worry about a female of yours giving up that there cunt
between her legs. You see, pussy will stretch a mile,
however it won't tear an inch. Give it enough time it'll
shrink back down to size. You hear what I say nephew?
Don't worry yourself bout that thang. It's hers to do what
she want with and trust me, when I tell you half the time she
don't want it. And last of all nephew, how you know pussy
and nothing of great importance? If it was such a hot
commodity, God would have kept it up there with him."*
Davonte always remembered those words and although
Uncle Ed was a jokester at times, he always told the truth.
The part that ate at Davonte is where did he lose control?
Whatever the case, until he figured that out, he would keep
the girls busy. They both had daily routines that he
oversaw and made sure wasn't missed. Each day consisted
of going to work, upon returning home jumping jacks, sit
ups, leg kick backs, lunges and frog squats. From there,
they would rotate weekly on the cooking. After showering
and eating, he had them devote an hour to reading
scriptures, sometimes the Bible and other times the Quran
of Muslims.

*"In order to overstand the weakness of humans, you must
know what they claim to believe and follow,"* he would tell

them. *"This will allow you to see what it is they're striving for."*

On Saturdays, they were quizzed on what they'd read and learned throughout the week. Because they were women, there was quality time that was needed to be spent with each of them. This he would do by assigning them days. There were two days a week given to them both. These were their individual days to spend with him. The weekends alternated so they each could be taken out to dinner and the movies. It was clear with the three of them that he was the boss and could pull rank when he felt, therefore changing their days whenever.

Whichever one was on her period, slept in a separate room during this time. This was something neither had a problem with, reason being, they felt it was like torture to hear the other having sex and were unable to join in. The two of them enjoyed him most when they had him alone. Davonte enjoyed them most when the three of them got dressed and stepped out for a night on the town and he having a woman on each arm, what man wouldn't enjoy that? Davonte would show out too with the ladies, kissing and hugging causing observing men to be envious. Sometimes other women would catch Desiree and Angie in the ladies room and ask them, what was it about Davonte? Desiree would simply smile and shrug her shoulders. Angie would always be chipper and wide-eyed when she answered, *"Because he's wonderful!"* She would exclaim smiling from ear to ear.

Although things appeared to be good between the three of them, there was still the personal thoughts and feelings they held inside. Desiree wondered were things really okay now with her and Davonte or would her mistake be one he wouldn't let her live down? She also wondered would there ever be a time with just her and Davonte again or would things go back with him having both of them but living in their separate homes? Along with these thoughts, she questioned how Davonte would act knowing how she had Angie sprung. Now that he was home, she was unable to indulge intimately with Angie the way she'd like, but when time did allow, like in the truck while they were supposed to be grocery shopping or out paying bills, she would get into Angie's world in such a way. Every now and then just to make sure she still had Angie where she wanted her. She would make her do daring things, like times when she wore a skirt and was driving, she would pull it up and have Angie go down on her throwing her left leg up on the dash between the steering wheel and drivers door. She would drive around while talking to her. Words added a different element to any situation especially when it came to a woman and Desiree made sure Angie stayed full of her seducing conversation. She had one more thing she was going to do to make sure Lil Ms. Angie was where she wanted her.

Was Davonte aware something was taking place? Yes, but he was unaware to what degree.

Now, Davonte's thoughts were also held for his own personal good. As for what Desiree had done would surely always leave a scar on his ego, but moving on was a must for him, along with getting them to realize that the way things were at the moment would always be. Davonte now had the two women he wanted with him together under the same roof and as far as he was concerned, they would all be growing old together.

Angie's thoughts were now a ball of overwhelming emotions. The man she loved was home and giving her what she wanted and needed, mental and physical stimulation, making her feel on top of the world all day everyday. He was undoubtedly the cause of her heart beating and the breath she breathed and if this wasn't enough, Desiree now had Angie blown away with the idea of having the best of both worlds.

Sometimes, Desiree would get Angie hot and wet with to die for foreplay, then send her to Davonte to be finished off. Other times, she would come behind Davonte and finish off what of her was left. Angie's each day was full and complete. She had all that was needed in life as far as she was concerned. All that had to be done was to keep both Davonte and Desiree happy and satisfied. As long as they were happy, she would be. It was obvious they both loved her. Angie had her hands and head full, a man who gave her according to what he knew was best for her, as well as guided her in the direction she needed to go, along with understanding her to the best degree a man could. That, and having Desiree to fill in the gaps of being a woman and knowing what a woman wanted and needed at times, made Angie's every yearning able to be fulfilled. When she thought about it, she felt so good she'd rather kill or be killed than be without either of them.

Davonte, Desiree, And Angie strolled along the walkway at Atlanta's Piedmont Park. It was late spring, 72 degrees and a lovely day with summer around the corner, there was nothing but love in the air. The exercises he'd had the girls doing was paying off and it showed. Both of their legs, calves and thighs were thicker, shapely and well defined.

Desiree strutted her stuff with a pair of form fitting cotton white shorts and matching top with a pair of tennis shoes. Her hair was in long thin twists that bounced and raised up on the sides as the wind gently blew. Desiree's waist was trimmed down, her breast perky with her ass and hips looking luscious. The aura of the day gave a feel of romance. There was a frisky energy Desiree felt ozzing throughout her body. You not only noticed it because of her red lace thong and bra you could very well see through her outfit. But also, by her seducing walk brought on by the sway of her firm ass and hips. You could see the glow on her face as she beamed radiantly and there was a tingling presence between her legs that made a smile stay plastered on her face, she felt naughty.

Angie wore a similar cotton short outfit, only it was a soft pink and beneath it she wore black lace high cut panties and no bra. You could see her breast well, but she didn't care, she too was consumed by the aura of the beautiful day. She walked with her hair pulled back in a long ponytail hanging down her back, a smile on her face and her breast bouncing carefree. Because of the friction from them brushing against the fabric of the shirt, her nipples were noticeably erect. Now, her walk was nothing short of being enticingly raunchy, her thighs and calves not only looked good on her short body, but you could see all she had to offer. Although her waist was also trimmed down and her thighs and calves were firm, Angie's ass cheeks were loose. They jiggled and jumped as she walked. There were signs of a gap being born at the lower curve of her ass right before you got between the legs, why? Because she just had to have it. She couldn't allow Desiree to have it all to herself so, Davonte being the giving person he was, gave it to her.

He overdosed her with anal sex, it was a weekly ritual. Sometimes taking place two or three times in one day. He kept her taking it on her back, legs in the air, on her knees doggy style, standing up bent over holding her ankles. There were times she wanted it so bad, he would just sit at the edge of the couch watching T.V. with his legs spread and she would anally ride him backwards bent over palms to the floor. Davonte told her the best way to do it is to continually find and hit spots that work for her and felt good, then work them until she felt she could cum from it. She followed his instructions and became an anal sex freak. A lot of times things were a shitty mess, but it didn't stop

Angie from wanting it or Davonte from giving it. From her ass regularly being stretched, in one way or another, it remained lose and jiggly. She welcomed the looseness of her ass cheeks along with the growing gap. It was all a sign of how she was getting it and Angie was with that. Not to leave out the fact she was already a hairy woman and Davonte didn't allow for her to ever shave her crotch, her shorts revealed the print of her hairy puss and two long winking lips. Angie loved how she felt inside and she flaunted it in her every step.

"I'm trying to make sure you two overstand and are clear when it comes to how things are going to be."

"We hear you," Desiree told Davonte. *"And you have communicated this to us on more than one occasion, so it's clear you're very serious about what you're saying."*

"I'm saying," Davonte said, *"By all means if either of you have a problem with this, let it be known now so it can be taken care of."*

"I don't have a problem with it baby," Angie said rubbing her hand on his lower back, then sliding down to palm his left butt cheek.

"Honestly, neither of you should have an issue with what I'm putting together here. All men have a preference and requirements when it comes to the type of bitch they are in a relationship with. It's a matter of comfort and what makes them happy. In my case, I want two bitches."

"Okay," Desiree said, *"The need to be happy is overstood, but I have to ask, do you feel you can handle two women? Not just sexually but all around emotionally and mentally? It's not like when you were in jail away from us, now you're home and have no choice but to deal with both of us on a daily basis and this will be for the rest of your life. Not one, but two, constantly."*

"The way I see it," Davonte said pulling them close to him and wrapping an arm around each of their waist. *"I've*

247

been home a couple months now and have been handling things well. Women always say, no two women are alike, so on and so forth. However, from what I've gathered the differences are small and very few. Not to mention, when the majority of woman get with a man, they either structure themselves around him and his life naturally or he molds them to do so. Those who don't or can't be molded because of psychological or emotional damage causing them to ego trip are usually by themselves. In short," Davonte continued, *"If you can handle one bitch you can handle ten. In my case I have two fine ass bitches that can and will be handled. Got it?"* He asked, meaning just what he'd said.

"We got it daddy," Angie chimed as she stretched up on her tippy toes and kissed him on the cheek.

"And you?" He asked Desiree while smacking her on the butt.

"I...I...It's all good. I mean you know I'm with it," she responded. Truthfully, Desiree had hoped things would have been somewhat different when he came home. *"One more thing,"* Desiree added, *"What's the deal with your way of talking to us?"* She asked taking note of how he spoke to them at times in a rather discerning way.

"What you talking bout baby?" He asked. *"The way I sometimes call or refer to y'all as bitch or bitches?!?"*

"Exactly!" She exclaimed looking over at him wide-eyed and curious.

Davonte had always had a touch of thug in him when it was needed but since he'd gone to jail, there seemed to be a totally different person in him.

"Listen," he said stopping in his tracks and pulling both of them in front of him, leaning forward he kissed Desiree on the forehead, then slowly on the nose, followed by a soft yet prolonged kiss on the lips. Angie squirmed and bounced on her toes awaiting her dose of affection.

"Heyyy," Davonte said in a stern voice noticing her impatience. He patted her softly on the butt. *"Easy,"* he told her, *"Ain't nobody forget about you."*

As he leaned in to kiss her she closed her eyes, she wanted to feel it all. Just like he'd done Desiree, he planted kisses with his soft lips on her forehead and nose by the time he reached her lips there were tiny explosions going off inside her body. Their prolonged kiss turned to darting tongue action. Desiree couldn't help but to smile, she knew how Davonte was capable of making a woman feel. She too on several occasions had felt the same explosions. Davonte pulled his lips away from Angie's and resumed talking. Angie stood there glossy-eyed. Desiree took her hand and tapped Angie on the lips so she would close her mouth.

"My calling either one of you bitch shouldn't be a big deal, so don't sweat it, and don't let it lead either of you into thinking I don't love you."

"I'll be your bitch!" Angie exclaimed.

He smiled. *"And as long as you both behave yourselves, you don't have to worry about me calling you bitch or going off on you in public or in front of people period. But don't get beside yourselves, because I will react, trust me."*

As Davonte talked, he rubbed a hand on each of their butt cheeks and slid his middle finger up and down their butt crack. They both stared into his eyes and played with his earlobes. People walking by looked on amused, but they paid no one any mind. They all knew once they got home that evening it was on. There would be a romantic, intense, sexual war taking place.

"Now who think they in shape?" Davonte asked with a touch of excitement in his voice.

"We do," they both said at the same time holding their hands in the air like models showing off their bodies.

"Well, let's race," he said getting in a runners position.

"Oh, its on like a mutha fucker!" Angie said turning ghetto and getting in position beside Davonte. Her words surprised both of them.

"What's up, babe?" He asked Desiree.

"Yeah, Desiree!" Angie yelled hyped like never before.

"If you can't beat'em, join'em," Desiree mumbled to herself. She didn't bend all the way down like Davonte and Angie, but she did put one foot in front of the other and bend forward preparing for take off. Seeing they were ready, Davonte started.

"Get on your mark!" He yelled.

"It's on now niggas!" Angie said. The way she gritted her teeth would have made you think it was the Olympics.

"Get set. Go!" He yelled as he and Angie took off like bats out of hell.

Desiree stood up straight, *"Shiiiit,"* she said, *"Bet I don't. A bitch just a little too sexy for all that thurr."* She giggled as she thought of a song. She sang it as she watched Davonte and Angie actually hauling ass down the walkway causing people to move aside. *"I'm too sexy for my shoes, too sexy for my shirt. Damn, that bitch fast!"* She said watching Angie keep up with Davonte. *"I'm too sexy. Here I come y'all!"* She yelled as she started to walk faster switching her hips hard as hell from side to side. *"My shoe came untied and I didn't want to fall!"* She yelled. *"Plus, I'm too sexy,"* she whispered.

The Day Went as well as predicted. From the park they made their way to the mall and window shopped after nagging Davonte, he let them both purchase a Coach purse. From there, they went and stuffed themselves on fish hoagies and curly fries. Afterwards, they caught an early evening movie and headed home. They flirted, kissed and teased one another in the car on the way home. Once there, they barely made it in the door before clothes were being ripped off and thrown on the floor from the kitchen, up the stairs, and to the bedroom.

Angie laid on the side of Davonte with her head on his chest. She was suddenly awakened by a tapping on the forehead, she opened her eyes. There was Desiree glaring down at her as she lifted her head up to gain focus from her exhausting snooze. She noticed Desiree motioning with her finger. As her vision cleared, she saw Desiree's lips moving, saying, *"You,"* as she pointed at her, then, *"Here,"* as she pointed between her legs. *"Now,"* Desiree added.

Angie looked up to see if Davonte was sleep. Then making her way under the cover like an earthworm, over and around Davonte, she went placing herself between Desiree's legs. Desiree saw the lump in the cover from Angie's head pause, figuring she needed more room to work, she spread her legs up and wider. Actually, Angie was wondering what it was with Desiree always wanting to get hit off by her after they'd already been getting down with Davonte. If it was a matter of her not getting enough, she didn't mind hitting her off. If she was just being greedy and wanting to be overdosed, again she didn't mind. But the part where she wanted Angie to make her cum so she could lick her and Davonte's cum up out of her was starting to be a bit much. This is something she would be talking about with Desiree. Pleasing Desiree was one thing, she really didn't mind doing. However, tonight Davonte had delivered on both of them another one of his Oscar winning performances. Angie still had semen running out of her, so she knew Desiree's cunt was full, especially seeing that he had exploded in her first. Then they both got two follow up explosions before things ended. The thing about it, Desiree only released a little, but Davonte's was thick and a lot. Mixed with Desiree's and all the bodily fluids, it made her stomach hurt once she swallowed.

Desiree interrupted her thoughts by tapping her on the head, threw the cover back, then she heard Desiree's mouth go, *"Slurp, slurp!"*

Continuing to make a heavy breathing noise as if sleep, Davonte cracked one eyelid and peeked to see what the happenings were. He'd been figuring something was up with the two of them. He laid there and listened to Angie getting started on Desiree. What he wondered was why they carried on as though they were sneaking, because he didn't mind them getting down. Hell, as a matter of fact, he felt they should roll like that anyway. He decided to wait until they got good into it, then pretend to be waking up. A few minutes past and Desiree began to make small jerking motions, her lips puckered as if she was smelling the top one and she bit down on the bottom one. Davonte watched as her body started to tense up. Right then, he opened both eyes, rose up and spoke.

"Hey, what y'all two doing?" He asked. At the sound of his voice, he and Desiree watched the lump of cover between her legs stop moving, raised up and slid over between Davonte's legs. Davonte felt Angie place his meat in her mouth and began working the head with her lips and tongue. As he came erect, it caused her head to rise higher. Desiree let her head fall back on the pillow with a look on her face that couldn't quite be explained. He figured it might have been because she was about to climax and Angie had stopped abruptly. But why? Was his question.

After Angie's vigorous performance, she exited towards the foot of the bed from beneath the cover. Without looking in either Davonte's or Desiree's direction, she headed to the bathroom. She'd had enough time to rinse and gargle. A second after she'd walked off, Davonte watched Desiree slide out the bed and head in the same direction. Entering the bathroom, she closed the door behind her seeing the light fade from the door closing. Davonte figured she must have needed to take a dump.

Sitting on the toilet, Desiree watched as Angie finished rinsing her mouth. Desiree told herself she was going to let bygones be bygones. But, she had lied deep down inside, she hadn't let go of the night Angie failed to confess up to Davonte what she too had done with the owners son from the restaurant. She wanted things a certain way all because of that and it seemed the work she'd put into Angie may be fading. So, as she sat on the toilet peeing and ego-tripping at the same time, she decided to put one more move into place. Angie turned the water off on the sink and looked at Desiree who told her, *"Leave that on."* Then motioned with her finger for her to come over.

"I know this girl don't want no more sex," Angie thought. *"Baby, I'm done for the night,"* she told Desiree.

"Now!" Desiree demanded in a whisper.

Angie walked over with wrinkles in her forehead wondering what Desiree's problem was and why she had her leave the water on unless she was going to wash her hands when she was done. Once Angie stood in front of her, Desiree didn't even wipe, just stood up and asked Angie, *"How you gonna play me? How you gonna stop straightening me out, knowing this what you need and just slide over and start sucking his dick?"* There was attitude in her words.

Angie was shocked by Desiree's questions, but before she could answer, Desiree turned to flush the toilet, then as she quickly spun back around to face her. Angie would have liked to move out the way just as fast as she'd saw it coming.

CHAPTER TWENTY-ONE

"NEXT MOVE"

Why He Was there, he really couldn't answer. But since he'd kept the phone number and address, he took it upon himself to call and drop by. Davonte sat on the couch waiting for the half naked Asian female to let Mr. Wonderful know he had arrived. From the outside of the house and from the looks of the neighborhood you would've thought Mr. Wonderful failed to have any income coming in at all. Then to see the brand spanking new candy apple red North Star Cadillac with the 20 inch vogue tires and rims parked in the drive way would have led you to believe the residence was getting a visit from wealthy relatives. Yet, stepping into the house was the kicker. At the entrance of the door was a 4X4 square foot area of high polished red oak wood, the rest of the room that seemed to be a living room was covered from wall to wall with an inch thick white carpet and if that wasn't enough, the room was decked out with white baby booty soft leather furniture. The couch and loveseat were large and said money. They were covered with red silk pillows. The walls of the entire room were mirrored. There was a huge fireplace. The trim and its base was red marble with white swirls. Over the fireplace, was a large 4x5 foot oil painting of Mr. Wonderful in a white tailor made suit with a red tie and large red pimp hat. On each side of him was a naked woman on their knees and in his hand was a leash, the end was attached to the diamond-studded collar around the female's neck. In their mouths were stacks of money.

"Take your shoes off please and come this way," a well-shaped white female told Davonte.

He did as he was instructed and followed her down a hallway. There wasn't much to the hall except for the studio lighting that lined it's ceiling. After making a right turn, they stopped in front of two kissing stained glass doors. As the white female stepped in front of Davonte to open the doors, he couldn't help to notice how large her behind was. She even had hips with a rather small waistline. All he could think is she had to have black in her blood. Motioning with her hand, she sent Davonte into the room. The lavish lifestyle of Mr. Wonderful was also extended into this room. There was no money spared as Davonte's eyes followed the in-wall fish tank that sat smack in the middle of the walls circling the whole room. Inside the tank were colorful salt-water fish, including small sharks and an octopus. There were all types of nick-nacks inside, small castles, a treasure chest, it was nothing short of an underwater kingdom inside the walls of Mr. Wonderful's sitting room.

Mr. Wonderful stood there observing his company. His appearance was far from that of the county jail where he'd first met Davonte.

No county blues with the words 'County Inmate' on them. No, today Mr. Wonderful stood dressed in black silk pajama pants and a matching robe that hung open showing his slender stomach and flat chest. On each pinky finger he wore large 14k gold rings with 2-carat diamonds that flickered like fireworks every time he moved his hands. Around his neck was a solid gold Gucci link necklace. At the end of it, in the center of his nappy chest was a medallion a 14k gold solid nugget about the circumference of a silver dollar and about an inch thick. It was covered with diamond chips. No question about it, he was representing *"That Nigga"* status.

"Come on in young blood!" He yelled, snapping Davonte out of his amazement. *"Watch your step now,"* he cautioned Davonte who caught on to what he meant once he looked in front of himself. The center of the room

dropped. It actually dropped down three steps. Davonte walked down the steps and greeted Mr. Wonderful with a manly handshake.

"M Dub," he said.

"Young blood," he returned, *"Have a seat."*

Davonte sat down on the smooth black suede furniture. The whole room was black and gold with the exception of the crystal nick-nacks in the wall unit curio cabinet. Pushing a button on a wireless remote microphone, Mr. Wonderful said, *"Bring us drinks."* He then turned to Davonte and told him, *"Yes, its real,"* making reference to the large leopard rug that laid in the center of the room. It was the leopard's whole body, head, paws, tail with the cat's claws still intact. Stuffed in his mouth, were bundles of hundred dollar bills. Mr. Wonderful could look on Davonte's face and see what he was thinking.

"Why, why I have this house in this neighborhood done up on the inside in such a way? Let me explain, in order to relieve your concerns. This house belonged to the mother of my bottom bitch before she passed away."

With a curious look on his face, Davonte inquired, *"Your bottom bitch?"*

"Yeah, Yolanda, the first female I coped and turned out. She's been with me longest, has made plenty money, has given me little problems and knows her place. So, when her mother passed and she asked me to purchase the house because it held many childhood memories for her, I said hell, why not?!?! Now, by all means, it needed work and I refused to live anywhere without my creature comforts, so here we are baby. Here we are."

Davonte smiled and nodded his head in approval to be in the presence of a real live pimp, it had a degree of excitement to it.

"So, how old was your first female or bottom bitch at the time you turned her out?"

Davonte really didn't care to know the answer to the question. It was asked moreso out of striking up more conversation.

"Well," Mr. Wonderful said with his head tilted back as though he was looking at the ceiling, *"Let me see... she's about forty-seven years old now and that was over twenty something years ago. So, I would say she was about 19 or 20 years old."*

"And still around?" Davonte questioned.

"Still around," Mr. Wonderful told him. *"And going nowhere. I'm all she knows, all she has and has given of herself all she's got. In short,"* he said with a rather mysterious grin on his face, *"I've made her all she is."*

"I bet you did," Davonte said under his breath.

Reaching for another remote, Mr. Wonderful looked over at Davonte and began reading him. No doubt there was something on his mind.

"So, what brings you here to my humble palace?" He asked while pushing a button on the remote, causing the smooth soft sound of jazz to fill the air. Mr. Wonderful started to groove to the sound of the music however it only lasted a hot second before a young lady walked in and announced, *"Here's your drinks daddy."*

Now Davonte had noticed a couple of very attractive naked women running around here and there and he had to admit they were fine, but when he asked himself would he pay to play? The answer was no. But this one who'd walked in with the drinks took his breath and when he asked himself the question of would he pay to play? This time the answer came quick, how much, how often, and should he get two jobs? The way she bent over when sitting the tray down was so natural yet so seductive, Davonte tried not to stare.

"It's okay," Mr. Wonderful told him, *"To look and appreciate what you see is to compliment me. So, by all means young blood, enjoy."*

It was clear to Davonte this young lady was born with this beauty and seductive demeanor. She stood 5 foot 9 with lovely even shoulders. Her breasts were very firm looking almost perfect, nipples and all, not too much and far from too little. As she turned her back to Davonte and spoke with the man she referred to as "Daddy". Davonte took in her hind sights, long legs, slightly bowed, shapely enough to win a prettiest legs contest and at the top of them where most women's legs smoothly connected to their lower ass, hers had a crease. She had teardrop shaped cheeks that hung with the greatest of sexual splendor and at the base of her lower back, just above her ass on each side sat two cute dimples.

"Turn around and say hello," Mr. Wonderful told her.

As she turned around she smiled and gave Davonte a gentle wave with the wiggle of her fingers. That's where Davonte continued to take in her tender beauty, her eyes showed strength backed by confidence and as she stood there butt ass naked, there was an innocence about her. When she flashed a glimpse of her lovely smile, Davonte saw her pearly white straight teeth. In the middle of the right front tooth, shined a small diamond. Truthfully, you would have thought a diamond on a woman's tooth would have been a bit much, but not on her, it only added to her beauty. Davonte let his eyes travel down her body, in her navel hung a butterfly shaped diamond clustered belly ring. He wasted no time looking directly between her legs at the goods. It made him weak, the hair was long but neatly shaved around the edges and panty lines. The small area just above and around the clit was shaved exposing it. In it, there was a lavish piercing, not a hoop like many get, instead it was a gold dumbbell, it stuck out the actual skin on the hood of the clit. The other end stuck out from under the hood with the clit on it without a doubt was a half-carat diamond. Her hips were mouth watering, the nails on her fingers and toes manicured and natural. Nothing was fake or added to her. To top it all off, she was covered from head to toe in the most beautiful chocolately brown skin. A blemish?!? No. Nowhere, never!

"All right, young blood, don't hurt yourself." Mr. Wonderful told him, *"Allow me to introduce you to this lovely tender specimen. Baby, this is Davonte, a.k.a. young blood. Young blood this is none other than my bottom bitch, Yolanda. You two say hello, if you will."*

"Young blood," Yolanda greeted winking an eye.

For a second there, Davonte was stuck, he couldn't believe this was a damned near fifty year old woman, not a wrinkle, not a sag.

"Hi there," Davonte finally belted out, adjusting in his seat, fighting back the urge of his nature wanting to rise. *"I'll be damned,"* he thought to himself, *"Yolanda was mistaken for an attractive woman when in reality, she was a "Goddess" and M. Dub had her selling pussy for over half her life."*

"Okay bitch," Mr. Wonderful said, while slapping her firmly on the ass, *"Ain't no standing around you know better than that. Go get them other bitches ready, it's about time for shift change and you need to be getting suited up your damn self, get out there and get it."*

Yolanda pouted and whined, *"Daddiee."*

Mr. Wonderful jumped up from his chair, his demeanor changed just that quick.

"Bitch!" He snapped, *"Don't play, put your mutha fuckin' lip in and get straight. To hell with that childish shit! You know what it is, ain't no kids around this mutha fucker. All that's around here is bitches with working pussies and money. Anything else has no place in my life!"*

Davonte was shocked he'd snapped the way he did.

"Now before you go," he said sitting back down, *"Give my man an encore."*

Right then, Yolanda turned around and stood with her legs shoulder length apart, which made for an amazingly stimulating scene. With little effort, she began doing a little bouncing motion gently up and down on her toes, as she did, her butt cheeks began to open and close like a lovely butterfly. There was also a clapping sound they caused to make a rhythmic beat. Davonte was definitely wooed.

"If I could just take her home," he thought.

"Alright, you long leg sexy bitch, you can excuse yourself."

Just like that, Yolanda stopped and headed out the room. Davonte didn't like the fact Mr. Wonderful called her a bitch, *"Not her,"* he thought. She was too beautiful for such degrading words.

Yolanda exited and Mr. Wonderful poured vodka into the two shot glasses and popped the bottle of champagne. He handed Davonte a glass and sat down.

"She's beautiful," Davonte said.

"Glad you think so," Mr. Wonderful said with a smile and holding his glass up for a toast. Davonte imitated the gesture.

"To whom or to what?" He asked. Then added, *"To you M. Dub."*

Mr. Wonderful smiled. *"Thanks, young blood. But I think this one will be to that game. That game called life and those who play to win."*

"Here, here," Davonte said. From there, they turned up their glasses.

"So, tell me young blood, what brings you to ole M. Dub?"

It Had Been two weeks, Desiree and Angie hadn't spoken a word to one another and Davonte had warned them they'd better not as much as look in the other's direction. They were to go to work, home, and in their rooms. Davonte would cook their food, then serve it to them in their rooms. If the phone rang while he was out, they weren't to answer it. He would have no sex, lovemaking, or intimacy of any kind with either of them. At night, he would sleep on the couch. They had really pissed him off again. After all the talking and agreeing on things together, here they turn around and take shit to another level and for what?

Mr. Wonderful Sat rubbing his chin, analyzing what Davonte told him. By now, they'd finished off all the champagne and was half way through the bottle of vodka. The music stopped, and they sat talking. Mr. Wonderful had given orders for a dinner to be prepared for him and Davonte, at that time, he had a high yellow young chick come into the room in a pair of high heels, a chef's hat and a tiny apron, a very tiny apron, that's all she wore. While she listened to what Mr. Wonderful would have her cook, Davonte gave her a leisurely look over. Her breasts were large and he hoped she wasn't going to cook that way. The way she stood and her ponytail, reminded him of Angie. He couldn't wait for her to return, not so he could see her again, but because M. Dub had her fixing a delightful feast. A romaine salad, topped with fresh steamed crabmeat, broiled lobster tail, breaded and fried calamari, along with tomato and basil pasta. She was also preparing fresh baked honey wheat bread. Davonte's mouth watered at the thought.

"You say y'all had not too long ago finished doing your thang?!?" Mr. Wonderful began, *"Then you dosed off for a minute, woke up to them having a little party of their own, so you said something and from there, the one that was*

*doing the other stopped, slid over and went to doing you?!?
Finished up, went to the bathroom where the other followed
and moments later, all hell broke lose?"*

"That's what happened," Davonte said, thinking back to
that night he'd jumped from the bed after hearing angry
screaming noises and loud bumping. When he first reached
the bathroom door, he thought the girls had took it upon
themselves to get sexual with out him, at least that's what
he assumed from the rough grunting sounds. But, after a
couple seconds, it was clear they were fighting and hard at
that. And to make matters worst, at some point they fell up
against the bathroom door and caused it to lock. Davonte's
banging and yelling didn't make them stop. He actually
had to turn the knob hard until it broke, then bust through
the door. By this time, they had fallen over into the tub.
Davonte yelled and pulled at them to stop, but being all
bent over in the tub, made it difficult for him to keep them
separated. So, he stood up and turned on the shower, once
he saw the cold water didn't work, he turned it off and
turned on the hot water. Within seconds after the water
touched them, they both leaped from the tub like two wild
cats. Davonte's anger made him start slapping at both of
them, catching them on their bare backs with his open
hand. He cursed at them, sending them into separate
rooms.

*"Don't worry yourself about it, young blood. What it
looks like is somebody's running game and the other ain't
wit it."*

Davonte looked at M. Dub with a puzzled look on his
face.

*"Whichever one you was with first, she done pulled a
move and it done backfired."* Mr. Wonderful was positive
about what he told Davonte.

"Are you sure?" Davonte asked.

A look of seriousness came over Mr. Wonderful's face. He looked Davonte straight in the eye and asked, *"This is the same two women we're talking about here, correct?"*

"Yeah," Davonte responded.

"Well, don't ever insult me in my own house with such a question again."

Although Davonte couldn't quite see it, what he knew, but was overlooking for the moment, was the fact Mr. Wonderful had over the years became an expert on women's thoughts and their behavior. And how right he was, Desiree had been running her little game on Angie for a minute and all was going well for a while, however, that night Desiree played her hand, but Angie wasn't having it. Or maybe, she'd went too far when she flushed the toilet, then turned around and slapped the shit out of her. The slap turned Angie's head like she'd been caught with a left hook from a boxer. It made her see a white flash. For a second, she thought she had been knocked out, then the sound of Desiree's voice awoke her saying, *"Answer me!"*

Angie's inner voice told her, *"This bitch done had you leave the water running, then she flushes the toilet so her slapping you couldn't be heard by Davonte. What in the hell is going on!?"*

At that moment, a thousand thoughts had gone through Angie's mind at the speed of light. But once she caught her self and got her head straight, she socked Desiree straight in the eye. From there, they tore the bathroom up.

"Like I said," M Dub spoke, *"Don't worry about it, she was running game, it didn't turn out for her. Honestly, now you're in an odd position if you leave things the way they are. The tension will be a bit much around the house for all of you. Eventually, someone will want to leave. Gotta ask, is that what you want? A broad gone be a broad no matter what and with that, they gone have their individual thoughts and ways towards and about one*

another, especially when it come to sharing the same man. But even with them being how they gone be, it has to be peace in your home, young blood. Oh yeah, everyone must be comfortable to some degree and you young blood need to be the only feared and intimidating factor in that house. That's the way it must be and that's the way they want it. Trust me, what I'm telling you."

While M. Dub was finishing his analysis on what Davonte should do, two females walked in. One was the chef who'd come earlier. She rolled a cart in with her. You could smell the food as soon as they entered the room. The other thick female was short and built like a stallion with her she carried placemats, table linens and a bottle of wine.

Davonte **S**pent **T**he entire day with the man he'd tagged M. Dub, a modern day pimp who played by old school rules. He had to admit, he enjoyed himself, the food, the music, and Mr. Wonderful's words of street wisdom and let us not forget the lovely women. M. Dub gladly called all of them into the room, lined them up and had Davonte point to one of his liking. At first, he looked for Yolanda, once M. Dub realized, he informed him she was out working, unfortunately, therefore, unavailable. With that brief let down, he settled on the short thick female who had come along with the chef to bring the food. As he pointed at her, M. Dub smiled and told him good choice, then looked at her and told her, *"You know what it is."* With the wave of the hand, he dismissed the others. Right before getting on her knees and unzipping Davonte's pants, the very curvy female told him, anytime he felt the need, just tell M. Dub to send for her and she'd come in a flash and cause him to do the same thing.

"Just ask for Chocolate Thunder," she told him.

Davonte didn't partake in all the goodies she had to offer, only her oral expertise, but he told himself he'd be back for her and Yolanda too for that matter.

As he drove home, he laughed to himself as he remembered all except Yolanda had their vagina's shaved completely bald.

"Man," Davonte thought, *"Life is strange and one's mind played a part in it."*

As the thought of M. Dub's stable of bald pussies caused him to think of all the hair that was on the bathroom floor when he'd bust in to break up Angie and Desiree's title fight. From the equal amount of hair on the floor and the scratches on their faces, it was hard to say who had won or got the best of the other. Pulling in the driveway, he tried figuring what tactic he would use to get things back to the norm? M. Dub told him what he needed to do was find out what sparked the fight and get to the bottom of that situation.

"Once you do that, you'll know exactly what you're dealing with when it comes to the two of them. That's your next move."

CHAPTER TWENTY-TWO

"STEPS TO MENDING"

Desiree Stood At the stove stirring a pot of tomato paste she was preparing for a spaghetti dish with fresh made Swedish style turkey meatballs. Although the dish was one of Davonte's favorites, Desiree didn't care to be standing over the stove today. She was on her monthly and cramping, not to mention it was hot as hell. Davonte didn't want the AC on because he didn't like cold air. Desiree was hot and bothered and in the worst way. However, she knew this dinner was all apart of his mending tactic, a dinner, a movie, and talking, plenty of talking. He was trying to get to the bottom of what had taken place and why? Desiree felt like she ought to tell Davonte.

"That bitch got caught up in the same type of predicament as I did, but she didn't let it be known like she claimed she would. I felt betrayed so I set out to pay her back."

That's what she wanted to do, but she didn't want to come off weak like she was hating. Then again, knowing them two, she'd tell him and Angie would turn into a little whining innocent brat. Desiree could hear her now, *"Oh Davonte baby, I'm so sorry. I don't know what came over me. You know you're the only man for me, the only man I truly love, blah, blah, blah."* Desiree placed a hand on her lower stomach as her thoughts were interrupted by a cramp. A grin of discomfort on her face was suddenly replaced with a smile or more less a devilish grin, as she had another thought, *"I ought to put a voodoo hex on both they asses."*

She remembered hearing her mother and grandmother talk when she was little about putting roots on people, which was quite common for their family seeing that their

266

roots were from the Deep South. One of the ways of
putting spells on folks, she remembered was by blood from
a woman's menstrual and mixing it in spaghetti sauce.

"That'll make a man love you forever," they would say
and the way she felt about it since Angie was so in love
with Davonte, if it worked on him, it would undoubtedly
work on her. Desiree stopped stirring, turned the eye on the
stove down a bit, walked over and reached for the phone on
the wall. Dialing the numbers on the phone, she decided to
call her mother and see just how much truth was in these
voodoo spells and she figured it'd best to find out before it
was time to serve dinner. *"Hey mama, what you doing? I
wanna ask you something."*

The Evening And dinner started off okay, late, but okay.
Late because Desiree sat on the phone with her mother for
over an hour. Davonte didn't care for his meal being late,
however, he tried to play fair. He was a lot of things and he
knew it, but he wasn't one to come between family
especially child and parent. Besides that, the evening went
on. He was pleased with dinner; fresh salad and garlic
bread along with the spaghetti was great. The sauce was a
tad bit runnier than he cared for, but acceptable. The
meatballs were on point and shredded cheese sprinkled on
top to set the dish off.

Desiree knew she had done well and it showed on her
face. She ate but not nearly as much as Angie and Davonte
did. Moreover, she enjoyed the fact that they enjoyed the
meal. They say music soothes the savage beast and a well-
prepared meal will bring even the most unsettled to ease,
and that's exactly what this meal had done. It allowed
Davonte to open the door to a much-needed discussion. A
discussion of how and why things had become what they
were? And by all means the floodgates were open.
Davonte wanted to know what was going on between

them? Now, he was far from being a fool and he was well aware that it was two black women he was dealing with, so the complete truth would not be told, especially if it would cause either of them to be placed in the wrong. Being aware of this, he knew he'd have to read between the lines and piece things together. He found the situation to be interesting, remained silent throughout most of the conversation, only occasionally posing the question from there, they'd have their say. Each of them talked around certain things Davonte noticed, but played along. Desiree spoke with aggression with her eyes oftentimes, darting back and forth between he and Angie. There was an unspoken code between women, a set of rules they followed and were taught while young by older women. Davonte could tell from Desiree's actions that Angie had somehow broken this. When Angie would speak, it appeared to be difficult for her to look at Davonte or Desiree directly in the eye for more than a brief second. And a few times, it seemed as if she wanted to cry, but fought with deep breaths and batting eyes to hold it back. From what Davonte gathered, there was some act of foolishness committed on both their parts causing emotional pain and distrust to both of them. At some point, Desiree attempted to approach things the way she felt fit, which let Davonte know she was the one affected most, however, Angie seemed to have followed along, that is, until she couldn't take anymore. And that led Davonte to know she too must have been guilty in whatever it was they were covering up that led to them falling out.

Davonte listened and heard both of them out, remaining calm and unmoved by anything either of them said, deciding he would sleep on it a couple days and put it together.

Meanwhile, since the lines of communication had been slightly reopened between them, he would watch, yet pretending not to be, in order to see how they now dealt with each other. This would allow him to assess just how bad things were between them. After that, he would devise a plan to put things back in its proper perspective. Loving him is where their minds should be and nowhere else. Because the way he saw it, for their minds to be on anything else was counter productive and a waste of valuable time.

The Ladies Spent the following days trying to mend what they had. Some days were better than others. They wanted to forgive and very much tried. They would speak, leaving out and coming in from work. To help with the healing process, Davonte had roses sent to both of them at work. A move to brighten up their day and it worked. When they got home that evening, they were both willing to discuss all the gossip surrounding them being delivered roses. They laughed here and there. Agreed several females were hating and jealous because they never receive roses, flowers, or anything for that matter. Yeah, all seemed to be on its way back to the norm, that is, until they went to bed at night. That's when they would stand in their individual bedrooms looking in the mirror. The scars from the fight were healing, but not fast enough to keep each of them from going to bed angry.

Days And Weeks passed, another month was coming to an end. It was April and the end of the week. The weekend marked the beginning of May and Davonte had yet to land him a job one with decent pay and benefits. One where he could stay at home and be able to hold things down at the house. This frustrated him because it wasn't like he couldn't get a job, it was a matter of one worth keeping. But his probation officer didn't see it that way, as far as he was concerned, Davonte could have a job cutting grass, laying brick or shoveling shit. It didn't make him none, but he'd better have one by April 9th or he would be getting violated and placed back in the county jail.

"I mean, it's not a seat in Congress, but it's a paying job and for the most part rather simple. You may have to exercise some people skills here and there, but other than that, it's gravy. So, what you gonna do?" M. Dub asked Davonte. *"Mildew or bar-b-que?"*

"It's Saturday," Davonte told him.

"No problem," M. Dub responded. *"Come through and we'll see about putting you on."*

"Alright, I'll be through there in bout an hour."

"Good, see you then. Oh, and uh, put on something casual, slacks, button down shirt, you know?!?" With that, M. Dub hung up the phone. Davonte didn't mind going by there, it would give him something to do because he knew he wasn't about to go looking for no job on the weekend. But the part that got him was, M. Dub offering to help him with a job, a man who has exploited women the greater part of his life.

"I hope he ain't on making me a pimp B.S." Davonte thought, mumbling to himself, talking out loud. *"Not that I would mind having a stable of women turning me in money they humped all night for. However, I can't see running that one pass my probation officer."*

He thought of M Dub's words, *"Exercise some people skills. Put on some slacks".*

"Hell, fuck it, let me slide through here and test my people skills, maybe he'll give me Yolanda's fine ass."

Davonte could see it now, her handing him a stack of money after being out sucking and fucking tricks all night. He smiled ear to ear, then it would be daddy's turn to get right. He envisioned himself licking Yolanda's butt cheeks, he couldn't help but laugh as he could hear her saying, *"I'm out with tricks all night, then come home to one."*

*"Well, **I** Apologize, I really do,"* Desiree told Angie. *"I mean, it was a matter of me feeling like I should pay you back. Not only because I felt betrayed by you, but also because you didn't get caught and I did."*

"I'm sorry too," Angie spoke, looking teary eyed, *"It all just happened so fast. I didn't know what to do."*

Davonte left out and told the girls he was feeling real frisky and wanted some all out raunchy sex when he got back home and it would be some three-way play. Something they hadn't done since the fight.

"So, whatever kinks y'all need to work out to make things right, do it," he told them before leaving out. *"Cuz I ain't gonna be for no crap later on when its going down."*

The girls had been talking and things, but a formal apology had not been done on either end. So, with the words of apology being spoken by each of them, they hugged and fought back tears. A tight embrace sealed it and Desiree rubbed her hands up and down the curve up Angie's back as she nuzzled the tip of her nose at the base of Desiree's neck. It appeared all may not have been lost.

*"**H**ey Turn That shit down!"* M. Dub snapped at Davonte. *"How you gone get your mind set on making money and you blasting that music?"*

Davonte heard him, but didn't hear him. He was too busy gloating in the limelight. M. Dub had let him drive the Caddy to their destination. It had just been detailed and shinned like new money.

"Turn right on the next street," M. Dub instructed Davonte.

Davonte slowed up and turned the corner in such a fashion he'd might as well been a pimp himself.

"You look good behind that steering wheel," M. Dub told him. *"You ought get you one and get rid of that truck."*

"I might do that," Davonte told him wearing a big smile. *"I might just do that."* Davonte took notice of them being on one of Atlanta's well known streets, Peachtree Street, heading towards the Buckhead area. It took money to play out here.

"So, where are we headed?" Davonte asked, knowing it had to be some pimp/hoe type situation. Seeing how M. Dub was dressed clean as a whistle with diamonds gleaming.

"I'ma take you by two of my top clients place, a father and son duo. I've even given the son a few pointers on how to get at these broads out here in these streets. Once he's done with them, he usually shoots them to me and I take it from there. They're big spenders and a couple of my girls say the son is as big a freak as he is a spender. I mean they say he does it all, lick, eat, the whole nine. He's paid Yolanda up to fifteen hundred for one night. Which isn't unusual for her. But, what she did find unusual about the guy, is he likes her to strap up and hit him off in his butt hole before he lays into her. Says it really gets him off."

"Damn," Davonte exclaimed.

"Yeah, you got some nasty suckers out here," M. Dub said. *"I tell my girls all the time when they tell me some of the stories that be taking place with they tricks, I don't see how y'all bitches do it. But when they tell me, "We do it for you daddy," I understand how they could then."* With that, he busted out laughing. *"Slow down young blood, we bout to have a turn in a second."*

After hearing M. Dub talk about his father/son clients, he knew a real job wasn't about to take place. But to hell with it, he told himself, *"I'll go along for the ride."*

"Turn up in here," M Dub said pointing a finger at a huge lot full of cars. The sun caused his diamonds to jump

off like a dozen bright stars. Whatever it was M. Dub was bringing him to do, Davonte hoped it would cause his fingers to end up dressed like his.

*"**D**avonte Said It's on tonight when he gets home. You with that?"* Angie asked Desiree. Their apologetic embrace had turned into a couple nibbles on the ear and a peck on the lips.

"Yeah, to be honest, I'm surprised he went as long as he did putting up with our shit." She told Angie, who had to agree.

"You right about that."

"Let me ask you something?" Said Desiree while looking Angie directly in the eye.

Hugging Desiree tightly, Angie smiled, *"Go ahead, what is it?"*

Desiree paused for a second questioning should she leave well enough alone. *"Were you really feeling me? I mean, was you really feeling me?"*

Angie said nothing, she simply took Desiree's hand and guided it down inside her cut off sweat pants she slept in. Once Desiree's fingertips reached the outer lips of Angie's split, she felt how wet she was. They had barely kissed.

"Does that answer your question?" Angie said happily.

"Yes, yes it does," Desiree said also feeling cheerful.

"Good," Angie told her, *"Now let's make something to eat, then we need to be getting ready for ourrr man's return home. And we'll start by taking a bath together,"* Angie added. *"How you feel about that?"*

"That's cool," Desiree said slapping Angie on the ass and heading for the kitchen.

"We ain't doing nothing though," she said looking out the corner of her eye at Angie's reaction.

"Don't start," Angie said looking only too sneaky.

Davonte Strolled Through the door behind M. Dub. A
couple things going through his mind, one what kind of job
was he about to try putting him on with, with a set of his
clients, one being a bi-sexual of some sort. And the other
thing on his mind was where had he heard the name of this
establishment before?

"Hey, there's my main man," M. Dub said to a tall
slender gentleman approaching. The two shook hands and
M. Dub asked about the guy's father, which let him know
this was the son, the one who took it in the ass. Davonte
figured the boy must have had some serious issues if
Yolanda's presence alone didn't turn him on.

"Well, let me introduce you to an associate of mines," he
heard M. Dub say turning to face him. *"This is Davonte,
Davonte this is Antonio. His father owns this place and he
manages it. What's up with that dish washer job you all
had available?"* M. Dub asked Antonio.

Part One. To Be Continued...

ACKNOWLEDGEMENTS

I WOULD LIKE TO ONCE AGAIN GIVE THANKS TO THE MOST HIGH AND TO LET IT BE KNOWN HOW GRATEFUL I AM TO HAVE BEEN GIVEN THE ABILITY TO WRITE.
THANK YOU ALL FOR CONTINUING TO READ MY WORK.
AND SO YOU KNOW, THE INTERESTING STORY AND THE LIVES OF DAVONTE, DESIREE, AND ANGIE STILL TAKES PLACE TO THIS VERY DAY. HOWEVER, I WILL ONLY WRITE MORE ON THE STORY OF THEIR LIVES AT THE REQUEST OF MY FANS.
IT'S ON YOU ALL, SO LET ME KNOW! ☺

DION JONES

Djnovelist@aol.com

Available Now!!

Mandingo Love

Turned Out (Mandingo Love Pt. II)

Player, Cheater, Or Damn Fool

Coming Soon From Penhouse Publishing!

Author Dion Jones

The Madam

Please

Author Erica Romero

As Cold As Ice

Author Melvin Adams, Jr.

From Hardwood 2 Concrete

*For Ordering Information Call 770-897-9990, Or Order
Your Book Online At The Following:*

Penhousepublishing.com

Amazon.com

Borders.com

Barnes&noble.com

Blackbooksplus.com

Waldenbooks.com

<u>DISTRIBUTORS</u>

A&B BOOKS

C&B BOOKS

LUSHENA BOOKS

SEABURN BOOKS